BURY THY BROTHER

The Gripping True Story of a Family Torn Apart
by the Civil War

by

Barbara M. Lord

Bury Thy Brother
Lord Skywriter LLC Book/published by arrangement with
Peacock Press LLC

Peacock Press LLC

First Edition
First Printing

ISBN 978-0-615-52936-3

PRINTED IN THE UNITED STATES OF AMERICA

Acknowledgements

There are so many people to thank; I hardly know where to begin. My younger sister Mary put in many hours of research for me from Augusta, Maine to the East Coast. Special thanks to Martha Constant without whose help this book might still be in galleys! Thanks also to John and Mike who helped me with computer problems -- frequently solved by asking Mom if the printer was plugged in! Patient sons. Thanks also to the Atlanta History Center and the Antietam and Spotsylvania battlefield rangers. So many friends and family encouraged me for years. Thanks to you all.

Thanks also to Penobscot Shaman Neptune who allowed me many years ago to hand copy a speech given by Chief Joseph Orono.

The picture on the front cover is Addison sitting at his mother's kitchen table. He was saying his farewell, not knowing if he would ever see his family again.

CHAPTER 1

Present Day

The ghost sat trance-like on the native gray granite base of the war memorial, his blue uniform and kepi indicating a Union soldier. His youthful face, blond hair, and blue eyes suggested a boy of perhaps eighteen or nineteen years of age. A cold early morning mist swirled around the tombstones and clung to the wet polished granite. Wild blueberries and strawberries dotted the patches of grass along the stony dirt paths that divided the living from the dead. Bitter clusters of sour red fruit weighed down the slim branches of the chokecherry trees at the edge of the cemetery. August in Maine could be brutally hot, but the sultry squally air, redolent with the sharp scent of pines, carried with it a hint of rain.

Addison Grant stared up at the overcast sky and remembered the summers of his childhood in Waldo County when he, his brother Lemuel C., and their father Joseph would lie on their backs in the hayfields and watch the "mares' tails" sweep across the bright blue sky and, like celestial

banners, announce a change in the weather. He
stared at the family hayfields and recalled the
sweet timothy haystacks and the sweat that trickled
down his arms as he pitched endless windrows of
hay onto the wagon drawn by the sturdy black
Percherons – Danny and Boy.

The girl now walking up the cemetery path
appeared to be eight or ten years old. Her slender
arms hugged bunches of colorful wildflowers –
queen anne's lace, black-eyed susans, goldenrod,
and numerous weeds that had caught her attention.
Addison had seen her several times before and
knew that she would walk toward the ancestral
plots – including the Grants – but something was
different this time. She laid the flowers and her
battered tin blueberry pail on the soft earth and
pulled a tiny notebook and a stubby pencil from
her pink-striped cotton apron pocket. As she
circled the tall polished granite monument in the
center of the Grant plot, she began to read aloud
and laboriously write down the names and dates
from the stones on the ground and the obelisk.

Addison leaned forward and stared hard at
the girl.

"Is it you? Have you finally come to me?
Please be the one. Oh please!" he whispered.

The boy soldier stood up and watched the
girl as she meticulously wrote down every word on
the Grant obelisk and every name and date on the
granite grave markers. As she had many times
before, the girl walked up the hill to the war

memorial behind Addison and quietly circled the monument, reading all the names. Addison stood, turned toward her, and froze as he heard her saying his name over and over again: "Addison Grant, Addison Grant, Addison Grant." Never before had he heard her say his name.

"Please be the one," he whispered. "Please, my little cousin, please be the one." The willowy girl shook her head and walked back to the Grant plot. Her long brown hair blew across her slightly flushed face as she leaned down to pick up the flowers, into which had crept a colorful hay spider. With one last caress of the obelisk, she turned away and again whispered Addison's name. Addison looked heavenward and wordlessly pleaded his cause.

The ghost stared back at the town war memorial for a moment and then back at this young girl. Was it too much to hope that at last his angel had come? She would have to search out the story and care enough to find the truth, to right the terrible wrong. The girl was young, but the soldier had a strong feeling that she would be true to the quest. After all, she was of the blood.

Addison Grant stared down at the green sprigs of timothy grass and looked one last time at his little cousin. He could only hope and pray that she would be the one. Time was so short.

"Craig Elachie, my little cousin, Craig Elachie," he whispered.

Addison wished that he could just blurt out the details and settle it once and for all, but the rules didn't allow that. He could only hope that one of his kin in this last generation would care enough to help him. As he stared out over the old hayfields, Addison was overcome with sadness and a great sense of loss. He had spent his brief youth in war. And the tragedies that followed – was he somehow to blame for all that? Unable to bear the thoughts, he concentrated on his childhood as he walked back to the monument and sat down, his contorted face in his hands. So many had failed him. He must find his champion.

As he stared at his cousin, Addison had an idea. He could not suddenly appear to her as a Civil War soldier without frightening her, but there was something better. He rushed past her to the old caretaker's shop that bore an uncanny resemblance to a mossy stone crypt. Addison morphed into the absent caretaker's form and stopped the little girl.

"Are you a Grant, young lady?"

"Not exactly, sir. The Grants are on my father's side of the family, though."

"And why are you so interested in Addison Grant then?"

"Well, sir, I've noticed that his name is on the big granite memorial in the Grant plot, but his name is not on the town war memorial. He was in the 7th Maine, Company B, the Grant memorial says."

Addison hesitated. The rules were clear. He could not say much more to her.

"Then perhaps you will be the one to solve the puzzle. It must be important to Addison, don't you think?"

He choked on the word "cousin." That would be too much. Addison longed to tell her the whole story. His father's cruel parting threats, his brother's taunting about the Grant badge, and his mother's silence when he announced that he intended to enlist. So many had failed him. He must find his champion.

"He had been to see the great death and found that, after all, it was but the great death. He was a man."

THE RED BADGE OF COURAGE,
Stephen Crane

CHAPTER 2
September 17, 1862

A foggy, misty morning greeted the troops as they prepared for yet another battle. Addison Grant hunkered down on the ridge with the rest of the 7th Maine Volunteers, Co. B., now reduced to fewer than two hundred men. Antietam Creek ran crimson with blood and body parts, the once merciful fog had evaporated, the sun glared a smoky blood red, and the roar of cannon and ordnance deafened even experienced ears.

The slaughter scene below him made the gorge rise in soldiers' throats even though they had seen such before in other battles. But never had they seen such carnage – thousands upon thousands of dead and dying. Watching the battle and waiting now for orders late in the afternoon made the scene below all the more macabre. A miasma of fear crept among the troops, and like two Bighorn rams smashing into each other, the battle had raged all day with neither side willing to give way. Unholy piles of bodies littered the battlefield and the Sunken Road near the Piper farm. Thick black acrid smoke choked the soldiers on both sides.

Addison watched Rebel sharpshooters slipping through the Piper farm and orchard, settling down to pick off the Yankees beyond the Sunken Road. Whispers rippled through the decimated 7th ranks as some wondered if their officers were seeing what was happening down there.

Addison leaned over to his Penobscot friend James Moody and worried aloud about this new development.

"Geez, I sure hope Major Hyde is watching this. The damn Rebs are gonna pick us off like pigeons if we're sent in there. I for sure don't want to be right smack in the middle of it, and there's not enough of us left to do any good."

The cries of the colorful Zouaves with the 9th New York echoed across the battlefield from the Harpers Ferry Road.

"Zoo, zoo, zoo!" yelled the bold Zouaves as they charged into immortality.

Major Thomas W. Hyde, scarcely older than his men, was watching. He saw Colonel Irwin of the 49th Pennsylvania and brigade commander for the 7th Maine talking to the Maryland battery commander. As the major rode over to the two officers, he heard the battery officer complaining about the Rebel sharpshooters near the Piper haystacks.

"We'll take care of that, commander. You just wait here."

Colonel Irwin then turned to his junior officer.

"Major Hyde. I want you to take your men and drive those Rebs away from the trees and buildings."

"But sir, I saw about two enemy brigades go in there! We have fewer than 200 men left, sir."

"Are you afraid to go, sir?" the Colonel snarled.

"No sir, I am not. You give the order loudly enough for my men to hear it, sir, and we are ready."

Colonel Irwin, unsteady in the saddle and with a noticeable slur in his speech, barked out the orders. With serious misgivings, the youthful major called his men to attention.

"Come on, men. Let's go! Let's show those Rebs what the Maine boys can do!"

Two young boys who carried the marking guidons pretended to go to the rear as ordered, but

the major soon saw them flanking the color guard.
Almost immediately, one boy – Johnny Begg –
lost his arm, and the other boy – George Williams
– was shot dead. The color corporal Harry
Campbell wept when the major reached for the
colors to give them to a sergeant.

"No, sir, please don't take the colors from
me. I want to carry them, sir."

"Very well then, corporal, you are now a
color sergeant. Carry on."

As the little cadre of soldiers approached the
Sunken Road, it was so filled with the dead and
dying that the major's chestnut Virginia
Thoroughbred stallion had to step on Rebel
soldiers in order to cross over. One dying soldier
shrieked in pain as the big horse stumbled and fell
to his knees on the boy's ruptured gut.

The 7th Maine charged across the road to the
right of the Piper farm where Major Hyde had seen
some enemy soldiers. Just as they reached the
trampled cornfields, the Maryland battery opened
up and immediately killed four Maine boys.

"Damn that wretched battery!" yelled Hyde
as he ordered his men double-quick into a little
valley. A round tore through the adjutant's big
white horse and the shattered animal collapsed
with a shrill scream as the Rebel troops rose up
behind the stone wall on the Hagerstown Pike and
poured rounds into the 7th Maine troops. Because
the Union soldiers were moving fast, little damage
was done. The major gave the command "left

oblique" to move the troops to a safer position behind a little hill. Hyde rode in front of his men and topped a ridge, where he saw Rebel troops hiding "at the ready".

"Left flank, left flank!" yelled the commander before his men showed themselves to the Rebels, and he led them past the Piper barns to the orchard. The 7th charged, and the Confederates who had been waiting there for the Maine boys, fired a number of volleys.

Twice, the major's horse was hit, and his rider slid off the back of the rearing, plunging animal. Blood spurted from the horse's mouth where his back teeth had been knocked out. Blood and tissue oozed from his wounded hip.

"I'm sorry, boy, but I need you. Steady now!" Hyde said trying to calm the injured animal.

As he swung onto his frightened horse he saw Confederate battle flags coming at him. One bore the title "Manassas".

"Damn! Just what I need!" the major whistled.

Surrounded by a number of Confederates, Hyde desperately looked for an escape through the fence. Just when he thought no help would come, he heard his own men rushing back with loud screams of "Rally, boys, to save the major!" They aimed their Windsors through the tall pickets and wire fence, and the major squeezed his lathered, bloodied horse through a narrow opening. Out of ammunition, the few 7th Maine survivors moved quickly down the valley, followed by the Rebel troops. Hit in the arm by errant grapeshot, Harry Campbell held his bloody stump up to the major and gathered up the colors with his other arm.

"Go on, sir. I'll be coming right behind you!"

Moments later, Major Hyde heard Harry cry out in pain, but he could not go back to save the newly minted sergeant or the colors. The scant remainder of the regiment formed up again and headed for the covering Vermont troops who had been told by their officers that they would never again see the 7th Maine boys alive.

As the exhausted survivors made ready for the night, Major Hyde learned that Colonel Irwin had been drunk when he gave the orders.

"Damned Colonel. Orders from old John Barleycorn. I wish I had been old enough or distinguished enough to have dared to disobey orders," the distraught officer said. He thought of all the young men who had been wounded or died. Only two men had escaped death or severe wounds. Weeping, the young major pulled the shared blanket over his head and tried to stifle the sobs. The stench of dead and dying horses and burning horseflesh made him gag. Through the night the rotting guts of both men and horses exploded in a sickening staccato. Bowdoin College hadn't prepared him for this.

*****

A deadly storm of shot and shell had whistled and whined around Addison's head as he fell on shredded bloody corn stalks. His father's prized Enfield rifle that he had carried earlier at right shoulder shift to avoid bayoneting the men pressed close in front of him lay in the bloody mire. Stunned, Addison tried to collect himself. He must have been unconscious for a while, he thought, because he did not remember being hit.

Addison summoned the courage to move and felt a limp bloody body stretched out against his right side. He spoke to the yellow camp dog in a raspy voice, but the animal did not stir. Slowly, Addison rolled over onto his left side and yelped in pain. He could see the inert yellow form and was grief-stricken when he saw that the dog had multiple gaping wounds. Many of the shots must have hit him as he cowered beside Addison. The little mongrel probably had saved his adopted master's life.

Since he could not help the dog, Addison examined his own wound. A warm ooze of sticky blood seeped across his belly, and he rolled gingerly onto his right side to survey the damage. As Addison pulled up his tunic and unbuttoned his trousers, excruciating pain stabbed his groin. Realizing that the meaty gaping hole was an exit wound, he reached gingerly behind him and found the entry point of the round that had knocked him to the ground. Addison pulled some moss off a fallen tree and stuffed it as best he could into the wound to staunch the flow of blood. A lone man stumbled toward him and fell beside the young soldier.

Penobscot soldier James Moody, and friend of Addison, was shot in the leg and half unconscious, but he put his arm around Addison and covered the boy's bloody body with his own.

"Stay down, Addison. This can't go on much longer. I'll get you out of here when the shooting stops. Stay down!"

The Indian warrior pulled more moss from a downed tree and stuffed it into both his and Addison's wounds. More rounds slammed into the body of the dog with a "thunk" like a sledge hitting wood. Another round hit James in the left arm and broke bones. He dug his fingers into the dirt.

"If I don't stay conscious, I will die," he said through clenched teeth. "I must stay awake. It's getting dark, and no one will come looking for us. Hang on, Addison, hang on. I'll get us out of here."

*****

All around them, men were still falling with sickening grunts. Some were shot in the back by their own panicked troops and some by deadly enfilading fire from the Rebs. Boys on both sides screamed and laughed hysterically as they reloaded and fired in frantic volleys – sometimes at point-blank range. Some tried to fire empty weapons or forgot to pull out the ramrod. Cannon and three-inch ordnance rifles blazed through the battered cornstalks in a lethal hellish chorus. Men fell dead in neat rows where they had hidden, harboring a false and fatal sense of invisibility.

When the shooting stopped, and ignoring his own wounds, James half crawled and half staggered as he dragged Addison from the battlefield to the medical tents, where both collapsed from loss of blood.

When Addison regained consciousness, he had no idea where he was or what had happened to him. A burning, sulfurous stench struck his nostrils, and he nearly passed out again. With clenched bloody fists and by sheer force of will, the boy remained conscious and took stock of his surroundings.

A desperate voice startled him.

"No, no, no! Don't cut on me any more! Let go of my leg! Don't take my leg! Help me! For the love of God, someone help me! If you take my leg, you might as well shoot me! Aaaahhh!"

A horse's shrill scream was a counterpoint to the man's. Eerie silence followed a rifle shot outside the tent.

All around Addison lay the dead and dying. Piles of arms and legs, hands and feet lay outside the blood-spattered tent. Musty mold attached itself to every dirty damp spot. A myriad of biting flies like tiny Harpies attacked the living and the dead, and covered the bloody arms of surgeons struggling to save the wounded who screamed and swore in their agonies.

The dark blue cloth attracted vicious black flies and savage deer flies. Iridescent bottle flies attacked the piles of human debris where they laid eggs that quickly became maggots feeding on dead flesh, crawling among rigid useless fingers that would no longer pull a trigger or caress a loved one.

As the orderlies lifted him onto a table dripping blood and gore, Addison could not help groaning. An abattoir would have been cleaner, he thought. There was little time to sanitize anything and precious little clean water. Antietam Creek ran red with blood, as did the waters of Egypt when Aaron struck the flood with his staff.

The surgeon sneered as he examined the boy's gaping wound.

"Shot in the back, boy, hey? Well, we'll get you fixed up anyway.   This is infected, orderly. Hand me a trocar."

It took a moment for the comment to filter through Addison's hazy brain. The doctor thought he was a coward and had run away! The young soldier nearly passed out from the pain of rough handling by the exhausted surgeon, but he gritted his teeth and didn't make another sound. He hadn't run away from the battle. He had never run away. As Addison faded in and out of consciousness, he thought he could hear his father's last words as he signed the under-age enlistment consent.

"Whatever else you do or don't do in this terrible war, Addison Grant, don't you get shot in the back. Might's well not come home if you do." Addison's friend N. S. Fales, who along with one lieutenant had miraculously escaped unscathed, found Addison weeping bitterly on a makeshift cot under a tree.

"Is the pain so bad, Addison? I'm sorry you were hit, but it looks like you'll be all right. At least we get to go home for a spell. The 7th took a wicked pounding. Most of the men didn't make it out, so I guess they'll be sending us home to recruit."

Addison gasped for breath and gritted his teeth.

"I'm not crying from the pain, Fales, although it's bad enough all right. I'm crying because I've been shot in the back for fair and true, and my father will think I'm a coward and that I ran. I didn't run, Fales! I didn't! I don't know how I got shot in the back, but I swear I didn't run. Where's my father's Enfield rifle? I don't see it here and I'd best not come home without it. Father sets great store by it."

N. S. Fales lowered his head. Many of their friends had fallen that day in battle. Cannon and ball and canister were coming from almost every direction, and word was already circulating that the colonel who had ordered the 7th into that meat grinder was "shot in the neck", "drunk as a skunk".

"Fales, where's James? James Moody, the Penobscot Indian? He must have dragged me off the field. I probably owe him my life. I know he was wounded. Can you find him for me?"

"Sure, Addy. I'll look for him. If he was badly wounded, he might already be headed for a train back to Washington, though."

Skirts rustled behind Fales, and he turned to see what female might be in the camp. A diminutive woman wiped her bloody hands on her apron and leaned over to examine Addison. Fales stared at her.

"What's your name, ma'am? I presume you're a nurse."

"Clarissa, young man. My name is Clarissa Barton, but my friends call me Clara. I shall pray for your friend. He's lucky to have you here to tend to him. Is there anything I can do for him, or for you, for that matter?"

"No ma'am. Thank you just the same. And thank you, brave lady, for being here amidst all this horror, and for bringing all those medical supplies. God bless you."

The nurse nodded and smiled.

"Far better than those filthy cornhusks you've been using and the boiled horse hair for sutures. There are more of us nurses here than you might know. God bless and keep you."

Fales reached out and touched her arm.

"Excuse me, ma'am, but do you know who those men are that are rearranging the bodies of the dead? And why, pray tell?"

Clara Barton, the barely five foot tall angel of more than one battlefield sighed.

"Yes, young man, I do indeed. That man over there with the camera is Alexander Gardner. He works for the famous photographer Mathew Brady. I suppose he started out wanting to show the world the horrors of war, but now he seems more interested in arranging dead bodies in a photogenic way. Perhaps he makes more money."

Fales gasped and simply shook his head.

"I've seen more horrors than you can imagine, young man," the petite nurse said. "More than you can possibly imagine. God bless you and your friend."

*****

Addison fell into a troubled, fitful sleep, calmed somewhat by the presence of his friend and a dose of laudanum that a sympathetic orderly had given him. In the forgiving fog, Addison Grant drifted back to his old homestead in Maine. He thought he heard his father's stern voice and his mother's soft weeping. He thought he could smell the sweet new-mown timothy hay and taste the strong switchel they carried to prevent thirst.

CHAPTER 3
Ten Years Earlier

Late one summer afternoon when the Maine weather was wrong for haying, Joseph Grant and his young sons Lemuel C. and Addison sat on a mossy stone fence at the edge of the cornfield. The boys watched the tattered scarecrow flapping idiotically in the breeze. Didn't scare the crows much. They were too smart. It did frighten the raccoons though when it rustled and clattered in the night breezes. A couple of tin pie pans tied together under the scarecrow's faded beige homespun shirt made a great coon deterrent when the corn ripened.

Farmers fought a constant battle with the elements and with Nature's children, and it seemed like a losing battle more often than not. Rarely did everything go right, and when it did, the old-timers would say that nothing worth having was ever won cheap. Something bad was bound to happen if the harvest was good, the critters sat at table elsewhere, and the weather held. Something bad

was comin', they would say. Ayuh, something
wicked bad was comin'.

As the boys shifted around on the stone
wall, a colorful copperhead swished off through
the piles of brittle pine needles.

"Good thing that wasn't a rattler you were
sittin' on, Lem," Addison laughed.

Copperheads wove through the stone walls
looking for field mice and baby rats, but seldom bit
people.

"Papa, tell us about great-grandpa Captain
James Grant again, would you, please?" begged
Addison as he chewed on a piece of sweet grass.
The farm produced just about the best hay in the
county and men came from all over when the hay
farmers were selling.

"Oh boys, you've heard the story about
Cap'n James too many times already. You can
probably recite all of the battles and doings
yourselves. Let's just watch those clouds for a
spell," he said as he lay on his back and stared at
the sky.

Maybe there'd be rain if the mackerel sky
was any clue, but Joseph usually bet more on the
mares' tails that brushed the scud from the sky as
they hurried past and warned of weather coming
up. When the rain came from onshore storms in
the summer, it sometimes ruined everything in the
fields. If the farmers were lucky, the rain passed
by to the south and ran the Penobscot back down
to the sea.

        Addison persisted. Again he begged for the
story.
        "Aw, Papa, please tell us again. He was
such a grand hero, serving in the Revolutionary
War and all. We want to be just like him. Tell us
the stories again. We can't hay, and the corn's not
ready yet by far, nor the blueberries either.
Please?"
        Joseph sighed and began to organize his
thoughts, although he'd told this story to his
children a hundred times or more. His grandfather,
Captain James Grant had served with distinction in
the Revolutionary War. The Grant family had a
tradition harking back to ancient Scotland that the
firstborn son would serve as a warrior/soldier, and
Captain Grant had honored that ancient calling.
One fierce battle took place right in front of his
holdings in Frankfort and Prospect, after British
troops and the Continental fleet had met at
Townsend.
        Commodore Saltonstall and Col. Paul
Revere were in the thick of the battle. The
Continentals had twenty-one ships of sorts in their
little fleet with the flagship being the frigate, *The
Warren.* Brigs, sloops, and a collection of
transports made up the rest of the revolutionary
armada determined to fight off the British invasion
and to prevent them from capturing and controlling
the Penobscot River, then subsequently all of the
northeast and part of Canada. From that vantage

point, the British could have controlled the eastern seaboard.

Again, to the delight of his two blond, blue-eyed sons, Joseph recited the saga of James Grant, recalling the fight for the Penobscot River and a fort that was lost due to Saltonstall's hesitation at two critical moments. He was from Connecticut, though, Joseph always explained with a grin.

Eventually, as the battle began to go the wrong way, *The Warren* was set afire by her own crew at Oak Point Cove just above Frankfort Village to keep her out of the hands of the advancing British.

Joseph was admittedly proud of his grandfather and all the Grants who had preceded him, back into the mists and myths of Scots antiquity, back through Peter Grant to the banks of the River Spey in the Upper Highlands of Scotland. The Castle Grant was the seat of the Laird, and part of the clan holdings ran up and down the west side of Loch Ness, home to the great loch monster some called Moray after the Moray Firth where she was first seen centuries before.

In a small hand-carved box on his desk, Joseph kept the Grant badge, an emblem of three mountains afire, emblazoned with the motto "Craig Elachie" that meant "Stand Fast". In times of war or danger, fires on the mountains signaled other clans. The oldest son would wear the badge into battle if, God forbid, another war erupted.

As Joseph lay on the cool grass and watched his sons climbing trees and racing each other around the hay fields, he thought about his brothers and the meeting they would have this night.

*****

The Grant brothers all sat around the old planked pine dining table lit with melting sweet beeswax candles and flickering, hissing coal oil lanterns. The fire crackled and snapped on the ancient stone hearth, and the air was redolent with cooking odors. A haunch of venison on the rack dripped fat into the spitting coals, making the men's mouths water in spite of the tension.

Hannah, their widowed mother, rattled cooking pots in the kitchen and the aromas of fresh bread, beans, and stove wood hung in the air. No one spoke for a long time, each brother lost in thought. Their mother and sisters chatted quietly in the kitchen, pretending not to be interested in the men's conversation. Finally, Joseph sighed, ran his slender fingers through his dark curly hair and spoke.

"I guess it falls to me, brothers. I'm the only one who's really interested in the farm, and Mother just can't do it alone. Our sisters wouldn't be a lot of help either. Just think about the time that Mary Eliza tried to milk that ornery old Guernsey cow, Matilda. Gosh! Milk, pail, stool, and sister went aflyin' every which way, 'member? Guess her hands were cold!"

His brothers chuckled at the recollection and then fell silent again.

"With Lemuel P. already down in Georgia building those railroads and doing fine for himself, I can understand why you are wanting to join him. Times are hard, and some of us already have families to support. If that's what you really want to do, then go with my blessings. It will be terribly hard though, especially when haying time comes. Maybe there'll still be some around needing jobs. I'll just have to hope my boys will be up to it. They're a mite young to pitch hay, but they can drive a team, rake windrows, and pick corn and blueberries."

Alfred, James, and George Grant knew they were asking a lot of their next-to-youngest brother Joseph. He had been only thirteen when their father died; Lemuel P. had been eleven. Of all the children, Joe and Lem had taken their father's sudden death the hardest, especially when rumors began that it was not an accident.

The brothers now looked carefully at Joseph, trying to gauge whether or not he was really ready for them to leave him alone with a widowed mother and two unmarried sisters. Winters in the North Country could be brutal and life uncertain on a Maine farmstead. A big gale that turned out to be a rogue hurricane hit New England in 1815. And all New Englanders still talked about 1816-1817 – the year without a summer. It snowed all summer long, the crops failed, the newly shorn sheep froze to death, and many people starved. A volcano somewhere or other, people said later.

"Are you sure, Joseph?" asked Alfred.

"Yes, go ahead. I may need some cash money now and again if anything happens to the crops. Blueberries should be good, and the corn and hay, but it's hard telling. We've had some wicked droughts from time to time, you know. There might not always be a good timothy crop. Guess Rosilla might be going, too? That'll just leave me, mother, Elmira, and Eliza."

The three brothers leaned on their elbows and stared into the fireplace. Each man knew that what he was asking of Joseph was risky. Of all the Grant boys Joseph was the least strong, the least sure of himself, more like his father that the others. The risks involved in going south and leaving Joseph to run the farm alone and take care of their mother gave all of them pause. Still, Lemuel P. was making a lot of money and investing it in land. Georgia was where the money was right now, and the railroads were building track at a great pace. Lem's experience as a rod man with the railroad in Maine had given him the credentials to do well for himself in the South.

Hannah appeared in the doorway and spoke sharply to her sons.

"Do what you need to do, boys. Times are hard and we can handle this farm without you. The neighbors have been good since James died,

and I'm sure we'll manage. If we can't, then one
or two of you should come back to help out. I
simply will not lose this farm that your father and I
worked so hard to get. James borrowed one
thousand dollars from my father to buy the land
and build this house, and I shall not lose it, no
matter what. Do what you need to do, and I shall
do what I need to do. Joseph and I can manage.
There's been enough talk for one night. Set the
table, girls."

Only polite conversation was allowed at the
table in this house, and the boys obeyed their
mother's rules. They talked some of politics and
crops and unusual weather, some of kinfolk and
cousins they hadn't seen in a spell. Nothing more
was said about the boys heading south to Georgia.
Contented sighs accompanied the sour green apple
pie and soft homemade cheese for dessert. The
boys would miss their mother's cooking.

"Well, that's it, then, I guess," said Alfred as
he rose from the table. Amid murmurs of
agreement the three brothers kissed their mother
goodbye, hugged their tearful sisters, shook
Joseph's hand and walked slowly to the door of the
house their father had built. Alfred looked out at
the two graves in the cemetery next to their
father's stone. Nathan Willard had died at
seventeen and their baby brother Wellman had
lived only five days after he was born. Mother
didn't have any more children after that, but no

one ever talked about it. Life could be short and the fates cruel.

As he closed the heavy door behind him Alfred whispered, "I wonder if I'll ever see my mother again."

CHAPTER 4
Frankfort, Maine, 1861

Joseph Grant sat down with an exasperated grunt and laid his son Addison's letter on the maple desk that he and his boys had made one soggy summer when rain kept delaying the haying. The stocky black Percheron draft horses had grown fat and lazy that summer. The hames and horse collars were a little tight on their thick muscular necks when Joseph hitched them up again. This summer Joseph could have used more help from his son, and wished that he hadn't wanted to spend time in Palmyra. Oh well, he had thought, the change might be good for Addison, but now he wondered who was behind this letter -- Addison or his cousins.

"Palmyra, Maine
        1861
        Dear Father,
        Perhaps you will be somewhat surprised at
the nature of this letter I am to write, but no change
of circumstance has changed my mind. I think
now, as I always thought, that if I were old enough
to enlist it would be the joy of my heart to do so.
There has been an enlisting officer here from
Augusta. There is a regiment forming there, and
there is a call for troops. He told me I was plenty
old enough, large enough -- and finally, just the
boy they want. He says a young man of moral,
temperate, and industrious habits cannot fail to
meet the approbation of the leading officers, and
has it not proved so with Lem?
        "But this is not what I look at most. Our
country is in danger. The liberties, advantages,
and blessings bought for us by the blood of our
fathers must not be annihilated for want of courage
and alacrity. And even if our country withstands
this present awful crisis, where are our Scotts and
McClellans coming from in future troubles? I
assert they will be found among the present heroes
of 1861. If the young men of the present age are
afraid to enlist under the banner of freedom, the
total annihilation of this glorious fabric must
ensue.
        "I, for one, stand ready to pledge my honor,
my service, my life, for the welfare of my country.
With me it is life or death. There is no alternative.

I had rather die than live under Southern despotism, and I can never remain at home and act the coward, while my brother and my countrymen are fighting for one of the best causes that man could fight for."

Joseph caught his breath and laid the letter down again, unfinished. Addison was so eloquent and so determined that Joseph felt his resolve slipping. What was he to do with the headstrong, patriotic son he and Julia had so lovingly and carefully reared? And had he not allowed Addison's older brother Lem to enlist a few months ago? With trembling hands and blurry vision, the distraught father picked up the letter that had been so carefully crafted and written with such a beautiful hand and glorious verbiage.

"Perhaps you will say that there are volunteers enough without me. But that is not the thing. How should I feel when our troops come home to hear it said: 'There goes Add Grant. He is a great hand to preach Republicanism but he is a coward after all, for he dared not enlist to fight for it.' Don't think that what I am writing is the impulse of the moment. I have thought of it ever since Lem first enlisted. I was just as determined then as I am now, and I am just as determined now as I was then. I am determined, so sure as the Seventh Maine Regiment leaves Augusta for the battlefield, so sure I shall go with them. But I had much rather go with your consent. I should not

feel right to go without it. But I know you will
give it. I never knew you to show partiality.

"I want you to weigh the matter candidly,
before you answer this. If you had made it a study
for three months as I have, you would think as I
do. All I am waiting for is an answer from you. It
will either relieve me from much anxiety or make
it still worse. If you answer me in the affirmative,
be assured you will make one soul happy; but if
the negative I shall be greatly disappointed, almost
broken hearted.

"For weeks and months the blood of
patriotism has burned within me until I can bear it
no longer. Now the chance for me to enlist, the
wish of my heart, presents itself; do, for heaven's
sake, let me put it into execution."

"Give my love to Grandmother, Mother and
all, and please accept this from your son.
Addison H. Grant"

As Joseph put the letter down again his right
hand lingered on the last page. Tears welled in his
eyes and at length spilled over, plopping on the
letter and causing the ink to run and bleed out to
the edges of the paper. How could he argue
against Add's enlistment when he had given in to
his elder son only a few months before?

A tradition handed down through
generations of Grants who had defended the lochs
and braes of the highlands had cast its shadow over
his first-born. The tradition had faltered with his
own father James, Jr. – first son of the famous

captain James Grant. James, Jr., a quiet well-educated man who had no interest in becoming a military man, hated the waste of war. After he married and had sons of his own, he worried aloud that his sons might question his courage. At the age of 47, he suddenly died – some in town said it was by his own hand. Some said he had fallen from the hayloft. Joseph and his brothers and sisters never knew which was true. Their mother never spoke more of it after the funeral.

*****

Joseph, like his father, hated war. He had prayed for years that no war would lure his boys off to the rumble and thunder of some distant conflict, or worse yet, one close at hand. Now his absolute worst fear had taken form. Here was war threatening to rip his nation asunder, and here was his youngest son determined to fight. Joseph was sure that Addison and Lemuel were good boys and brave, but word had trickled back to the rural towns and villages about the new weapons of war and the carnage they were wreaking among the young bloods of the warring sides.

Shuddering at the thought of his sons in the midst of some hellish battle, Joseph groaned and pounded his fist on the table.

"No, Addison, no!" he wept with his head cocked back and tears streaming down his rugged, weathered face.

Alarmed, his pretty wife Julia hurried from the kitchen.

"Joseph! What on earth is the matter, dear?" she said hovering in the doorway, putting distance between herself and whatever horror her husband faced. "Surely it's not Lemuel? Is it Lemuel, Joseph?" she said in a trembling voice that fell to a whisper by the end of the sentence.

"No, not Lemuel, dear. The letter is from Addison. He wants to enlist."

Julia froze and her long slender "piano" fingers curled into small fists. Her knuckles blanched and her delicate frame trembled.

"They shall not have both of my sons. They shall not!" she wailed as she slumped against the doorframe. "Who is responsible for this? Surely Lemuel has not tried to recruit his brother. Who then?"

Joseph shook his head in mute resignation. Recruiters were everywhere, and the young men and women were excited by the talk of war, great battles, and noble causes. Not one of them had seen a man blown to pieces by cannon shot, or run through with a saber or bayonet. Joseph himself had not seen such, but the Revolution had rent the country not long ago, and many good men had died for both sides of the cause. Some died for freedom, some for loyalty to the crown regardless of who was wearing it.

The next morning Joseph sent for his younger son, insisting that Addison come home at once. He was needed for the haying now that the rain had stopped, and frankly Joseph wanted to have an earnest talk with his headstrong, patriotic son. A raw chill in the air signaled the onset of unsettled weather, and Joseph had one more important errand before travel became too dangerous even with a good driving horse like his black Morgan mare.

*****

"Julia dear, I have to go to Bangor for a day or two. I should be back about the time that Addison gets here from Palmyra. I'll take some of our good meat from the smokehouse, some of your delicious bread, some apples from our orchard and a jug of water. The carriage blankets should keep me plenty warm enough, and I have a horse blanket for Jewel. Don't worry about me, dear. I shall be very careful and won't tarry. I love you."

"But Joseph, look at those storm clouds. Do you really have to go now? Can't it wait 'til after you speak with our son?"

"No Julia," Joseph said rather more firmly than he intended. He coughed into his scarf and a bit of blood trickled down his chin. Joseph turned away from Julia and wiped the blood away. "I really must go now. I'll be back before you know it."

Joseph chirped to his mare and she stepped out smartly.

*****

Julia just watched as her husband disappeared from view. Bangor wasn't that far, after all, but nasty winds sometimes blew off the

Penobscot River. What could be so important in Bangor that made Joseph feel that he had to leave right now?

*****

Addison arrived at the farm just before his father returned, and mingled his mother's tears with some of his own. He knew how difficult everything was for her and how she worried about Lemuel. Addison heard his father's mare neigh a greeting to his horse long before Joseph was even in sight. Addison had walked his gelding Ranger cool and bedded him for the night in clean straw. The tired dapple-gray horse had dozed standing with his right rear leg cocked until he heard the mare that he had not seen in months. Out of the same dam, they had grown up together and kicked up a great fuss whenever Addison or his father would leave the farm with the other horse.

Addison went out to help his father back the carriage into the shed and unhitch the mare. They worked in silence until the horse was cool and dry, both animals had a portion of hay, and Ranger had a little clean water in the heavy oaken bucket that hung on a rounded iron hook. The mare's condition warranted taking her water out of the stall for a while and waiting on the oats until she had completely cooled down. The men would come out later to grain both horses and give them water before the family retired for the night. For now, both horses seemed content with their hay, a warm dry bed, and each other's companionship.

"Mind the grain room door, Addison," his father said, coughing with a raspy grating noise. "Wouldn't do to have the horses get in there. Especially with the mare not really cooled down yet. Latch it good. I know that Ranger has a mind of his own and can get out of his stall if he wants to bad enough. He's a stout rascal."

Addison nodded, secured the latch on the door, felt the mare's chest and neck, and shook his head as he adjusted her stable sheet.

"Going to be a spell before you can water the mare, father. She's still warm even after we rubbed her down."

Joseph just nodded. His sons knew horses and there was no need for him to check the mare himself. Both men turned their collars up against the gathering storm and leaned into the wind as they made their way back to the house.

*****

Addison and his father ate dinner without speaking a word to each other, and Julia's efforts at conversation were wasted. The ghastly tension between her husband and her younger son terrified her, and she feared the outcome of their conversation when it finally took place. Not a day went by that Julia, a petite pretty woman from one of the best families, did not agonize over her absent son Lemuel. She hid from the post rider when he came with the mail, which he did as a courtesy to the families with sons or husbands in the war.

Most of the time, a family member would rush out to take the prized letters from his outstretched hand, but sometimes he would dismount, tie his horse to the post, take off his hat, and inquire if the husband or a grown son were perhaps at home. Women frequently swooned when they saw the rider take off his hat and walk toward the door. The news was never good.

*****

At length Addison and Joseph rose from the supper table, walked into the parlor and stared into the fireplace. Neither of them wanted to begin the discussion, and dreaded the outcome for different reasons. Addison wondered if he had made a mistake writing that letter to his father. By invoking the history of his Grant family in a previous letter, he had risked much and now had all but called his own father unpatriotic if he didn't allow Addison to enlist. His father's stern visage made Addison swallow hard before he spoke.

"Father," Addison began and cleared his throat. "I know this is difficult for you and for my dear mother, but I beg you to hear me out. I must tell you that I have decided that I will enlist with or without your blessing, but I would rather have it than not."

For nearly an hour Addison pleaded his case while his mother hid in the larder. His father leaned on the massive hewn maple mantel, gripping it with both weathered, calloused hands and clenching his teeth as his son repeated the patriotic rhetoric of the day. Addison gestured and implored like a seasoned orator as his grandfather had been.

"Father, please listen to me. Here is the heart of the matter. You let Lemuel C. enlist underage and the town is proud of him. So are you, whether you choose to speak of it or not. Why am I any different? Must I sit home and hide from the townsfolk? Can I not wish that you would be proud of me as well?"

"Addison, my son, it is the tradition of the Grants that the oldest male in each generation goes for a soldier. Your elder brother Lemuel joined the army although I was reluctant. Son, the point is that traditions are important, but as the scriptures say, if I may quote the Lord himself, 'The law is made for man, not man for the law.' You do not need to die to prove that you are a man, Addison."

Addison kicked the logs in the fireplace with such force that his father startled and stepped back.

A heavy silence hung palpably in the air. The man-child knew he could lie about his age and enlist as so many of his friends were doing, but the Grants did not lie. The headstrong young man also knew that his father was thinking about his own brother, Lemuel P., in Georgia, and agonizing over the conflict between patriotism and family.

Addison thought, too, about his gentle mother Julia who had endured the deaths of two babies and now walked in what seemed to some to be a dream state much of the time.

Both Addison and his father stood staring silently into the fireplace. Neither of them ever looked forward to these discussions. Addison could not give up, and his father would not give way.

Finally, in desperation, Addison turned to his father with perhaps the only weapon left to employ.

"Father, how can you insist that I sit out this war when our entire family has such a proud history of fighting for liberty? From the Revolution back, we Grants have always been willing to fight and die for our freedoms. Even back in the history of Scotland, the Grants were known as warriors.

"Craig elachie", remember, Father? Our family crest is three flames on a mountain. Does that mean 'look out for yourself and run'? It does not. It means 'stand fast'."

Addison knew he had played a dangerous card. By bringing in the entire family history he risked infuriating his father with such an obvious tactic. Still, perhaps it was working. With an anguished groan his father grasped the mantel with both hands. His knees began to buckle, and his son instinctively reached out to support his father.

"No, Addison, no!" his father wept. "I cannot bear the thought of losing both of you. Who would carry on this proud name whose history you invoke here? Who would take care of your precious mother if I die first, as I am likely to do? No, Addison, do not ask this of me. Please do not ask this of me," the older man begged as he collapsed in a fit of coughing. A tiny trickle of blood appeared at the corner of his mouth when he turned his back to Addison.

Torn between the hint of success and the sense of shame that flushed his face when he realized that he had at last worn his father down, Addison knew that victory was within his grasp. Emma would be so proud of him. Now no one in town could ever call him a coward. He would be a soldier like the Grants before him. He would be like Lemuel.

Addison turned back to his father and saw tears streaming down the older man's contorted face.

"I must go and do my part, father. I know that you would go yourself if you could, but they won't take you and Mother could never bear your leaving. She needs you. Let me go and be with Lemuel. Together we'll look after one another. I'll sign up with the 4th, too, and we'll be great Scots warriors, Lem and I.

"I've brought my enlistment papers, hoping that I could persuade you to sign here. Will you sign, father? Please let me go and make all of you proud. If you don't let me go, the war will be over before I have my chance, and my Emma will never want to marry me. No one will want to have me if they think I'm too cowardly to go. Shall that be my lot, my inheritance, father?"

*****

Joseph knew that he was beaten and his gentle heart broke. There was no answer to his son's pleadings and protestations of patriotism and family honor. There was no place to turn to avoid what must be. Wearily Joseph sighed and weeping, laid his face on his son's shoulder. With his tears he baptized him, with his sobs he ordained him, with the stroke of a plume he opened the door to liberty and death.

As Joseph staggered to the barn to be alone, a cold wind bit through his coat. Although he could tear up the papers, he knew that would not end it. He had to let his beloved young sons face death and destruction unimaginable in their time. Joseph's retching and vomiting was observed only by the black mare that nickered anxiously to her master. She pawed the ground briskly and snorted at the dust she had raised. The gelding laid his head across her back and stared at the sobbing man who had collapsed to his knees. Looking past the bent shaking form, Ranger watched his own master hurrying to the barn. Addison knelt beside his father in the straw and wept with him, then shivered slightly as though someone had walked on his grave.

CHAPTER 5
1861

Before he spoke with his father, Addison
had thought he knew what his enlistment would do
to his mother, but the fervor of patriotic slogans
and calls for all able-bodied men to come to the
defense of the Union was more than he could
stand. One after another, his brother, his friends,
and his cousins had enlisted. For miles in every
direction, Addison was nearly alone among his
male peers. The young women of the town and
nearby farms had begun to look askance when he
passed and had begun to whisper behind his back.
Even his dearest Emma had taken his hand one
afternoon as they stood on the banks of the
Cattamawawa Stream.

"Addison, will you enter the lists? Will you
answer the call to arms?" She nearly swooned and
fanned herself as she held her breath and waited
for his answer. "You would look so very
handsome in a uniform. Dear heart, the war will
be over before you know it. It surely can't last
much longer. If you don't enlist soon, you will

miss your chance. I will write to you every day, I promise."

"Emma," Addison had said softly. "I shall, of course, enlist as my brother Lemuel has done, but I fear that my dear mother will take it ill. She is so full of fear for the safety of Lemuel that she seems to be walking in a dream much of the time. I must wait a little while until I have talked with Father about it. Just a little longer, my sweet."

Emma stared at her beau and then frowned. She fanned herself vigorously as she pictured him in a dashing uniform, then snapped her elegant black feather fan shut. She lowered her eyes as she turned toward him and took both of his hands in hers.

"Are you afraid, Addison? I know war is a fearsome thing, but our cause is just. Almost all of the boys in town and even the married men have enlisted. Several more units have formed since your brother Lemuel enlisted."

She shyly raised her eyes to his and held her breath. They were so close she could feel his breath on her face. Something she had never felt before stirred in her and warmed her nether parts in a way that was most disconcerting. She wanted Addison to kiss her even though they were not yet bespoken. He had always been shy and very much the gentleman, exactly as she imagined the knights of old must have been. Here stood her Lancelot, her knight in shining armor. Images of battle flags and men clashing with sabers and muskets flashed through her mind's eye. She could nearly smell the smoke and hear the battle cries as she grew faint and started to sink to the ground in a swoon. Addison gripped both of her small hands and steadied her.

"What is it, Emma? Are you ill? Shall I take you home?"

"No, Addison, I'll be fine. Just hold me for a moment, please."

What little Addison knew about women he had learned from his sisters, and that wasn't much. He did know they were given to vapors and fainting and were delicate in nature, but he also knew they could be strong. He put his arms around her and drew Emma's trembling body to him. As he did so, the closeness of her and the attar of roses in her hair aroused him. He kissed her softly on the cheek and nuzzled her curled blonde hair, blowing a wisp from her flushed face. He pulled her arms around his waist and held her against him. After a moment's struggle to free herself, Emma sighed and yielded. She looked behind her and saw that no one was watching.

Addison pulled away from her, raised her face to his, and stared down into the intense blue eyes that mirrored his own. She was so beautiful, he could scarce believe that she had promised to wait for him if he went off to war. What if some soldier came back from the war before him and swept her off her feet? He couldn't bear the thought.

Addison led Emma to the little copse of trees that grew along the bank. He leaned back against an old willow tree whose graceful branches like a ballerina *en plie* brushed the surface of the stream and reached after the ripples that drifted freely down the slow current.

The boy drew the girl to him and kissed her throat and neck, like a determined but inexperienced and awkward young stud horse courting a filly coming into her first breeding heat. Addison's manhood rose, pulsating, growing hot. He was sure she could feel it even through their clothes, but he didn't care anymore. He knew she was a maiden as was he, but he was losing control. Her hot cheeks flushed and Emma raised her face to his and kissed him full on the lips. Addison felt her heart pounding against his chest, nearly matching his own, beat for beat, and wanted her so badly he groaned.

"Oh Addison, what are we doing?" Emma gasped. "This is wrong, my love. We must wait until we are married. I promise I will wait for you, I promise!"

Addison knew she was right, but how he wanted her. He could imagine their bodies entwined in passion. If he went to war and died, then this passion he felt for her would never be consummated. Surely that could not be right.

The sudden pain that he felt in his lower belly dropped him to his knees, and he rolled in a ball on his side. Frightened, Emma knelt beside him and cupped his youthful flushed face in her gloved hands. A mischievous breeze nudged her feather fan that had fallen on the creek bank. The fan slid into the water and floated downstream, brushing against the smooth hard river rocks, turning coyly around them, teasing with quivering plumes.

"Addison! Are you in pain? Are you ill? Shall I run and get help?"

"Ooh, oh, Emma. I shall be fine. Just give me a moment."

Manhood thwarted is a frightful thing. Addison had heard of this malady from some boys who lived along the river in town, but had never suffered it himself. In a few moments he recovered, the fire of his passion quelled. He stumbled to his feet, adjusting his disheveled clothes. Somewhat abashed, both Emma and Addison straightened their clothes and brushed off the willow leaves. Addison turned his back to his sweetheart and tucked in his shirt. He smiled at the thought that a few minutes ago, he would gladly have shed his clothes, but now he didn't even want her to see him tucking in his shirt. Passion was surely a powerful thing. He promised himself that he would learn to control it until they married after the war. That should only be a few months. He could wait. They walked hand in hand back across the bridge toward town.

"Sorry about your fan, Emma. I'll buy you another," Addison said when he saw what was left of the bedraggled feathers lodged in a tree root.

"No need, Addison. It wasn't expensive," Emma lied.

She would wait for him to return from the war in a few weeks, and then she could give herself to him. She shuddered as she thought about how close they had come to committing a sin, and with a new respect for this part of her being, she promised to be less judgmental of young women who had given in.

CHAPTER 6
The Enlistment

Addison and other boisterous, boastful young men full of patriotic bravado packed the train that rumbled off to Augusta where they would join other units from their home state. The 1st Maine Cavalry was already in the war along with several other Maine units, and still more were forming to fight in the Great War to Save the Union. Flags flapped and people cheered in every town they passed. Women rushed to the windows at every stop, thrusting food and drinks into their outstretched hands. It was marvelous. They were instant heroes. Addison wondered how he would find the 4th Maine and Lemuel. Oh well, he thought. I'll just tell them that I'm supposed to be with my brother Lem. Someone will surely tell me where to go. At best, the trip was uncomfortable. The men were packed in tightly, like sheep in a winter fold, Addison thought as he looked for any familiar faces.

"Hey there, Josh," he yelled to a friend across the car. "Didn't know you were in here. Going to war, too?"

"Ayah, Addy my boy. Hope it ain't ovah afore I git theah, reckon? I'd sure hate to miss such a grand kerfuffle, eh?"

Addison shook his boyhood friend's hand a little too vigorously, and neither seemed inclined to let go right away. Finally, they dropped their hands to their sides and stood awkwardly looking out the dusty window. August in Maine was usually sweltering hot, and this year held no promise of an exception.

"Skeered much, Addy?" whispered Josh.

"Naw, not too much. My brother Lem is in the 4th and they're doing OK. He was at some place called Bull Run or something, and it was pretty bad, but he's ok as far as I know. Don't think he got shot or anything bad. Besides, Lem and I are great shots. We'll look after each other. We'll make the town proud of the Grant boys – that's for sure. I'm sure you will, too, Josh. You'll be great. We'll all be great. Think how the girls will act when we come home heroes from the war. We'll have our pick of the ladies, but of course I'm promised to Emma. I want her to be proud of me, and I want to make her father proud, too. Then he'll let me court her properly."

*****

Josh nodded absently and stared at the living mural sliding past the windows. He wondered

how long it would take to get to Augusta on the
train. It was his first train ride, and he was out of
his element. Usually Josh was the town braggart,
but due to his friendly smile and glad hand, no one
paid much attention to his wild tales. Monster
black bears and charging bull moose generally
evaporated in the light of day. Josh had to find
some other outrageous adventures to act out for
friends and the ladies. This time, though, he had
an uneasy feeling that he wouldn't have to
exaggerate much. Those Rebs were a fearsome
bunch, and the edge nearly always went to the dog
on his own porch.

*****

The troop train rumbled into Augusta and
squealed and screeched to a stop at the edge of
town. Its engine blew thick black smoke and
cinders into the air. Stirred by the fluttering flags
and blaring horns, the young men whooped and
hollered as they stepped off the train. Addison
thought for a moment that they all sounded like
western wild Indians as he imagined they would
sound during a war dance.

The Grants were friendly with local Indian
tribes like the Penobscot and often visited their
villages, trading wooden items or tools for the
Indian crafts. Visitors had to canoe across to
Indian Island where many of the Penobscot lived.
Addison loved to watch the women weaving fancy
baskets, and marveled at their dexterity as the
women's fingers quickly wove useful items,

mostly from basswood inner bark or ash splints and sweet grass.

When he stepped off the train Addison recalled one day when he was visiting the Indian village before he left for Augusta. The chief's daughter had approached him.

"Friend of my people," she had begun softly. "We wish you would not go to war, but we have a small gift for you. My sisters have made a little abaznu'de for you. Perhaps you will think of us when you use it. Your ancestors and mine were friends many, many years ago, even when the white men and the Indian were not always friends. Please take this small basket with our prayers for your safety. We will ask the Creator to watch over you."

*****

The recruiters wasted no time lining up their prospects and getting them signed on. Addison clutched his underage endorsement and stepped into a line on the back side of the crowded noisy train depot. He looked around for friendly faces, but seeing none but Josh, he stood at attention and stiffened his back as an officer strolled past. The officer's boots were shiny and looked new. Addison wondered if the man had seen much action or whether his job was just to recruit boys like himself.

Addison's heart began to race. He was overcome with the desire to step out of line. His life seemed no longer his own to command, and he thought about his mother and father and how upset they were with his decision to join up. What if they were right? What was one man more or less to this war effort? Some wealthy men had even hired poor men to serve the army in their stead. Addison began to tremble and sweat with a terrible premonition. What if both he and Lemuel should be killed? He gasped at the thought. What would this do to his father and mother?

The officer walked down the line again, and stopped squarely in front of Addison.

"Where you from, boy? You look young."

"From the town of Frankfort, sir, and I am young, but I'll be a good soldier just the same. See, here is my father's signature. My brother Lemuel is already fighting in the war. I don't rightly know exactly where he is, but he's with the 4th, sir. I'd planned on joining the 4th, so we can be in the same unit."

The recruiter frowned slightly and looked south, as if picturing the location of the 4th Maine Volunteers.

"It doesn't work that way, boy. The 4th is already in the fight, and we're forming the 7th right here. Doesn't mean you and your brother won't end up together, you see, but we can't put you in a unit that's already gone. You'll most likely end up seeing action together, and I'm sure that you'll both be fine soldiers. Your father must be very proud of his brave sons, and your mother, too, of course. Mustn't forget your dear mother."

As the man smiled and strutted down the line, Addison felt a bit of panic starting. Why couldn't he just join up with Lem? He didn't know anyone, hardly, that was here to make up the 7th. He didn't know that he really wanted to trust his life to strangers. Maybe they didn't even know how to handle their weapons. Maybe someone would accidentally shoot him before he ever got a chance to show what a good shot he was. He rubbed the stock of the Enfield rifle that his father had given him when he left. He thought of home and his father's warning.

"If you're determined to fight, son, then at least take a decent weapon with you. Don't know what the army has for the men that sign up. Take this Enfield and at least you'll hit what you're aiming at," his father had said with a noticeable catch in his throat. The older man turned away abruptly and hid the tears that suddenly spilled down his cheek. Joseph cleared his throat and bent down to brush some lint from his pants.

Addison, silenced by his father's uncommon emotion, had stood quietly, awkwardly, not knowing what to say. Somehow things had changed. He had sensed his father's unbearable pain and now wondered if he was doing the right thing.

*****

"Say, Addy, do we get a bonus or sumpin'?" Josh whispered as he appeared beside Addison. "Wonder if that officer has ever seen any fightin'.

Ain't he just too purty and shiny now? Maybe
he's just here to impress the ladies."

Addison was preoccupied with his own
thoughts as the men still in line shuffled past him.
He wondered if he and Lemuel would ever again
just horse around, wrestling in the lofts and
playing king of the hill on the haystacks. His
cheeks hurt as he remembered his mother's sour
green apple pie. He could remember the texture of
his grandmother's soft summer cheeses, smell the
rich heady tang of the fall apple cider and feel the
rough salty rind of bacon and hams curing in the
smoke house. The thoughts made his eyes tear and
his mouth water. Addison wondered what on earth
he was doing in this line. How did this happen?

"What did you say, Josh?" the boy-soldier
mumbled. "Do we get some kind of bonus? The
recruiters in Frankfort said something about that,
but no one here has mentioned it. They're not
going to let me into the 4th, Josh! What am I going
to do now? I want to fight next to Lem. We could
take care of each other and make sure we get home
to Mother safe and sound like I promised her.
Who, for the love of heaven, do we know in this
outfit?"

Josh shrugged and stepped up to sign his
name on the troop roster. Like Addison he was
underage and to boot he had no papers, but no one
seemed to care. The quartermaster looked him up
and down and handed him a mostly blue uniform.

"Your boots look okay to me, boy, and we're a little short on footwear at the moment. Those'll do. Have ya got your own weapon, boy, or do we need to find you something' to shoot them Rebs with?"

"Don't got a rifle, Mister. Guess I'll need one, huh?"

"Unless you want to throw rocks at the Rebs, boy."

Josh stared up at the tall square-jawed man and down at the uniform. He raised his leg and slung his foot over his knee to look over his boots. First the right leg, then the left. Finally he sighed, asked about an enlistment bonus -- which question was met with a shake of the head -- and wandered off to find a weapon. He never looked back at Addison who was beginning to tremble slightly as his turn came at the table.

"Next in line! Step up here and do it smartly!" rumbled the quartermaster whose dark brown eyes looked cold to Addison. The quartermaster stared at the boy and looked him over like a man buying a plow horse or a milk cow.

"You'll do, boy. What's your name?"

Addison's hand shook like a schoolboy about to be smacked with a ruler as he signed his name. No one asked his age. His life was no longer his own.

CHAPTER 7

Crammed like cattle on troop transports, the Maine recruits suffered in silence. Addison, Josh, and the others sweated profusely in the August heat.

"I'm wet as a swamp rat, Addy. I'm afeared we'll all die of heat stroke afore we get wherever we're going. Where are we goin', anyhow?"

Addison stared into space and didn't answer. Soon enough the boy soldiers arrived at the camp where they were sorted and drilled and turned into some semblance of troops before being shipped off to the war.

Geez, Addison thought to himself. Most of these boys don't know one end of a rifle or musket from the other, and some of these men look dumber than a bucket of rocks. This will be like herding cats. I hope I don't get shot by one of my own. He shuddered to think of a round slamming into his back. The last thing his father had said to him before he left home now sent chills down his spine.

"Whatever else you do or don't do in this war, Addison, don't you get shot in the back, boy. If you're going to insist on enlisting in the war underage, so be it. But you carry the Grant name into that war. Don't you get shot in the back, hear? Might as well not come home if you do. Should have said the same to Lemuel C., but I forgot. He's older, though. I expect he knows how I feel about cowardice. Besides he's pretty much out of harm's way as a commissary sergeant."

*****

One of the men on the train headed to the training area died from food poisoning. Rumors flew that somehow the Rebs were poisoning the food or some of the people who were handing food in through the train windows were Rebel sympathizers. Might have been true in Maryland, Union officers muttered among themselves.

Pretty sad to die of food poisoning before I ever get to the war, Addison had mused. Guess I'll be more careful about accepting food. Wouldn't read well in the paper if they had to report my death not due to some heroic act in battle, but from food poisoning. That would be so embarrassing for my family.

*****

Time passed as if in a bizarre dream, and the leaves were falling when the troops were finally ordered to prepare to leave for the battlefront.

Some of the soldiers were sharing their crusts of bread with the birds that were milling on the ground around the troops. Male pigeons cooed and strutted around with puffed-out breasts. Females looked for food and tried to evade the determined males who bowed and turned, showing their best plumage.

"At least the birds have enough to eat here," Josh laughed as he threw a crust of bread toward a small flock of pigeons.

The birds flapped and struggled to control the food as a few grackles joined the little flock and pushed the pigeons aside. Their glossy black wings glistened even though the day was overcast and rain threatened. The birds on the ground had not looked up into the trees, so they didn't see the large hawk as it hurtled toward them. He had picked his target carefully. The fat posturing pigeon never saw his attacker until it was too late. The hawk dove, hit, and heaved himself back into the air with the stunned prey in his powerful talons. The men around the attack site froze in silent amazement. Many of them had never seen a hawk up close before, and only one or two had ever witnessed such an attack. Silence dropped over the men like a shroud. The pleasantry of feeding a few bits of bread to some birds had been shattered. Slack-jawed, Josh stared at the hawk as it flew off with its prize.

"Geez, Addy, did you see that?" he whispered.

"Yep. Did. What kind of hawk was that anyway, Josh?"

"Dunno. Prob'ly a red tail. Got lots of them Down East. Expect that they have some of them here, too. That was amazing. That hawk didn't even care that there was a bunch of us standing around, neither. He just picked a pigeon and nailed it right in the middle of the flock. Bam! All that's left of that there bird is a few feathers and some blood on the grass."

The men shuffled onto the transport and looked around for some place to stow their heavy packs and haversacks. Since it had rained the night before, many of the bedrolls were wet. No one was looking forward to the trip. Seasickness hit most of the men before they arrived at their destination. Every space along the ship's rails was occupied, so many were forced to vomit where they stood. The slimy vomitus made it hard to stand, and some slipped and fell in the stinking slop.

After the troops moved to Washington, nothing much happened. Nasty winter winds bit through their coats and britches, sparing neither enlisted man nor officer as the brutal cold froze their toes and fingers. They still had no ammunition.

In March they left for the front. The ensuing skirmishes and battles tired the men, many of whom had become quite ill. Some called it swamp fever, and some just called it ague. Whatever it was, it drained a man's strength and will. The doctors treated the men the best they could, but supplies were still erratic, and the frustrated generals told the men to find whatever they could to treat themselves.

Addison had some knowledge of herbs and poultices, but many plants around him looked strange and maybe poisonous. A doctor once told him not to count on the birds either. Birds could eat some things that would kill a man. Old wives' tale, he said, that man could eat whatever birds or even other animals could eat. The bewhiskered old man had spat on the ground for emphasis as he said it. The water they had to drink was frequently dirty, and Addison was sure that had something to do with the dysentery and other illnesses that sprang up among the troops.

*****

The names of the places where they had fought stuck in Addison's brain like a horrible collage, a nightmare from which he could not awaken. Yorktown where he found Lemuel and the 4th Maine, Williamsburg, White Oak Swamp, and recently Crampton's Gap and South Mountain. Now at some place called Antietam, Addison had a sense of foreboding that he could not shake off. He had learned that this was to be a major battle that Lee could not afford to lose. The Maine men, exhausted from the battle at South Mountain, needed rest and recuperation, but there was no time.

Addison squatted in silence under a tall tree that reminded him of the trees on the farm in Frankfort, but he had no idea what kind of tree it was. Exhausted, hungry and sick, men collected in little groups here and there. A couple of Indian soldiers sat together in silence, staring into the woods. Having not seen them in previous battles and curious about them, Addison finally moved over and sat near them.

"I guess you speak English?" Addison said as he leaned toward one of the men.

"Perhaps better than you do, "the Indian said, his dark brown eyes nearly black like his hair.

"What are you men doing in this war anyway?" Addison queried, puzzled.

The man nearest him just stared into space for a minute and slowly pulled a folded piece of paper from his pocket. The paper was yellowed and somewhat tattered along the edges, but otherwise readable.

"We're Penobscot actually. My name is James Moody. What's your name?"
Surprised by the Christian name, Addison hesitated and then gave his own name and town.

"Addison Grant of Frankfort. Do you live on Indian Island up in Old Town?"

"No, Addison. I live in Brunswick with my family."

"And your real name is James?"

"Yes. My father is a doctor in Massachusetts."

"A doctor? Really? Gosh. That's something to be proud of. I figured you'd have some Indian name like Standing Bear or Tall Tree or something. How come you're called James?"

The Penobscot soldier smiled and looked at the ground.

"How come you're called Addison?"

"That's my Christian name, of course. Addison Grant. Friends call me Addy."

"Well, Addy, my Christian name is James Moody."

Wondering if this man was taunting him, Addison simply stared for a moment.

"Why is an Indian carrying a Christian name, James? Don't you have some kind of tribal name?"

"Tribal name? You mean a Penobscot name? In fact I do, but the missionaries gave us all Christian names a long time ago, because they couldn't speak our language or pronounce our names. They couldn't pronounce the name of my people either. The real name is Penawahpskewi. Can you say that, Addy? Not many white people can. Or maybe they don't care to learn it. And actually my tribal name has nothing to do with bears or trees, and Penawahpskewi means 'water that runs over rocks'."

James waited for the expected guffaw from his new friend and sat patiently. Addison just stared at him.

"You're not teasing me are you, James? That's your real name."

"Yes."

James was holding an expensive looking weapon and Addison was curious about it.

"What's the rifle you're holding, James? It looks like it cost you dear."

"I'm a sharpshooter, Addison. With Berdan's unit mostly. That's why my uniform is green. Makes us harder to see, I guess. Just attached to the 7th for now. The weapon is a Colt 1855 Revolving Carbine. I bought it myself. Only one man I know about has one of the new Sharps. His name is Truman Head but everyone calls him California Joe and he's a great shot. At the Camp of Instruction in the Capitol, the sharpshooters put on daily demonstrations of their skills. President Lincoln visited that camp several times as did the local citizens."

"Have you killed many men with that rifle, James?"

"I'd just as soon not talk much about it. Just remember, Addison, soldiering is a job. It's not who you are. My first encounter with a Reb was at a creek. Both of us were going to fill our canteens. We stepped out of the brush on our own side of the creek, saw each other, and ran like scared rabbits. I was embarrassed and didn't tell anyone that I had run from a Reb, but it made me think. Why should I have wanted to kill that boy? I didn't know him, didn't have any grudge against him."

"Guess you're right, James. Never quite thought about it that way. What's that paper you're holding?"

The Penobscot man fingered the edges of the paper and reverently touched the words written upon it. For a moment, he was silent. Then he looked hard at Addison. There was an awkward silence as neither man spoke.

"Well, Addison Grant...," James began and hesitated. Again he looked thoughtfully at the white man who could just as well have been his enemy as his comrade.

"Go on, James. I really want to hear what's on the paper. Read it to me, please."

"Well, Addison," the sharpshooter began again. "This paper helps me remember why I joined the army. It's a copy of a speech that a great Penawahpskewi chief named Joseph Orono gave to his people when they decided to help your people fight the British who were coming up the Penobscot River. It's a great speech, although I can't help wondering if he would have felt that way if he had known then what would happen to our people after that war."

The Penobscot man looked again at the fragile piece of paper and chose to share what was written on it.

"The Great Spirit gives us freely all things. Our white brothers tell us they came to the Indian's country to enjoy liberty and life. A great sagamore is coming to bind them in chains, to kill them. We must fight him. We will stand on the same ground with them, for should he bind them in bonds, next he will treat us as bears. Indian liberties and land, his proud spirit, will tear away from them. Help his ill-treated sons. They will return good for good and the law of love runs through their children and ours when we are dead. Look down the stream of time, look up to the Great Spirit. Be kind, be valiant, be free. Then are the Indians sons of glory."

James Moody carefully refolded the paper and put it back in his pocket. For a long minute he stared at the ground, then raised his eyes to meet Addison's. The Penobscot man had been greatly moved by the speech. Tears carved a path through the dirt on his cheek and he did not wipe them away.

"Gosh, James, that was a powerful speech. I wish I could have heard him give it. Maybe we would not have won that war without your people. My great-grandfather was a hero in the battle to stop the British from coming up the Penobscot and taking over this part of the country. His name was Capt. James Grant."

James smiled a wry smile and looked into the eyes of his new friend as Addison related the family story of the heroic Capt. Grant and the battle for control of the great river that the Indians so revered and loved.

When Addison had finished, James sat
quietly for a moment. When he spoke, it was clear
that he was choosing his words very carefully.
"My friend Addison. The story that has been
passed down in your family is not quite true. The
Indians were there, too, and saw the whole battle,
if you can call it that. The British chased your
ships up the river until they were becalmed.
Perhaps your people were not paying attention to
the tides or had forgotten that the great river is
attached to the sea and moves with the tides of the
sea. Their ships had no wind and began to drift
down with the outgoing tide toward the British
ships that were waiting for them at the mouth of
the river.

"Fearing to be captured, your men sank their
ships and swam to shore. Some ships were set on
fire. Then the men ran into the forest. Even your
great hero Paul Revere, afraid to lose his ship and
his property, refused to pick up men from the
water. I'm sorry if I have ruined your family story,
but Indians do not lie and this is what happened
that day."

Furious, Addison gritted his teeth, turned
away, and decided not to argue. Over his shoulder
he told his new comrade that he would see him
later and walked back to his tree.

"Stupid Indians. What do they know about
wars?" he grumbled. The small yellow camp dog
that had attached himself to Addison lay down
next to him, snuggled up to his thigh, and laid his

head on Addison's leg. The boy put his hand on the dog's head and whispered to him.

"We'll be ok, dog. Stay close to me. You remind me a lot of my dog Bull at home, but he's bigger than you. I'm glad he's not here. He's not as savvy as you are. Wonder where you came from? Guess it doesn't matter. You're mine now. Let's get some food and rest. Tomorrow will be here soon enough."

*****

The Penobscot sharpshooter rose and walked over to a small lake. The eerie song of the loons reminded him of home. As the sun set over the water, the loons began to call. Then an owl hooted nearby.

"I hope you're wrong, wise bird. Do not call my name. I do not wish to die," James whispered to the quivering trees.

CHAPTER 8

As Antietam raged…

The young heifer, frightened by the roar of the nearby battle, ran in and out of the herd of older cows and their calves, not knowing what to do about the pain in her belly. She was carrying her first baby, a near-term calf sired by the farmer's best bull, and her time was near. She looked frantically for her mother who had tolerated the heifer's nursing longer than she should have, but could not find her. The war had interrupted many of the local farmers' usual practices, like separating calves at the proper time. And there were the hungry wild hogs, vultures, and packs of dogs. At least there was some safety in the herd, so the farmers left them together.

The pain intensified and the young heifer lay down in the grass. Vultures in the trees along the edge of the pasture were watching with their cruel yellow eyes. As the heifer struggled to birth her firstborn, the vultures floated into the air, circling, circling the scene below, waiting. Their activity attracted more of their kind, and soon the vultures that had been at work on the battlefield, joined their companions in the air above the young cow. The air was black with them.

Suddenly, as if by a prearranged signal, the flock began to circle lower and lower, closer and closer to the bovine victim below. The birds had learned from experience to recognize the coming event, and cocked their heads and stared intently as they flew, wings scarcely moving, riding the updrafts created by the heat of battle.

The heifer pushed hard and the calf began to emerge, nose tucked down on its front legs in what should have been a proper birth, but there was another force at work this day. The vultures, whose keen eyesight and sense of smell, alerted them to the emerging calf, dropped onto the struggling baby and began to tear it to pieces, eating it alive. Exhausted, the young cow tried to get to her feet, but the calf was not fully birthed, and she fell back on her side. She bawled for help from the herd members who had bunched together to protect their own young.

The defenseless calf mewled in protest at the horror he could not prevent, and succumbed. The heifer pushed one last time and bawled again for help from the others who only watched, chewing their cuds. They had seen it before. Some stopped staring and began to eat. Since the deafening noise of war began, the cows had seen the big black birds attack the newborn calves.

Had the heifer been older, she might have felt an urge to hide her travail in the woods, but even there the vultures usually found their victims, and claimed the calves and afterbirth as their own. The war had started this bizarre ritual, and the farmers were mostly helpless to stop it. Their weapons and ammunition had been confiscated first by one side and then the other as the battles surged back and forth across the farmlands, trampling the crops and ravaging the orchards. Hoping for an end to the war, the farmers kept breeding their cows and sheep and goats. The horses were gone. Confiscated. Most of them were dead, victims of the war.

CHAPTER 9

The Grant brothers did their best to keep in touch with one another, but mail from Georgia was slow to arrive in the North Country. Occasionally, the southern branch of the family sent money home to their mother, but as they each married and began families of their own, the money came less and less often. Joseph worried about the farm and his own family.

His brother Lemuel Pratt Grant had done very well for himself despite the fact that he was only nineteen when he left home to become a rod man for the Philadelphia and Reading Railroad. He showed mathematical genius even though he had almost no formal education. Eventually he became the Chief Engineer of the Atlanta & West Point Railroad, and was regarded as one of the brightest and ablest engineers in the South. That reputation led to the presidency of more than one railroad. A few years later, rumors of war began to drift about Atlanta like wisps of smoke from the engines of the trains whose tracks now crisscrossed the Deep South.

CHAPTER 10

After the slaughter at Antietam, the 7th
Maine – or what remained of it – was sent home to
recruit more men and remained in Maine until the
end of January.

*****

Julia had written often to her son Addison,
and believed that he would dread coming home to
face his father who had not written to him even
once during his recuperation in the field hospital.
His mother apologized to her wounded son for his
father's callousness, and told Addison that she had
heard the reports about Antietam. She knew the
firing had been horrific and thousands of boys had
died that day. At least Addison had not been
killed. Perhaps he would stay home now and help
with the farm. His father seemed weaker than
Julia had ever seen him before.

*****

When Addison's train arrived, his mother
and one sister met him at the railroad depot. As he
stepped down from the train, he grimaced in pain

and looked around for other friends and his father. No one else met him. Not even his sweetheart Emma. Her letters had tapered off quickly after he was wounded, and he could guess why. Emma's father had been a military man himself and from a long line of patriots and fighters. He often said he could not abide cowardice in any man. Addison assumed that Emma's father thought he had been running away when he was shot, and that her father probably was the reason why Emma had stopped writing.

Days dragged on into weeks of boredom and sadness for Addison. He could not bear to hear that his sweet Emma was forbidden to see him or come to the door when he stopped by her father's house. Her mother had died when Emma was young, and she had been raised to obey her father without question. Emma's father was polite to Addison's face when he told him that Emma could not see him, but cruel behind his back.

"Damned coward," he would snarl, closing the door on Addison's back as he sadly limped down the porch steps.

Julia grieved for her son's situation and angrily denied whispered rumors in Frankfort that Addison was a coward. Gradually she went to town less and less and worried more and more about Lemuel. A commissary sergeant, he was frequently away from the fighting, unlike his brother Addison who always seemed to be in the middle of it.

Addison grew distant from his father and scarcely spoke to him. They worked the farm together of necessity, but did not speak much. The horses remembered Addison and worked hard for him, never giving him any trouble, except once when a black bear wandered onto the edge of the hay fields looking for blueberries. Even then, though trembling at the dreaded scent, the Percherons hawed around and trotted off as Addison urged them to move away from the hungry beast. The horses carefully backed around and did not step over the traces that would have tipped the hay wagon. The bear ignored the horses' snorting and stamping and nosed around the edge of the field looking for wild fruit or anything else edible. Winter was approaching and she had a need to feed. She would birth cubs during the snows of winter while she slept in her den high on the hill.

One day in late fall, Addison heard that Emma was being courted by a banker's son who had returned as a wounded veteran. He had lost his left arm but still could ride a horse and drive a team. Addison went to his knees in grief and despair in the barn the night he heard the news. He just had to try once more, so he hurried to Emma's house. Her father let Addison stand on the porch for several minutes pounding on the door. Finally, he opened the door, drew himself erect, and told Addison to leave.

"Emma does not wish to see you, Addison, and neither do I. Please leave at once. You are no longer welcome in this house, sirrah. You are a coward and have no place among the fine people of Frankfort – certainly not with my daughter who is now betrothed. You may not see her."

At the word "coward", Addison roared with anger and grabbed the older man by the lapels.

"You weren't there, sir! You weren't there! I was not running away from the battle. We were in a crossfire. Was her fiancé shot from behind? Was his arm blown off from the front or the back? No one knows if he was running away, do they? I was not running away. Emma! Emma! Come down here! I must talk to you. Don't do this! For the love of God don't marry this man! I love you!"

Emma stood at the top of the stairs, covered her ears, and wept while her father and her younger brother heaved Addison bodily down the steps.

"I forbid you ever to see or talk to that man, Emma! Do you understand me?" her father bellowed. "Never, ever again! No man will have you if you disobey me or if you jilt your fiancé."

Emma retired weeping to her room. She would obey her father, but she would never love her fiancé as she loved Addison. If only she hadn't urged him to enlist, perhaps they could still have been together someday when the war was over. After all, with Lemuel already in the war,

Addison could have stayed home to take care of
the farm and his parents. Maybe this was all her
fault. She sobbed into her pillow until she finally
fell asleep.

Addison began to make new plans, as did
his mother. T. Cushing, a wealthy businessman
and friend of the Grant family wrote a letter that he
hoped would effect change in the minds of the
townspeople of Frankfort regarding Addison.

"23 Feb., 1864
To His Excellency
Gov. Cony
Dear Sir,
        Will you please take the following case into
consideration and if possible confer upon the
meritorious young man the favor he asks which is
a commission as Lieutenant, first or second in
some company now forming.
        Addison H. Grant now in his 22nd year,
enlisted Aug 13, 1861, was 18 months in service.
Has been engaged in ten battles, severely wounded
at Antietam, and lay in Hospital four months. In
consequence of this wound, received an honorable
discharge Feb 10, 1863 and had a pension settled
upon him for life. He now states that he has fully
recovered, although he has a rebel bullet in his
thigh, and he has given up his pension and
reenlisted Dec 31, 1863, I think in his old
Company B, 7th Me. Reg, and is now at or near
Brandy Station.

He intends to make the profession of arms his future vocation. He is a very good writer and has a fair common education. He is ambitious to excel in the profession of arms and has given good attention to the theory as well as the practice of military tactics.

Aside from this he is the son of parents who are in a great measure dependent upon him for support. I should rejoice to see such real merit rewarded by his being first in the line of promotion.

I am sure you will be glad to do for him all you can.

Most respectfully,
T. Cushing"

CHAPTER 11

Christmas had been joyless for Addison. He was not invited to the usual rounds of holiday parties and socials. Emma's father had been adamant about Addison not seeing his beautiful Emma and had announced her betrothal at an elegant Christmas engagement party. That was it, then. He could never again take her in his arms to whirl around the dance floor. He would never again walk with her down the backwoods lanes and pick brown-eyed susans or help fill her basket with sweet blueberries from the family farm. The wild ones often grew best at the undisturbed edges of cemeteries. The tame ones were fine, but not like the wild. It was as though the smaller wild berries became sweeter with the struggle to nourish themselves and cast their fruit at the end of the season. They propagated in quiet, secret places and cast their tiny seeds upon the earth.

New Year's Eve was fast approaching and the recruiters were in town again searching for young men they might have overlooked. The 7th

was recruiting again, too. A few of Addison's camp mates who knew the truth of his injury came to visit him and begged him to come back to the war. They needed experienced soldiers, even if they had been wounded. With his own kind, Addison knew that he could again hold his head high and feel like a man. His father scarcely acknowledged his presence in the house. When the haying was done Addison went to Palmyra to visit his cousins. Some also had been shot at one battle or another, and all had horrible and brave tales to tell.

One day just before the New Year came, Addison made up his mind. His cousins had pushed him too far. One too many teasing remarks. He bundled up against the cold and headed for Frankfort. His cousins apologized and begged him to wait for a break in the weather, but Addison refused. His stout gray gelding Ranger snorted and tossed his head every time the wind blew snow into his nostrils, and steam rose from his chest at the effort to break through the drifts. Addison pushed the big horse like a man possessed. Occasionally the horse stopped dead in his tracks, heaving and gasping for air. Snorting and shaking his mane the horse nearly went to his knees from exhaustion. Addison closed his eyes and kicked the horse mercilessly until he pushed on through the heavy wet snow. His cousins hadn't helped. Even they wondered if he had run away at Antietam. After all, he had been shot in the back of the hip. A little teasing pushed him over the edge.

"Damn all of you!" he had screamed. "I didn't run at Antietam! None of you were there! Fales was there. He can tell you! I'm going to Frankfort to re-enlist. I hope I never see any of you again, you miserable curs. I should have known even my own cousins wouldn't support me!"

When Addison arrived at Frankfort, he headed straight for the barn. He unsaddled the gasping, trembling horse who stood spraddle-legged with his nose nearly on the floor trying to catch his breath, gulping in great draughts of icy air. Ranger had nearly fallen over when Addison stepped down. Sweat dripped like foamy soap from the exhausted animal and his flanks were sunken in from dehydration.

Addison stared at the horse for a moment, and then was overwhelmed with shame and grief at the way he had treated his beloved Ranger. The young soldier knew he had nearly broken the horse's wind or even killed him. How could he have done this? He would never forgive himself if anything happened to the horse due to the ill treatment. While a new snowstorm raged outside the barn, whistling through the cracks in the old walls, Addison spent an hour tending to the horse, brushing his rough winter coat with straw and rags until it was nearly dry, then covering him with a heavy stable blanket against the winter chill. He gave the horse a few sips of water and waited a while before he gave him any more.

"I'm so sorry, Ranger" he said as he threw his arms around the horse's neck still sticky with half-dried sweat. "Please don't get sick and founder on me. I couldn't bear it. I nearly gave you the heaves as well."

At length, Addison gave the horse a small portion of hay and a few more sips of water. He would come back out after supper and finish taking care of Ranger. Right now, he had urgent business inside. He moved the water bucket away from the horse's stall and fought the strong wind as he struggled to get the barn door closed. Leaning into the wind, Addison pulled up his collar and pulled his hat down over his forehead. The cold, blowing gale force wind was giving him a headache.

*****

Ranger was content for a while with his sips of water and his bit of hay, but there was no grain in his manger. He was terribly hungry and now he was thirsty, too. The door to the grain room stood ajar, tempting the big horse. He knew where the feed was and backed against the wooden gate that kept him in his stall. After trying the stall door a few times with his muscular haunches, he pinned his ears like a mad cat and kicked the stall door into kindling wood.

Addison had not tied him in his stall so that he could lie down and rest from the hard ride. Ranger backed out of his stall, pushed the grain room door open with his nose, and inhaled the delicious smell of oats and bran.

His dinner was already mixed for him in a bucket and a bran mash stood beside it. Ranger eagerly ate the oats and the bran mash and then knocked both buckets on the floor. He grabbed the burlap sack of oats with his strong teeth and like a terrier shaking a rat he tore it open, spilling several quarts of oats on the floor. He turned for a moment to find the water bucket and drained it. Then he turned back to the great feast on the floor and ate for a long time.

At last, thirst slaked and appetite satisfied, he headed back to his stall to finish his hay. As he stepped into the stall, he suddenly dropped with a groan and rolled violently from side to side. A stabbing pain and pressure in his belly accompanied the fever that now raged through his body, but the pain in his feet was the worst. Ranger moaned in agony and lay gasping on the floor. Jewel nickered to her brother and pawed the floor. Outside, the snow and wind had begun again, and lights from the house cast distorted tree shadows across the glistening snow crust. Inside, another kind of drama was unfolding.

*****

"Father, you couldn't stop me before and you shall not stop me this time either! My unit needs me and there's nothing here for me. You hardly talk to me and neither does Mother anymore. My dearest Emma is betrothed to another man who simply lost his arm in the war. I had the misfortune to live with a wound that is a curse to me. Everyone here thinks I was a coward and ran away. Since my unit is here, ask them, Father. I am not a coward. Else I should have run away many times in many battles, but I did not. I am going to re-enlist.

"There is a bounty of two hundred forty dollars for re-enlisting and I shall give it all to you to help you with the farm. Maybe you can hire some man who was wounded in the war and can't make a living for himself. I shall no longer be a bother to you nor a target for the sneers of the townsfolk. Perhaps the fortunes of war will allow me to somehow prove my worth again and clear my good name. Please sign here, father. I'll go with or without your signature, of course, but it would be good to have it."

Joseph simply sighed this time and quietly signed the underage enlistment document. His nephew Augustus witnessed it. He was home on furlough for Christmas, and not much was happening at the moment on the battlefronts – at least not for the Maine boys.

Supper passed in silence and Addison regretted his sharpness with his father, but reasoned that his father deserved no more. He should have defended Addison against the charge of cowardice, but allowed it to go on. Even Lemuel could not believe that the people in town would assume the worst about his brother. The fact that he had served bravely in many battles seemed to matter little. The wound at the back of his hip had become a badge of dishonor.

     After supper, Addison stood at the door looking out at the falling snow. The Maine winter chilled the heat of battle and numbed the warriors to the point that little happened during that winter at least. Perhaps somewhere men were dying, but Addison chose not to think about the war for the moment. As he looked out the door his eyes wandered to the barn and he gasped. He had heard some thumping noises in the barn but had ignored them. Now he grabbed his coat and hat and raced out the door. Joseph's question fell on deaf ears, so he also put on a coat and followed his son to the barn.

     When Addison neared the barn door, he could hear the horse groaning and snorting and knew something terrible had happened. As he shoved the door open he saw the open grain room door, the torn burlap sack, and the smashed stall gate. Addison fell to his knees by the big gray and sobbed.

     "Oh Ranger! What have I done to you?"

     Joseph looked at the shattered stall door and the empty torn sack of oats on the floor and put his hands on the horse's hooves.

     "It's too late, son. Ranger is dying. He's probably got the colic, but he's definitely foundered. I'll ride to town for the blacksmith. Perhaps he can do something for him. There's too much heat and pain in his feet for him to stand, though. I'm afraid that…"

Joseph could not finish the sentence and quickly saddled the black mare and rode to the smithy. After hearing the story, the smithy shook his head, gathered a few things, and saddled the stout part-draft bay that was the only horse able to carry his huge muscular bulk. He checked to see that his pistol was loaded, then followed Joseph back to the farm.

When they entered the barn, the blacksmith stared for a moment and again shook his head. Addison had wrapped the horse's feet in wet rags, desperately trying to stop the founder that was killing his horse, but it didn't seem to be helping.

"Smithy, please do something for my horse. I'm afraid I've killed him. I rode him too hard and didn't stay out here long enough with him. While I was in the house, Ranger kicked down the stall door, got into the feed, and drank a whole bucket of cold water. Can you help him?"

The blacksmith worked for an hour or more trying to undo the damage, but the horse had colic and was foundered as well. There was an old Indian remedy he might try, but it hadn't worked in the past. If he could stop the colic perhaps that would buy some time to do something about the founder. Perhaps I'll be lucky, thought the blacksmith.

"The longer the horse stays down, the worse it is, you know. I don't know if this horse can bear the pain if we try to get him up, Addison."

Grimly, Smithy set to work again. He was sure the horse was dead and just hadn't figured it out yet.

"Addison," Joseph said quietly as he laid his hand on his trembling son's shoulder. "Addison, we have to put the horse down. He's suffering terribly and there's nothing to be done for him. He's got the colic bad and his feet are foundered. It's not kind to let him go on like this. We have to do the right thing by him."

"It's my horse, Father, not yours. I was hurt this bad or worse and they didn't shoot me. I survived the pain. Why shouldn't I give him his chance? Besides, this is all my fault. I can't just shoot him and walk away. I have to try everything. What else can we do, Smithy?"

Smithy looked at the horse and knew it was beyond his ability to save him.

"Well, Addy, there's an Indian medicine man visiting the parson. It's not far to his house. I'll go and get him. Maybe there's something he knows to do for the horse. I'll hurry."

Smithy hurried to town and banged on the parson's door until he woke up everyone in the house. The shaman was indeed visiting his friend, and agreed at once to see the horse. He picked up a bag of herbs while the parson hitched up his sleigh. They followed the smithy to the Grant farm, threw a carriage blanket over the driving horse and hurried into the barn.

By this time the horse was becoming shocky and responding to very little. The parson prayed over the horse while the shaman examined him.

"Very sick. Not much I can do, but I'll try."

The shaman touched Addison's arm gently and looked into his eyes.

"I'll try. The Great Spirit will decide."

The healer kneeled by the stricken horse and ran his hands slowly down the horse's side from shoulder to haunch, then put his ear on the belly and listened. He put his ear on the flank and listened again. He rose and raised his arms, praying for the horse and asking guidance from the Great Spirit and from Glooscap the creator of animals. The men backed away from the horse so as not to interfere with the shaman's attempts to heal the animal and all knelt again and began to pray in silence that God would intervene in this tragic illness and save Ranger.

"Much fever in the feet, friend Addison. Pray hard for your horse. I do not know if the Great Spirit wants this horse to live. He is a brave and beautiful horse. Perhaps the Great Father wants this horse for himself. I do not know."

*****

Addison wept. If only he could turn back the grandfather clock in the house and do it over, do it right. This shouldn't have happened. At least

he should have waited until morning to leave
Palmyra.

*****

The smithy knew that the horse was almost
certain to die, and was glad that someone else
would be the last to treat him. At least he had tried
everything he knew how to do. Perhaps the great
medicine man knew something more and could
heal the horse, but Smithy doubted it.

*****

Again and again, the gray-haired healer ran
his hands down the length of Ranger's body,
praying and speaking softly under his breath. No
one could understand what he was saying but it did
not matter. He was speaking with the Great Spirit,
imploring Him to let Addison keep the horse. He
prayed until dawn showed slightly in the black
eastern sky. The night had been bitter, but at least
the snow had stopped.

The shaman spoke more urgently, again
begging for the horse's life. Whereas the horse
had scarcely moved during the night, he was now
swishing his tail and moving his feet slightly.

"Stand back," the shaman said as the horse
stirred. "He must not get up until he has come
back from the place where his spirit has been. He
might fall."

Ranger raised his head slightly and looked
at the men. He sighed, put his head down and
made no further effort to rise.

"Your horse is strong, Addison. He is a great horse, but I do not know if the Great Spirit is going to let you keep him."

By the time the rising sun had brightened the Dixmont Hills, the horse was showing possible signs of recovery. Then, as swiftly as Ranger had seemed to be improving, he suddenly took a turn for the worse. He groaned and tried to roll onto his back. A few neighbors had come to help and several men tried to stop him, but even in his weakened condition, the gray horse managed to roll over and crashed against the stall wall with his feet leaning against the wooden slats.

"He's cast! He's cast!" yelled the smithy. "Get him back over or we'll lose him for sure!"

The men grabbed Ranger's tail and pulled him away from the wall. As the horse thrashed and fought, he kicked one man in the head and knocked him unconscious. The smithy dragged the man away from the horse's flailing shod hooves and checked his pulse.

"Is he alive?" whispered the parson.

"Yes, parson, he's alive. Just knocked out is all. I think he'll be okay later. I'll watch him. You men see to the horse."

The blacksmith shook his head as he watched the men struggle with the stricken animal.

The old medicine man stood up and with tears in his eyes took Addison by the arm.

"Addison, my friend, I believe the Great Spirit wants your horse for himself. Ranger is in terrible pain and there is no more I can do. You must decide what to do next."

The boy dropped to his knees and sobbed.

Joseph walked over to his son as the other men tried desperately to keep the horse from rolling over again.

"Addison, your horse is in terrible pain and none of us here know anything more to do for him. You must put him down. You must do it now."

*****

Addison bowed his head and rocked back and forth, burying his face in his hands. Even though he had seen much death and destruction and countless dead and dying horses, he didn't know if he could shoot his friend, a horse that he had helped train.   Smithy started to draw the pistol from his pocket, but Joseph laid his hand on the burly arm and shook his head.

"No need, Smithy, I've my own here. I didn't think any of us, not even our friend the shaman could save this animal. Would all of you please step outside, friends? I thank you for your help. This is something Addison must do himself, and I'm sure he wants a few minutes alone with his horse."

Joseph handed his son an 1851 Colt Navy Revolver, put his hand on the boy's shoulder and stood by his side for a moment, then without a word he walked outside. Addison wept bitterly. Sobs stuck in his throat.

*****

"I'm so sorry, Ranger. I'm so sorry. You've been such a good horse. You didn't deserve this; you didn't deserve this. Oh, Ranger. Forgive me for causing you so much pain. God help me to do this right. I'm afraid, Ranger. I've had to do this before in the war, but this is different. God, please help me do this right. Help me."

Addison stood up and stared at his groaning, thrashing horse. What if he missed? What if there wasn't a clean shot? He wiped his eyes on his jacket sleeve and stepped into the next stall away from the flying hooves. With shaking hands he raised the pistol and took careful aim. As he did so, Ranger groaned, looked at his weeping master and lay still, his wet sides heaving.

*****

Outside, the men waited, almost collectively holding their breaths.

"Can the boy do this, Joseph? Do we need to help him?" whispered the blacksmith. "Ah, I hate to bring this up, but remember Antietam."

"Yes, Smithy, Addison can do this. He has to do this. He's to blame, no one else. Nobody must try to help him. And you're all wrong about Antietam. I spoke with some men from the 7th while they were up here recruiting. My boy is no coward."

The shaman nodded and raised his hands to heaven, softly imploring on the boy's behalf, summoning the powers of the ancestors and the kindness of the Great Spirit.

Bang! The shot echoed in the barn, and all the horses that the men had taken outside startled and jumped. The black mare neighed and pawed the dirt, straining to get back inside to her brother. Joseph and Smithy stood outside the barn door waiting.

"Joseph? No chance that Addison... I mean that in the state of mind he's in...you know...there's no chance, is there? Should we go inside?" whispered the blacksmith as he twisted his black wool cap around in his chubby hands.

"No Smithy. No. There's no chance. He did the right thing. Let him be. We'll just wait out here."

"Um, Joseph, I'm that sorry that I couldn't save your horse."

"You did your best, Smithy. No one faults you."

Smithy nodded and stared at the ground. Minutes passed and still Addison did not emerge from the barn.

Joseph sighed.

"Gentlemen, I thank you for all of your help. I'll take care of things from here on. I know that Addison will thank you personally. Give him a day or two, would you please? You've all been most kind, and I'm sure you're all very tired."

The weary father walked over to the shaman to thank him, but the man just pointed over

Joseph's shoulder to the barn. The men all turned
around and saw Addison coming from the barn
with tears streaming down his face, and his breath
coming in labored, tortured gasps. The smoking
pistol dangled at the end of an arm numb with
grief.

    "Thank you all so very much. Please
forgive me, but I'd like to be alone. I'm sorry.
Here's your pistol back, father. Thank you. God
helped me and I only needed one shot. Don't
know if I could have fired a second shot. Ranger
seemed to know that he had to help me, and he lay
still just long enough for me to put him out of his
pain and misery."

    Addison walked toward the house where his
mother was waiting. She wept when he told her he
would re-enlist. The next morning he was gone
with the troops the 7th Maine had gathered up.
Along with Addison were a number of Indian men,
including an older married man named Samuel
who was a sharpshooter.

*****

    Samuel's mother did not care much for
making anything except mats and baskets because
materials took much time to gather, and baskets
and mats were useful. When her son wrote to her
that he badly needed mittens and woolen
underdrawers, she spoke to the old women of the
tribe. One old woman showed her something that
few women remembered anymore. The mane of
the moose had soft gray wool at the base where it

grew out of the neck. If Samuel's mother wanted a
yarn with which to create mittens and
underdrawers then she should collect that fur and
roll it on her thigh with an open palm. The fur
would mat into threads that could be used to make
clothing.

It didn't take long for Sam's mother to
collect enough fur to begin making a kind of yarn.
The missionaries in the area showed her how to
knit the yarns and even gave her some wooden
needles. Sam was overjoyed with her gifts and
thanked the Great Spirit for such a good mother
and the wife who had borne him children.

Sam had been interested in Addison's family
when they were visiting prior to leaving for the re-
enlistment. He was surprised to discover that both
of their fathers were named Joseph. Perhaps that
made them some kind of brothers, but Addison
thought otherwise. There was no Indian blood in
his lineage, he was sure. Sam just shook his head
and didn't try to explain.

One night while the unit was camped near a
lake, the Penobscot man heard loons crying in the
dark. Some people thought it sounded like a
woman in childbirth, but Sam loved the sound.
There were many loons in Maine, and these
beautiful black and white birds reminded him of
home. Loons could dive so fast that it was
impossible to hit them with gun or arrow. They
dove at the sound of the string or shot. Sam
admired the birds for their intelligence as well as

their beauty, and loved to watch the babies riding around on their mother's back. There they were safe from predator fish and turtles, but not entirely from the air. Mother loons always lost some of their babies every year. Sam wondered if they knew the names of the lost ones or if they mourned. Did they know, like chickens, which ones were theirs? Did they, like broody hens, peck to death the ones who were not? Perhaps that was the real meaning behind their cries in the night.

Samuel wiped down his expensive rifle stock with a rag and wished he didn't have the skill to use it. A sharpshooter took deliberate aim at another man – didn't just fire at a group or a line of soldiers. He had lost track of how many men he had killed. Being older than most of the men didn't help. Sometimes he was with the 7th Maine and sometimes he got detached and sent to another unit that needed him.

All of Berdan's sharpshooters moved around depending on where they were needed most. After a while, it all seemed to matter very little where he was. The night air was cold and his breath steamed in front of his face. He preferred to sleep outside on the ground when he could. He knew there were poisonous snakes around when the weather was warmer, but they got in the tents, too. No matter. If the Great Spirit was displeased with his part in this war, He would take him. Many of the Indian men had already died or been captured. Sam wondered aloud how many were dead or

dying or horribly wounded, and how many would
be left to return to Maine at the end of this war.
Everyone had thought it would be over quickly,
but there seemed no end in sight.

With a yawn Samuel stretched his arms to
the night sky and silently asked the Great Spirit for
His blessing. Tomorrow would be another day.
Perhaps he would die. He could not tell. A Great
Horned Owl stretched his wings and thrust his
head forward. The yellow eyes stared at the man
as the bird turned his head almost all the way
around to watch him return to his tent.

CHAPTER 12

After the formal engagement had been announced, Emma sank into despair. She tried repeatedly to talk to her father, but he would raise his hand in warning and leave the room.

"Father, I need to talk to you. Please. I just do not love Gilbert. He frightens me sometimes, Father. Gilbert can be so mean. I love Addison. Why can't you see that?" she would begin.

A stern widower, her father would glare at her and refuse to discuss the matter. She must not know of his weakening condition. He had sworn Dr. Blessing to secrecy. Before his heart gave out, Edward would see his only daughter safely wed. Gilbert did seem to have a dark side to him, but his father was a banker after all, so Emma would always be well cared for. There would be money.

On a sunny afternoon when the birds were twittering in anticipation of spring, such as it was in Maine, or "mud season" as the people called it, Gilbert drove to Emma's house and tied up his bay carriage horse that was dripping sweat. The horse tried to drop her head to catch her breath and stretch her back, but the cruel checkrein prevented it, and Gilbert couldn't be bothered to give the animal any relief. He never warmed her up, drove too fast, and didn't cool her down properly. Everyone in town had learned to get out of his way if they were about to meet him on the road.

"Damn fool!" Dr. Blessing had muttered earlier as he dodged Gilbert's flying carriage. "I've got a baby to deliver, for heaven's sake! That young idiot darn near ran me off the road. Doesn't do any good to talk to his father, either. I brought the boy into the world. Sometimes wish I'd let him just stay blue and die. Hard delivery for his mother. Harder rearing him. Not like his older brother at all. Oh well. There's always a black sheep.

"Come along, girl," he cooed to his old chestnut mare. "Don't know what I'd do without you. Many's the time you've brought me home safe and sound when I had fallen asleep and dropped the reins, you old rascal. Aren't you glad that I don't put a fancy checkrein on ya to keep your head high! Stupid idea. Horse can't breathe right and their backs get sore. C'mon, Gertrude! That baby won't wait much longer. Let's go.

"Guess Gilbert was going to see Emma. Wish her father hadn't encouraged that courtship. I've never liked that boy. Still not quite sure what happened to the Reynolds girl years ago. Gilbert was the last one to see her alive."

Dr. Blessing sighed and chirped to his mare. "Don't borrow trouble, Gerty. Don't borrow trouble. Sufficient unto the day and all that."

*****

Gilbert walked up the steps and opened the front door. without knocking.

"Emma! Come down here. I'm taking you for a buggy ride. Hurry up."

Edward Long stepped into the drawing room and stared at the unannounced intruder.

"You might have knocked, young man. I'm not accustomed to finding people standing in my front room."

"Well, Edward, I'm practically your son-in-law, am I not? You'll get used to it."

Emma brushed her hair and smoothed the dress her mother had made. Since her mother had died birthing her, it was one of the few things she had of her mother's. Gibby hadn't said anything about a carriage ride today. She stared into the mirror behind her vanity table. Her mother had made the pretty pink coverlet that lay on her bed and reflected in the glass. Emma stared at the reflection and thought about her gentle mother. Her father had told her much about her mother. He had loved her dearly. Sometimes Emma wished that the birthing bed fever had taken her as well. Did her father blame her for her mother's death in childbirth? With a deep sigh, Emma brushed back a wisp of blonde hair and turned to go down the narrow stairs.

The old house had been built to accommodate servants who came and went by the back staircase. Emma's room was at the top of the brown painted wooden stairs and would have been a maid's room if they could have afforded servants. The high dormer window admitted daylight unless the sky was overcast, and then the room was dark and gloomy. She would have preferred the sunny room in the front of the house, but her father would not allow it. That had been his wife's sewing room and nothing in it had changed since the day she died.

"Hurry up, Emma, for heaven's sake! Let's go!" Gilbert bellowed.

"My daughter is not accustomed to being shouted at like a stray animal, Gilbert. You will not address her in such a rude fashion!" said Edward as his face flushed in anger.

"I'll address her any way I please, old man! She's about to be my wife and you'll have nothing more to say bout it," sneered Gilbert. "I'm the best she's going to get after having been bespoken to Addison Grant, the coward. And my father is rich. Remember that, old man."

Emma appeared in the doorway.

"It's alright, father. Next time I'll hurry. I didn't know you were coming today, Gilbert. I'll just get my wrap," Emma said as she stepped off the last step onto the multi-colored rag rug her mother had made years ago.

"You don't need a wrap, Emma. Just come on! I want to go right now," Gilbert said as he reached for the door.

When Emma hesitated, Gilbert grabbed her arm and pulled her toward the door. Emma sighed and tried to ignore the uneasy feeling that had been growing over the last few weeks. Sometimes Gilbert frightened her. He could be so rough and rude. She didn't love him. She was sure of that. Emma couldn't help thinking about Addison nearly every waking moment. He invaded her dreams like an impatient lover. Why couldn't her father see how mean Gilbert was to her? Why couldn't she marry the man she loved? He and Lemuel would inherit the Grant farm one day, and it had always provided for the family.

"Get in the carriage, Emma! Hurry up!" Gilbert yelled as he walked to the right side and stepped up into the carriage, leaving Emma to fend for herself. "You're so damned slow! Like a sick cow! Get in the carriage!"

Emma struggled with her dress, trying not to catch it on anything or to soil it. Suddenly, the horse shied and the buggy lurched backward, throwing Emma to the ground.

"Oh for the love of heaven, Emma! Can't you even get in a carriage without falling down? Get up, get up!"

Emma heard the ripping sound as she fell and was horrified to see the long tear in her skirt where the wheel had caught it. Perhaps if she folded the material just right, no one would see it. Gilbert did.

"I suppose now you'll have to change your dress and that will take hours," he barked at her. "Oh just get in. Maybe that will teach you to be more careful. When we're married, there won't be any extra money for dresses. If you tear something you'll just have to wear it."

Emma grabbed the handrail and climbed onto the seat. She wasn't even settled in her place when Gilbert whipped the horse into a brisk trot and nearly knocked her down again. They rode in silence, and Emma wondered why Gilbert had shown up without telling her in advance.

The horse's hooves clattered across the old bridge over the Cattamawawa Stream as Gilbert drove the mare at a reckless pace. Stone-faced, he said nothing to his bewildered fiancé until they reached the edge of the woods and he stopped the sweaty, heaving horse.

"Get down, Emma," Gilbert said as he walked to the edge of the stream and stared into the water. He didn't offer to help Emma down out of the carriage and he hadn't even dropped the anchor to tether the horse. Emma held her breath and prayed that nothing would frighten the horse as she climbed down out of the seat.

Emma walked over to her fiancé and stood quietly, utterly at sea as to Gilbert's intentions.

"What is the matter, Gilbert?" Emma whispered. "Why are you so angry?"

Gilbert spun on his heel and glared at her. "I've heard that you've been writing to that piece of trash, Addison Grant. Is this true?"

"Good heavens, no, Gilbert! I've not written to Addison since my father broke the engagement. Where on earth did you hear that?"

"It doesn't matter, Emma. I've heard it. Tell me now. Do you still love Addison? Do you love me?"

Emma realized that Gilbert must know she still had feelings for Addison, and that since her father had arranged this marriage, she did not love Gilbert.

Her silence as she tried to think what she should say gave him his answer.

"I thought so, Emma! You still love Addison, don't you! You're wearing my ring and you still love Addison!" Gilbert yelled at her.

Emma quickly put her right hand in her pocket to hide the hammered silver ring that Addison had given her before he went to war. Gilbert grabbed her left hand and shook it in her face.

"You're wearing my ring, Emma! You belong to me! Get back in the buggy. Now!"

As they drove back to Emma's house in silence, Emma could feel her heart pounding in her chest. She could hardly breathe. Gilbert was crimson-faced and sweating profusely, and she hardly dared to look at him. Who had told him that she was writing to Addison? It wasn't true, although she wished she could. And why would anyone say such a thing? Panic began to set in as they drove.

Gilbert yanked the horse to a stop in front of the Long house and waited for Emma to get out.

"I'll be back tomorrow. Be ready by noon," he said, barely giving her time to climb down from the carriage. "And don't wear that shabby dress. Wear something nice for a change."

"Yes, Gilbert. I'll be ready at noon."

*****

Edward Long stared through the lace curtains his wife had made for their house and watched his future son-in-law jerk the driving horse around and drive off as though the devil was after him. When his daughter came through the door with her torn dirty dress and shattered look, he feared the worst.

"What happened, Emma! Tell me at once! Did he touch you?"

"No father, it's just that someone told him that I'm still writing to Addison. It's not true! I don't know who would say such a thing or why. Gibby is coming for me at noon tomorrow. Papa, I'm afraid. I think he's dangerous."

"Nonsense. If he thinks you're still pining over Addison, then of course he'd be angry. It will pass. Perhaps he has a nice outing planned for tomorrow. Don't worry, dear," Edward said with more confidence than he felt.

*****

When Gilbert came for Emma the next day, it was as though he were a different man. He smiled at Emma, shook her father's hand, apologized for his manners the previous day, and even helped Emma into the buggy. He complimented her on her pretty dress. "I brought a picnic lunch that I bought in town at the baker's, Emma. And here are some flowers. I hope you like them. I'm so sorry that I was awful to you yesterday. I guess I'm just a jealous fool, my dear. You're so beautiful. I can't bear the thought of anyone else in your lovely head. Let's go down to the stream and have a nice picnic."

Emma didn't know whether to believe him or not. Too many times over the last few months, she had seen his dark moods and flashes of anger. Was this the real Gibby or was yesterday's man the real one? Perhaps if she were just quiet today and listened to him without comment, he wouldn't be angry with her again. Perhaps it was her fault after all.

As they neared the stream, Dr. Blessing passed them going back to town.

"No baby yet, Dr. Blessing?" Emma called over to him.

The doctor stopped his horse and shook his head.

"It's her first one, Emma, and sometimes those babies take a long time deciding. I'll go back out in a few hours. Have to catch up on my other patients in town first. Have a lovely day children. I brought both of you into the world, so I guess I can call you my children, right?" he said with a chuckle. "Come on, Gertrude. Let's get back to town, girl. Gee up!"

Gilbert drove to the grove of trees downstream from the bridge. Emma stared at the spot, thought about Addison and turned her head away, afraid the bright roses on her cheeks might betray her. She took Gilbert's arm when he offered it and walked close to the stream. There had been a heavy rain a day or two ago and the water was higher then normal, roaring over the mossy rocks where normally a gentle stream flowed.

Gilbert walked into the woods away from the road and made a great show of laying out the blanket, the picnic basket and the flowers. He had even brought a vase for the flowers, and he filled it at the water's edge.

"Oops! I almost fell in, Emma! The bank is slippery. Water's higher than usual," he said with a nervous laugh.

"Do be careful, Gibby! We've come for a picnic, not a swim! This food looks delicious! What a treat!"

Gilbert handed Emma a plate of fried chicken, corn on the cob, and potato salad garnished with thin slices of tomato. She declined the sherry that he urged upon her.

"Do you think I mean anything improper, Emma? Can't you indulge me for once and share this expensive bottle of sherry with me? What can it hurt? Just this once? I feel so awful about yesterday. Please have just a few sips with me."

"Well, I don't know, Gibby. What would my father say? Our family doesn't drink spirits."

"Oh pish posh Emma! Sherry isn't spirits! It's just a special kind of wine. Here, hand me that glass from the basket. Just have a little taste."

*****

Emma felt that something wasn't right, but she wasn't sure what, exactly, was wrong. She didn't trust Gilbert and she didn't want the wine. She fussed over the flowers and rearranged them while her fiancé poured a small amount of sherry into her glass. She had never drunk it and didn't know what to expect, so she was pleasantly surprised at the fruity taste as she slowly raised the glass to her lips.

"Oh Gilbert, this is very good. I can see why your family likes wine. May I have a little more, please? It's quite delicious!"

*****

Gilbert poured a little more into her glass and watched her as her face flushed. He looked back toward the old wooden bridge and watched for a few minutes, listening for the sound of hoof beats on the road. He had driven his buggy out of sight into the woods, and his horse – with her checkrein undone – was happily munching on the sweet timothy grass.

*****

Emma felt a little giddy and she knew her face was flushed. Perhaps she should not drink any more, but it was so good. Only just now she noticed the strange, almost bitter aftertaste, and she realized that Gilbert had not touched his glass.

"Do you like the laudanum, my sweet? I've practically lived on it since I lost my arm in the war. Doc gives it to me whenever I run out. Sure kills the pain. I put a little of it in your drink."

"What is laudanum, Gibby? I'm sorry. I feel so strange. I think I'll just take a nap for a moment. Why didn't you drink any wine?"

"I didn't need it, Emma. But it's lovely, isn't it?"

Emma fought the fog as long as she could. Something wasn't right. She was afraid. What was happening to her?

"Just lie down for a few minutes, Emma. You'll feel better soon. I'll wake you up in a little while. There, there, just lie still. Don't you feel wonderful?"

"Gilbert! What's wrong with me? Am I dying?"

"Hush now, Emma. Just let it flow over you. Isn't it a lovely feeling?"

Emma tried to sit up and regain control of her senses. Her heart raced and she could feel her own pulse in her throat. When she tried to stand up, she lost her balance and fell back on the blanket. Panic became fear as she stared into Gilbert's eyes.

"Emma, Emma, my dear, don't struggle so! Just lie still and the feeling will pass. Trust me. I wouldn't harm you, my dear!"

"Gilbert, take me home this instant. I want to see my father. I don't love you, Gilbert. I tried to, but I just can't. I still love Addison. I can't marry you," gasped Emma.

"Really. So it's true that you've been writing to Addison. I thought as much! How dare you play me for a fool, you whore! Well, my dear, if I can't have you, no one will!" said Gilbert, his lips curled like a snarling dog.

"I haven't been writing to Addison! I just know that I still love him. You frighten me, Gilbert. I don't want to be your wife."

As Emma tried once more to rise, Gilbert hit her hard with his right fist and knocked her out. He looked around to see if anyone could see him, and then dragged her deeper into the woods. He'd have what he wanted and he'd have it now. As he started to remove her clothes, he heard the clip-clop of a horse's hooves approaching the bridge. Gilbert grabbed the pillow he had brought and put it across Emma's face and leaned on it. The doctor's horse-drawn buggy clattered across the bridge and disappeared down the road.

"Damn!" Gilbert said. Unsure of himself and what he should do next, he continued to lean on the pillow until Emma was completely unconscious.

"Can't let her tell the story to her father," he muttered. Well, it had worked once before when he was younger. It would work again. After listening carefully for any other horses and hearing none, Gilbert dragged Emma to the riverbank and pushed her in. Just as he did that, he saw the diamond engagement ring sparkle like an errant star in the pristine water. He rushed into the stream, scattering black ducks as he reached for Emma's limp hand. He straddled her body and held her arm under the stump that had been his left arm, while he wrenched the ring off her left hand. In his hurry he failed to see the silver ring on her other hand as he let her body drift down the stream.

His britches were soaked but that was fine. They would just convince everyone that he had tried to save her. And this time there were no bruises on the girl's neck. He'd learned that lesson with the Reynolds girl.

Just as Gilbert clambered up the bank he heard the now-familiar clip-clop of Dr. Blessing's mare. Gilbert made a quick decision, timing his bedraggled appearance just as the doctor's buggy approached the bridge again.

"Doctor, Doctor!" Gilbert yelled. "Stop, please! There's been an accident! Help me! Emma's fallen in the stream!"

"What's that you're saying, Gilbert? Emma's fallen in the Cattamawawa here? How did that happen? Good heavens, man! Help me get her out! She might be drowning! How long has she been in the water?"

"Just a few minutes, Dr. Blessing! Just a few minutes! I couldn't hold her with just my right arm, sir! She just slid down the bank, sir!"

The pudgy doctor huffed and puffed as he waddled along the bank like some fattened goose. He could see Emma, but the stream was higher than normal and was running faster than he could manage along the slick bank. Annoyed, the doctor snarled over his shoulder to Gilbert who didn't seem to be in much of a hurry.

"Hurry, man, damn it! Hurry! What's wrong with you?"

"I, um, I turned my ankle, Dr. Blessing, when I was trying to get hold of Emma. Must have been amongst the rocks. I'm sorry. I'm hurrying as best I can."

"Bah," snorted the elderly doctor. "Just hurry up, Gilbert! She's getting away from us!"

In desperation, the older man finally started shedding his clothes. That's when he noticed that Gilbert still had his boots on. And all of his clothes. His britches were soaked to the knees, but nothing else was even damp. He'd have to check

that later. Right now it was urgent that he catch up
with the girl whose limp body, like a waterlogged
rag doll, was bumping along downstream, headed
straight for some unseasonable rapids. If she
wasn't already dead, he thought to himself, she'd
certainly drown in the white water.

"Help me, Gilbert, damn you boy! I'm
going in after her. Run ahead of me and try to stop
her from going over the spillway by the mill!
Hurry!"

Gilbert made a show of hurrying along the
bank, and dragged his left leg for emphasis. The
doctor threw himself into the stream, reasoning
that perhaps he could swim faster than he could
run. When he hit the cold water, he gasped and
swallowed some of it. His wire-rimmed spectacles
fell off, and he could hardly see.

A large rock loomed ahead of him, but the
doctor could not avoid it, as the swirling eddy
turned him around. He floundered, trying to get
past the rock, but he spun headfirst into it and
cracked his head on the mossy stone.

"Help me, Gilbert! Help me, please! I can't
see and I've smacked my head on that rock. Help
me get out! We'll have to run along the bank
instead. The water's too fast and I'm too old."

Gilbert hesitated for a moment and then
smiled. This was perfect. He grabbed for the
doctor who was desperately hanging onto the
slippery boulder, and pulled him to the shore.

"I'll go after Emma, sir! You rest here and catch your breath."

Gilbert ran along the bank, forgetting to drag his leg as he tried to catch sigh of Emma.

"There she is in those rocks," he gasped as he ran to her.

He could scarcely believe what he saw, but her eyes were open and she was trying to speak to him with her arms stretched out to him. In an instant, he jumped into the water and he pushed her head under water until she stopped struggling and he was sure she was dead. Then he put his arm around her waist, being careful to keep her face in the water just in case.

"Help me, doctor! I've got her! The current is so strong I don't know if I can hang onto her with just one arm! Help me!"

Dr. Blessing lurched to his feet and stumbled along the bank. Blood trickled down his forehead. He pressed his hand against the cut to stem the flow of blood. Age had slowed his gait and he could hardly breathe when he got to the rocks above the spillway.

"Hang on, boy! I'm coming! Don't let go of her!"

Gilbert had pulled Emma's face back out of the water just before the doctor got there, and began sobbing and crying, calling her 'beloved" and "Dearest Emma" as he hung onto her, slyly watching her face for any sign of life.

The two men wrestled Emma from the clutches of the Cattamawawa and dragged her onto the grassy bank. The doctor turned her onto her side and thumped her on the back. He listened for a heartbeat and felt for a pulse, but there was nothing. Her eyes were fixed and lifeless, and the good country doctor had seen death often enough in his lifetime to recognize it now. The only hope was that she had been in very cold water. He did not feel *rigor mortis* yet.

"Help me get her into the buggy, Gilbert. You follow me to town in yours. Hurry! Perhaps I can still save her, but I fear the worst, boy, I fear the worst."

Gilbert took a minute to look around at the scene of the crime. He picked up the wine bottle and the glasses and stashed them under the seat in his buggy.   He left the picnic blanket and the food where it was.

"Hyah, Gertrude! Yah, yah! Run, mare, run for all you're worth!" the doctor shouted at his usually docile animal. Startled, the mare took off, and galloped straight for the doctor's office. The buggy careened onto one wheel as they flew around the general store.

"Get out of the way! Get out of the way everyone!" the doctor screamed.

People scattered like free-range hens, and women picked up their skirts as they scampered out of the street.

"What is it, doctor?" the constable hollered as the buggy flew past him.

"No time now! Come to my office," the doctor yelled over his shoulder.

Several men were already waiting by his office door when he pulled the heaving, sweaty mare to a halt.

"Someone take my mare and unhitch her! Cool her down! You other men come and help me with Emma. Help me get her into my office!"

When he had Emma on the table, he shooed the men out the door. Almost at once a little knot of concerned friends gathered outside, and an anxious hush fell over the cluster of people. Emma's father ran to the doctor's office and shoved open the door. Red in the face and out of breath, he gasped out his question.

"What's happened to Emma, doctor? What is it? Is she going to be all right?"

The doctor shook his head and sent him outside.

"Just wait, Edward, just wait. I don't know yet."

Gilbert drove up to the doctor's surgery and pulled his horse to a halt.

"Someone take my horse, please! Take my horse!" he yelled with uncharacteristic concern. The liveryman scowled and spat at Gilbert as he unhitched the horse and walked it down the street. As he approached the barn, he called to his stable boy, gave him a coin, and told him to walk both horses cool and dry. Then he headed back to the doctor's office.

The doctor would not let Gilbert inside, and Edward Long looked carefully at his daughter's fiancé. Just this morning, she had told him that she was afraid of Gilbert. Had Gilbert harmed Emma? All Edward could think about at the moment was his beautiful daughter, his only child. He had promised her dying mother that he would take care of her. Had he failed?

*****

Dr. Blessing listened intently for any signs of breathing and held a small mirror over Emma's mouth, hoping to see even the tiniest cloud of breath. Nothing. There was a faint odor of something familiar and he closed his eyes, trying to identify it. Something that shouldn't be in this young girl's mouth. The old man held her left hand as he stared into the youthful face and tried to think what it was he smelled. As he cradled her face in his hands, he thought back to the night she was born. He remembered saying to himself that she was the prettiest baby girl he had ever delivered and had the sweetest face.

Rigor mortis was creeping through the girl's body, like an unstoppable plague, robbing her limbs of life, stiffening her fragile fingers, setting her blue eyes with the unmistakable flat stare of death. She was dead.

"You can come in now, Edward. I'm sorry. Emma's dead."

"What about me?" Gilbert said, a bit too loudly. "Can't I see my own fiancé?"

Edward looked over his shoulder at his almost-son-in-law and gritted his teeth.

"You can come in when I've seen my daughter. You can see her when I tell you that you can see her."

"But…but I want to see her now!"

"Get out of my way! You could have saved her and you let her drown!" Edward screamed with a rising flush in his otherwise clear skin. His handlebar moustache quivered and stood straight out like a snarling dog's whiskers as he pushed the younger man out the door

Gilbert thought briefly about fighting his way in, but there were too many people standing outside the office. It didn't matter anyway. He had what he wanted, tucked safely in his waistcoat pocket. He would just bide his time and pretend to be overcome with grief. There was one other thing he needed from the doctor, because he had used up the bottle that Dr. Blessing had given him just two days before. Time enough for that later, when there weren't so many people about.

Gilbert managed a few tears while he waited and a few appropriate sobs. Some people were sympathetic, but some just glared at him. Many had already made up their minds. This morning the girl was alive. This evening she was dead. And then there was the Reynolds girl. Several people in the back of the crowd were already whispering and looking sideways at him. The women just looked down and shook their heads.

As the shadows began to creep cat-like along the tree-lined roads, Gilbert waited. There would be time soon enough.

*****

While Edward held Emma's hand, he noticed the little silver ring. He stared at it and then tried to pull it off for closer inspection. The flesh was starting to swell slightly now that the body was not in the cold water, and Edward could not remove the ring. Then he looked at her left hand and looked up at the doctor.

"Look at this, Dr. Blessing. Where is the diamond engagement ring? I don't know what this silver ring is, but the other ring is missing. Did you see it when you and Gilbert dragged her out of the water?"

"No, I don't think so, but then we were pretty worn out from the tussle with the stream. Maybe it fell off when she slipped into the cold water. That would have shrunk her fingers. I'm sorry, Edward. We can look for it tomorrow in the daylight. I promise I'll help you look for it. By rights, it belongs to Gilbert, of course. He doesn't seem concerned about it, but maybe he hadn't noticed it either. I'll ask him when he comes in to visit Emma".

With a deep reflexive sigh that seemed like the last endless gasp of a drowning man, Edward patted Emma's face and tried to arrange her hair.

He smoothed her dress and folded her hands across her hand-stitched blue bodice. This morning she had been full of life and excited about the picnic. Tonight she was dead.

Edward stepped out into the street and glowered at Gilbert.

"You can see her now, boy," the distraught, weeping father said to the fiancé. "Don't stay too long. The doctor has some things he needs to do for her."

Gilbert opened the door and hesitated. The doctor motioned him inside and shut the door slowly behind him. Something just wasn't right, and when he looked at Gilbert, the doctor began to recognize the odor on the girl's breath. He was sure it was laudanum and sherry. What was this girl doing drinking such a thing? Her father would never have permitted it.

"Did you give this child laudanum and sherry, boy?" the doctor said with rising rage.

"Why, I guess she might have drunk a little of mine, doctor. I didn't give her any. Perhaps she poured herself some when I went into the woods to relieve myself. Maybe that's why she fell in the creek, sir. She was probably drunk. By the way, I need some more laudanum."

The doctor stifled the urge to strike the smiling boy, and with clenched fists turned his back.

"I think you'd best leave now, Gilbert. And quickly. I just gave you a bottle of laudanum the other day. I have to keep what I have left for my other patients until the next shipment arrives."

Gilbert stood looking at the doctor's back for a moment and considered his next move. Without further thought, Gilbert raised his fist and struck the old man on the back of the head as hard as he could, felling the doctor and rendering him almost unconscious. When he stepped across Dr. Blessing to get to the medicine cabinet, the doctor grabbed the boy's ankle and yanked him to the floor. As Gilbert hit the floor, the ring fell out of his pocket and the doctor snatched it up.

"I knew it! I knew it! Here's the proof, you sorry excuse for a human being! You drowned her like you did the Reynolds girl years ago! You couldn't even leave the ring on Emma's finger!"

"Help, help! Someone help me!" the doctor yelled.

Gilbert tried to run out the door, but Edward grappled with him and pinned him to the ground. Two men took Gilbert and held him while Edward rushed into the surgery to answer the doctor's call for help.

"What is it, Dr. Blessing? Did you fall? Did Gilbert do something?"

"Indeed he did, Edward. He murdered you daughter. I'm sure of it now. Here's the ring. He took it off her hand. It was in his pocket and it fell out on the floor when I grabbed his ankle. He knocked me down, because he was after more laudanum. By the way, Edward, I smelled laudanum and sherry on your daughter's breath. I think Gilbert drugged her and tried to have his way with her. If you'll step outside for a moment, I can tell you for certain if he succeeded. If she was conscious, I'm sure she fought him to preserve her honor."

Edward staggered outside in a state of shock as though he could hardly believe what he had just heard.

In a few minutes, the doctor opened the door and motioned for Edward to enter.

"She has not been dishonored, Edward. I'm sure of that. But it wasn't for lack of intent. Her pantaloons are down around her knees and some of the buttons are undone. That monster intended to rape her as he did the Reynolds girl years ago. I've been suspicious for a long time but couldn't prove it.

"And then there's the sherry and laudanum. I know you would not permit her to drink that, so it must have been Gilbert. He had the brass to suggest that Emma was drunk! Best have the constable with me when he puts Gilbert in the jail. Otherwise, someone might accidentally kill that bastard! Might do it myself. I brought him into the world, God help me. Maybe I should take him out of it. An overdose of laudanum would do it. Stay here with your Emma. I'll be right back. I'm going to get his father."

*****

The constable accompanied the doctor to the Pilkington home and pounded on the door. Gilbert's father had heard the commotion, but stayed seated in his chair by the fireplace. His wife answered the door.

"Pilkington! Where are you, you coward, you sire of jackals! Come out here and see what your murderous spawn has done this time!" the doctor roared.

*****

Sarah Pilkington sank onto a couch and covered her mouth with a lace handkerchief. She had heard similar charges before, but the family had status in the town and nothing had ever come of it. Nothing had been proven – not with the girls in another town, and not with the Reynolds girl. This time, she would not be able to protect her boy.

*****

The constable grabbed the banker by the collar so hard he ripped it off. Gilbert's father staggered out the door, dragged along by an irate doctor and the grimly silent town constable.

"There he is, the parasite!" hollered a woman at the back of the crowd. "He foreclosed on my farm after my husband was killed in the war! Now his boy has drowned Emma! Get him! Somebody get him!"

The crowd turned into an unruly mob, bent on attacking the banker, as though he himself had drowned Emma.

"Here now! Move aside," the constable said. Move back, I say. Let the law handle this! He'll get his due and so will that whelp of his. This time we have the proof. Stand back and let us through!"

The doctor opened the door to the surgery and motioned for the banker to approach the body.

"Is she dead, doctor? Is she surely dead?" he whispered.

"Yes, you fool, she's dead, and Gilbert did it. He had the ring in his waistcoat pocket. It fell out when he attacked me and tried to get more laudanum. I guess he thought he could get out of town before the people got him. Guilty as sin. Yes sir. No doubt about it. He drugged Emma, tried to rape her, and then drowned her in the creek."

The constable dragged Pilkington out the door and headed for the jail.

Dr. Blessing stood quietly while Edward Long said a tearful goodbye to his daughter.

"I'll bury her next to her mother. Now I've lost them both. What will I do? How can I bear it?"

"I can give you something that will ease your grief somewhat, Edward. Take this powder I've wrapped in a piece of paper, and put it in a half glass of water at night. It will help you sleep.

"I guess I'd best write to Addison. I don't think his mother is up to it. I know his father isn't."

"No, doctor. I'll write to Addison. It's the least I can do. I should have left them alone."

"Yes, Edward. By the way, that little silver ring was a gift from Addison before he re-enlisted. She sneaked out of the house one night to meet him at my office. It was all proper. I was in the other room. They were so in love. You're right, Edward. You should indeed have left them alone."

CHAPTER 13

Near the end of January, Addison's unit rejoined the Brigade and Division at White Oak Church, Virginia, and stayed there for the better part of the winter. In April, the war began again, and the time for resting and refurbishing ended. Major battles ensued at Chancellorsville, Franklin's Crossing, Maryes Heights in Fredericksburg, Salem Heights, Banks' Ford and Franklin's Crossing through mid-June. The soldiers were granted a brief rest and headed for Gettysburg.

"What a nightmare," Addison wrote as he began a letter home to his family. "The fierce battle has raged for days until the dead have nowhere to fall but stand in multiple mute rows of corpses at stone walls, immobile soldiers who are now just something for the living to hide behind and whose bodies are beginning to fall to pieces from shot and rot.

"It seems to me that the universe has scrolled in upon itself," Addison scrawled with the stub of a pencil. "The noise is deafening. I feel it in my belly and back, and there is no end to it. Men are falling everywhere, and it's hard to tell the living from the dead. Lem's unit got here a day before we did, I heard, but I don't know where he is. God help him. God help me. I doubt that many of us shall survive this horror. The cannon fire at will, and I have seen more death and destruction than any man should ever witness. I wish that it would end and we could all go home. Pray for us, father, and please pray that one of us at least survives to return home to our dear mother. God bless Mother. Hug her for me. I hope that the rest of you are all well. The Rebs are a fierce lot. Must be some Scots among them. Your loving son, Addison"

The 20th Maine was spoken of in awe after the dust and blood settled to the earth. Of course, they had Chamberlain astride his great gray stallion, "the Staples horse" as he was named, a gift from friends in Brunswick. Still the 20th was a brave lot. Little Round Top held and the 20th turned back the Rebels with yells and mostly empty rifles and muskets.

*****

What desperate determination, Addison thought. What heroism, what models of manhood held that hill.

*****

Addison was exhausted and slightly wounded at the end of the battle, but many of his brethren had fallen, dead or mortally wounded. Many more lay retching and gasping with fever and severe diarrhea that nothing seemed to abate. Only Addison's mother ever answered his letters, and those were becoming fewer and further between since she wrote of Emma's death. Her letter arrived the same day as Edward Long's did. That day marked the point at which Addison no longer cared if he lived or died.

*****

GETTYSBURG ANGELS

Thousands of men from both Union and Confederate sides lay in crumpled heaps on bloody ground. A mulatto woman drove her wagon piled high with food, clothing and other goods along the edge of the battlefield at Gettysburg searching for any who might still be alive. A young Confederate soldier, badly wounded, called out to her.

"Woman, woman! Over here! For the love of God, help me! Please help me. Do you have any water? Or maybe a bite to eat?"

The woman smiled for a moment. She was not used to being called "woman". Her employer and benefactor, attorney Thaddeus Stevens, called her "Madam" and left her $5,000. when he died. She had now nearly spent all of that money caring for wounded soldiers.

Lydia Smith stepped down from the wagon, gathered up some medical supplies, food, and water. She did what she could for the soldier, wrapping his shattered arm and giving him some fruit and water.

"Thankee, lady, thankee much. Are you a runaway slave?"

"No, soldier. I'm just a widow lady trying to help out. I'm looking for wounded men and the field hospitals. I'll leave you some food and this canteen of water. God bless. If we're lucky, perhaps the war will end soon. God willing."

Her skirts rustled as she walked back to the wagon that creaked as she climbed up on the seat. She didn't tell the soldier that she believed he would lose his arm to the infection that was turning his arm an ugly dark color. The wound was crawling with maggots.

Lydia chirped to the horse and said farewell to the young soldier.

*****

Lemuel Grant had not seen his younger brother Addison since the battle began, but knew from camp talk that the 7th was there somewhere in the hellish scene that lay before him. He and

Addison exchanged letters as often as they could, but when battles raged the mail service was erratic at best and non-existent at worst. Lemuel sat on a fallen tree and tried to figure out where the 7th was likely to be. He knew where the 20th Maine was, because they had defended and held Little Round Top.

When his mother had written to tell him that Addison had enlisted again, Lemuel shuddered. Why hadn't his willful younger brother stayed home with their parents? He was desperately needed to help with the farm, and he had paid the price for his freedom from this monstrous thing that threatened to devour the entire country. Lemuel was sure that he himself would have stayed home, given the opportunity. Being a soldier, he thought, is your job in this war. It's not who you are. He remembered having heard that from some Indian sharpshooter, or maybe something Addy had said. No matter.

As he sat and stared at the massacre that lay stretched out before him, the tired older brother realized that the wound in Addison's back would never let him have any peace, and that the town wouldn't either. He could only imagine what Addison had gone through when he returned home, shot in the back. Only the soldiers understood that the shot and shell and buck 'n ball flew from every direction, and many who were good and true men had been shot in the back. The minie balls and grape shot didn't much care which way you were facing. They would find your body and ravage it.

Lemuel took off the Grant crest that he wore pinned to his uniform and stared at it. Was this badge worth dying for? Was the Union really at risk if the South won? The recruiters constantly harped about the southern despots and slavers, but there were slaves in the North, too, and some of the men who had written the Constitution themselves had had slaves. There was no magic line above or below which there were or were not slaves. Lemuel sighed and pinned the badge traditionally worn by the eldest Grant back on his jacket.

*****

Having sat on the document all summer, Lincoln had officially freed the slaves in the South right after Antietam – much to the frustration of his cabinet. Nothing much had changed, Lemuel thought. Maybe the Rebs were a little more desperate, but that was all that Lemuel could see. He wished he could just go home. What would one man or dead body more or less matter in this war? He knew his cousins and probably one or two of his uncles from Atlanta would sooner or later be on the same battlefields on which he and Addison would be fighting, but he hadn't seen them for years and doubted he would recognize any of them. Maybe Uncle L. P. or his son John. Maybe not.

Exhausted and covered in dirt and blood, Lemuel groaned and stood up. His back was sore, and he had bruises and sores over most of his body, but couldn't remember where he got them. Being a sergeant wasn't all it was cracked up to be. Commissary sergeant was even less exciting. He often was stuck on a hill watching the desperate struggles on the field below him. Sometimes his commander assigned him to the artillery units, but too often Lemuel Grant stood on the sidelines aching to get into the battle. What stories would he have to tell his children when they asked what their father had done in the Great War? Oh well, he would say, your father made sure that the soldiers had enough to eat and sometimes he helped fire the big cannons.

Letters from home were scarce and Lemuel didn't know if his family was just not writing or if the letters were getting lost. He was amazed that the mail got through at all with the number of hands it went through. Sometimes the money enclosed made it to the soldier's hand and sometimes not.

He thought about his sweetheart Annie and wondered if she was still waiting for him. She probably was, but he couldn't be sure. Once Addison had told him that word had leaked back to the folks at home that Lemuel was dead. Rumors flew when information was withheld for military reasons. Most people at home didn't know for sure where their sons, brothers, and husbands were. Lemuel shook his head and realized that often he himself didn't know exactly where he was either. The Union had one name for battles, and the Rebs often had another. Bull Run, Manassas – who cared.

*****

Addison stared up at Little Round Top and wondered if the 4th was up there somewhere around the 20th. He sighed and curled up on the ground intending to rest for only a few minutes. He was so very tired, and the officers were already talking about moving on. Why couldn't they just rest? The Rebs surely were as tired as they were, and what could be accomplished now that couldn't wait a few hours? What was going to happen to the thousands of bodies and the dying men strewn across the battlefield? The pitiful cries of wounded or dying men begging for water and gibbering in the dark of night was more than he could stand.

He personally had shot several horribly wounded horses whose shattered bodies lay among the human remains. All the poor animals could do was to groan and roll their eyes in agony. Exposed rib cages, protruding intestines, gaping holes, and sometime missing legs were more than Addison could bear. At least that was something he could do. He could put those brave warhorses out of their misery. More than once a soldier lying near a dying horse had cried out to Addison to shoot him, too. Addison had wept and walked on past. He couldn't even bring himself to shoot a Confederate who struggled to raise his still-loaded musket and threatened to shoot Addison. The soldier's arm shook violently with the effort and he dropped the weapon.

"Damned bluecoat! You'll shoot a horse but not a man to put an end to his sufferin'. Damn you! Damn you, you yellow-bellied coward! Damn all you bluebellies!" screamed the wounded soldier.

Addison turned at the word "coward", looked back at the Rebel, and raised the Springfield rifle that he had taken from a fallen soldier. He took aim and hesitated. Just as he was about to fire, his attention was drawn to a macabre scene. He could scarce believe what he was watching. The vultures, dogs, and hogs were bad enough, but this was incredible. Two men were wandering among the bodies, wrenching out the teeth of the dead and even some of the dying or just wounded soldiers! What on earth was this new horror?

As he watched the men at their grisly work, Addison lost his temper and fired at the nearest human vulture. The man shrieked in surprise and pain as his leg shattered under him, and he plunged onto the body of a Union soldier. A Reb whom he had just tried to rob of his teeth was lying next to the blue-clad body and still alive. The Reb grabbed the ghoul by the throat, silently throttling the life out of him.

"Good job, Yank. We got him. Now if you can just hit that other one, it'll be a job of work well done."

As the dying soldier spoke, the other scavenger was jumping and stumbling across the dead and dying like a giant spider, clutching his bag of teeth, and screeching in fear. Addison took careful aim, fired, and dropped the man.

"What on God's earth are those men doing, Johnny Reb? Why are they stealing teeth?"

The Reb gurgled a laugh and coughed hard as blood trickled out of the corner of his moth.

"Why, my bluebelly friend, don't ya know? It's for them European high falutin' folk with bad teeth? They pay a fortune for strong young teeth to be made into falsies. Best place in the world to find 'em is on a battlefield. General Washington's were made of wood, I hear, but that's not good enough for them rich folk in France or wherever! Nosiree!"

The man gurgled again and fainted. Addison couldn't tell if the man was still alive or not, but was concerned that he himself might be a target in the gathering dark and he hurried off. He didn't know exactly why he was walking the battlefield, except that he hoped he might find a Maine boy to save. He probably owed his life to a Mainer when he fell at Antietam. Maybe Fales had dragged him off the field, or more likely the Penobscot man.

Another horse groaned near him and tried to get up. His intestines spilled out on the ground and the horse fell back. Addison held his breath as he put the horse down and thought of Ranger.

On the 4th of July, the 7th Maine moved from Gettysburg to Fairfield, then to Funkstown. In the fall, it was Bristoe and the Rappahannock. By spring they were fighting from the Rapidan to the James. On May 8th, they approached Spotsylvania Court House.

*****

In the middle of the night, the rain began again, an incessant pounding fusillade from the heavens that seemed frantic to stop the slaughter. Hope seeped into the weary brains of the combatants. Perhaps there would be no battle in the morning. Perhaps they could just rest for a little while. The march toward Spotsylvania Court House had exhausted man and beast, and no one was exactly sure whether the Rebs or the Federals would get there first. The heavy undergrowth, the rain, and the fog obscured everything, and the men crouched in fear and fatigue.

"Hey, Addison…pssst…over here, boy!"

Addison turned toward the sound of a familiar though raspy voice, and wept at the sight of his older brother Lemuel crouching in the brush.

"Lemuel! They said you were dead! Thank God you're alive! What's going on out there? They say Lee's already there. What have you heard about that? What are we gonna do?"

"Don't rightly know about Lee, brother Addy, but the 4th came across a freshly cut road through the forest and figured it was the Rebs that chopped that road through the woods. Don't know if the regular army went thataway, though. The rain has flooded the trails pretty bad. Don't see how we can do much good in such heavy rain, but the officers have told us to stay ready. We may be moving before dawn. Damn the rain! My boots are full of water. How you holding up, Addy?"

"Um, okay I guess, Lem. Pretty scary stuff, though, you know? The mail isn't getting to us very regularly either. How about you? Heard anything from home lately? Just from Annie, huh? Guess you heard about Emma?"

Lemuel stared at the ground, then quietly leaned back against the huge oak tree that must have stood a hundred years. He wondered if some Indian might have rested here once, or maybe even one of the Rebs that had helped cut the road.

"Haven't had many letters myself, 'cept from Mama," Lemuel whispered. "I'm sure sorry about Emma."

Addison stared blankly at the muddy ground and nodded.

"It was that bastard Pilkington that killed her. Drowned her, Mama said. Good thing they hung him or I might have run off home and done him in myself. Doc told me that Gilbert tried to rape her, but he's sure that he didn't succeed. Guess I'll try even harder to keep myself pure.

Maybe that counts for something in heaven. I may find that out pretty soon. The Rebs are getting pretty desperate.

"Hey, Lem, why don't you join up with our bunch here. No one would know. We could fight together, and maybe neither of us would get killed that way. We're both good shots and we could look after each other."

Lemuel smiled.

"Nope, Addy. There's comfort enough in family and good weapons, but it would be desertion. I've already come across some boys who shifted units to be with friends or family. Some of the Kingsbury cousins showed up in the 4th Maine, and some of the 1st Maine Cav boys ended up in the 4th Maine's medic tent with swamp fever.

"Drove the officers crazy trying to keep track of everyone. Most were where they were supposed to be, unless they didn't trust their officers. Especially on pay day, they were where they were supposed to be."

Lemuel smiled at the memory of men sneaking back into camp the night before payday.

"Addy, here's a funny one for ya. During the last big battle, we found some of our officers hiding in haystacks! Geez, brother, imagine that, for cripes sake! Officers hiding in the haystacks! Should of shot them, I say. Some general or other came along and found them. Threatened to start firing his pistol into the stacks, he was that mad!"

Like a fawn stalked by a predator, Lemuel who was squatting in the brush froze and held his breath. With his neck hairs bristling, he inched around on his boot heel and peered behind him into the forest. Shadowy figures crept silently past on a parallel line with the Union boys, and moved without cracking a twig or rustling a leaf.

He touched his brother's arm and held a finger to his lips. Without a sound of his own, Lemuel shifted his rifle to port arms and stared intently at the shadows that just as suddenly evaporated into the fog.

"Addy, did you see that? Who were those men in the woods – ours or theirs? Or someone else! Who could be out here, especially n all this rain. Damn me, I gotta get back to the 4th and tell my officers! Better tell your sergeant about that, boy. Could be the Rebs scouting us or somethin'! Addy, I got a really bad feeling about today. We got to stay in touch somehow. At night we'll call each other like we called the cows, remember? 'Hoo, hoo, hoo', like a barn owl. That way we'll both know that we're okay."

Addison turned his back to his brother and sniffed back a few tears.

"Well, Lem, I'll confess that Antietam is still on my mind some. They say lightning can't strike twice. Wouldn't be fair for me to get shot twice, now would it?"

Addison turned back to his brother, but Lem was gone.

*****

The boy started to stand up, but remembering the shadows in the woods, he thought better of it. Crouching, he sloshed through the deep puddles and the mud as he made his way to the nearest sergeant.

"Sir, sir! I need to report something, sir!"

"Go ahead, soldier. Permission to speak."

"Sir, I just saw some men sneaking through the woods off there, sir. There were at least twenty or thirty of them, I'd judge, and they didn't make a sound. Stopped now and again like they were counting us, maybe, but then they disappeared into the fog, sir."

"Well done, soldier. We'll send out scouts."

"One more question, sir?"

"Yes, boy, what is it?"

"Can the sergeant tell us anything at all about what we'll be doing today, sir? Some of us were just wondering, trying to get ready, sir."

The sergeant frowned and started to snap out an answer, but as he looked at the anxious young face, he softened. His own son was about that age and had begged to enlist. He tried not to smile as he turned away for a moment, then looked again at the worried face in front of him.

"Where've you served, boy? Seen much action?"

"Yes, sir! I was wounded pretty badly at Antietam and re-enlisted, sir. I've seen plenty of action with the 7th, though not as much as the sergeant has, sir, I'm sure."

"Well soldier, I can tell you this much. You'll see action today and tomorrow for sure. Get some rest, eat some food, check your pack and your rifle. And say your prayers, son, say your prayers."

*****

About the time that Addison finished his brief report, Lemuel was looking for his officers. Upon finding one, Sgt. Lemuel C. Grant snapped a salute and asked to report.

"Sir, I need to report something I just saw in the woods over there a few minutes ago."

The officer frowned slightly.

"A few minutes ago, soldier? What were you doing in the woods that it took you so long to report to me? Where were you exactly?"

Lemuel held his breath for a moment and frantically searched for the right, though not truthful, answer.

"Soldier, I asked you what you were doing over there? You're not a scout, judging by your uniform and you're sure not one of Berdan's men, so what were you doing?"

"Um, begging your pardon, sir, but I was relieving myself, and I had to wait until the men I saw in the woods passed me by, sir."

The officer hid a smile behind his hand, coughed, and asked for the report. Lemuel told him about the strange, silent shadows he had seen in the woods over yonder, and wondered if the Captain thought it might be important.

"Thank you, Sgt. Grant. Good job. Our scouts will check this information and get back to me. Dismissed."

An uneasy feeling had settled in Lemuel's soul, and would not be dismissed easily. He considered Addison's invitation to switch units, but abandoned the idea. He wondered again about the shadow soldiers or whatever they were. Maybe they were ghosts. There must be ghosts around these parts. Too many men had died horribly for there not to be ghosts. They moved like Indians. Rumor had it that both sides had recruited some Indian scouts from the west. Maybe so, maybe not. He really didn't care anymore. He just knew they gave him the willies. Like ghosts, though, they appeared and disappeared, never making a sound. No human being should be able to walk over sticks and leaves without a sound. It wasn't natural. Lemuel shuddered.

*****

Lee had been right to spend the manpower slashing a road through the wilderness. It gave him the advantage he needed to prepare for a major battle. The crossroads at the courthouse were crucial to his campaign, and both Lee and Grant knew it. Whoever got there first would have a decided advantage. Lee arrived first and immediately ordered the building of earthworks and a salient that projected out three-quarters of a mile deep and half a mile across the base. The soldiers called it the "mule shoe" due to its shape. By the time Grant got there, Lee's army had already constructed strong defenses comprised of deep trenches and traverses, gun emplacements, and abatises of felled trees and sharpened branches.

Grant studied the layout when he arrived and immediately regretted anew the loss of one of his best and most beloved officers, General "Uncle John" Sedgwick, the VI Corps commander. Sedgwick had fallen shot through the head by a Rebel sniper, moments after he had scolded his soldiers for flinching every time the snipers fired at them.

"Heavens, men, those Rebs couldn't hit an elephant at this range!" he had roared.

No sooner had Sedgwick made that remark than a sniper's bullet slammed into his face just below his left eye. Nothing could stop the blood, and with an amused look on his face – as though his brain could still judge the irony of it all – the great general fell and died, the victim of the Confederate sniper's favorite weapon: the British Whitworth sniper gun, which had a range of 1,500 yards when outfitted with a glass sight.

The soldiers heard of the loss of their beloved and trusted leader and were frightened anew. Word had quickly passed through the ranks to the 4th and 7th Maine units, partly because Maj.

Thomas Hyde had been in the area where
Sedgwick had been shot.

"Hey Josh," whispered Addison. "Where
the heck are you?"

"Right here, Addy. Behind the big oak tree.
Whatcha want?"

"I'm that scared tonight that I just can't
sleep. Must be about four in the morning. Do ya
think we'll fight today with all this rain and fog?"

"Dunno. Hey, did you here them Rebs got
Uncle John Sedgwick? Heard they got the General
right through the eyeball and splattered his brains
all over the colonel next to him. Nearly got our
Major Hyde, too, I heard.

"Them Rebs is damn good shots. Not sure
we got any ary as good as them snipers. How fast
you figure they can reload them rifles?"

"Gosh, damn me if I know. I hear they got
glass-scoped long guns. They just sit up there in
trees or on hills picking us off like squirrels. I've
heard they can shoot several times a minute."

Addison squatted miserably in the endless
downpour. Not a stitch of clothing anywhere on
his body was dry, his boots were full of water, and
the good gray wool socks his mother Julia had
knitted for him before he left Maine were sodden
and squished every time he moved. Fires were
forbidden this close to a battlefield, so the only
food was stale hard biscuits and a little dried meat.
Coffee grounds in a cup of cold water had to make
do for coffee, and there was no comfort.

Addison's thoughts turned to home, the warm fire on the big stone hearth, the smells of his mother's cooking, and the aroma of new-mown timothy hay blowing sweet behind the horse-drawn mower. Somebody had invented a baler a few years back, but the Grants didn't have the money for one of those yet. They grew some of the best hay in the state of Maine, by golly, he thought. When he was young, he griped about haying in the summer, but right now he'd give anything he owned to be back home getting ready for the haying. May, he thought. Too soon to hay, but maybe in June if the weather held. First cut always had some weeds and was sold for cattle feed, but every cut after that was pretty much purely sweet timothy, and how the horses loved it. The big black Percheron draft horses ate nearly fifty pounds of it a day in the winter, crunching the sweet stems and drooling green foam from the corners of their soft velvety mouths.

Addison's reverie was interrupted by voices down the trail from his unit. The ranks of soldiers slowly rose to their feet, stretched their backs, and shifted their packs. Depending on how lucky they were they might or might not have to be worrying about keeping their powder and shot dry. In a moment a ripple of grumbling and shuffling and splashing reached the men around Addison and Josh, and rolled on past to the units that stretched behind them in the dank darkness.

"Josh, what's going on? Where are we going at this hour? I can't see a thing! We could run right up on Johnny Reb and never know it!"

Josh grunted as he shifted his pack and steadied his rifle. He had tried to pour the water out of his boots, but had only succeeded in losing his balance as he hopped about, and plunked his already soaked sock foot down in the mud.

"Damn this rain!" he snarled as he tried to wash his dirty sock in a puddle. There was nothing for it but to stand barefooted in the mud and muck as he rinsed out the sock. He wrung out the sock, rinsed his blistered bleeding muddy foot in the murky puddle, and put the gritty sodden sock back on his dirty foot. The stretched-out sock drooped and sagged as he tried to pull it on.

"I'll have blisters bigger'n a toad by the time we get wherever the hell we're going, Addy. I wish I was home."

Addison straggled into line with the rest of the troops. No point trying to look smart when they were all so bedraggled. Their boots didn't all match, buttons had fallen off, pants sagged from weight loss, and every man jack of them was tired, wet, and longing for hot food and a fire. Surely the commanders weren't intending to fight this day. Maybe they'd just get into position and wait for the weather to ease up. Lee was already ahead of them. They couldn't see through the fog. Why rush?

A couple of officers rode down the line, and disappeared into the mist behind them, hissing at the men to shape up and look alive. Addison felt the hair stand up on the back of his neck. The officers only acted like this right before a battle, trying to get control of the stragglers and slackers. With his heart pounding in his chest, Addison tried his best to stand straight and look like his brother Lemuel in that picture he'd had made for Mama.

Of course Addison's uniform was too dirty and worn to want to have a picture done right now, but when he got home again, he'd have one made for his mother. She'd love that. He wished that he'd done that before he re-enlisted, but his mind had been on other things. Addison tried not to think about the war, but it was no use. It was all around him, even at four in the morning. The sun hadn't even climbed over the hills yet, and they were marching through the woods to God knew what.

The relentless rain hammered on man and beast, and fog shrouded everything, but scouts were able to slip in and out of the enemy positions and check for gun emplacements and guess at the numbers of troops. The Maine boys hunkered down when ordered to rest, but no one really wanted to sit on the ground that had become a quagmire, nearly sucking their boots off.

"Cripes, this reminds me of mud season back home, Josh."

"Yeah, Addy, except that there weren't no cannons back home. I got a bad feeling about this here. I sure don't want to charge through that fog, not knowing what's there. Got a wicked bad feelin'. Course, General Grant's out there somewhere. Guess that's a good thing for our side. 'Cept I hear that Lee is out there somewhere, too. Geez. This ain't gonna be no easy thing. Addy."

"Battle of the Titans," muttered Addison.

"What's that? Titans? What's a Titan?"

"Yeah, Josh, something my father read to me when I was a boy. Something about giants and gods and whatever. I don't rightly remember just now."

Fog hung like a shroud over the battlefield, and the men had too much time to think about what might be coming.

Abruptly at 4:30 a.m. General Grant turned his big stallion Cincinnati toward the Rebel defenses and ordered an attack at the point of the salient, testing the Rebel defenses and watching for cannon fire out of the fog. The Maine units shuffled closer together, excited and terrified, waiting for the order to charge. Trying not to look through the trees at the battlements, they checked their weapons and hitched up their pants.

Wouldn't do to have your britches fall down during a charge, thought Addison as he pulled in his belt a notch or two. As he buttoned his tunic, he fretted about the missing button near the top but shrugged it off. By the end of this foggy day, who would care? Antietam was never far from his mind, and no matter how firmly he tried to set aside the memory, it would sneak back to the forefront and taunt him.

A wave of excitement and nervousness suddenly swept over the troops. They stood at attention, watching their commanders who were peering through the fog and whispering to the scouts who came and went with reports on the Rebs.

A colonel rode up beside the Maine boys, and told them to get ready. His warhorse was in a lather from excitement and the sounds of weaponry muffled by the fog. The officer's bay stallion snorted several times and tossed his head. His brown eyes shone and foam dripped from the curb bit in his mouth as the rider jiggled the curb rein while he talked to the men.

"You men! Listen up! Straighten up those lines and let's get us some Rebs!"

Addison could barely see who was talking to them, but he knew they were about to charge through the fog into rifles, muskets, bayonets, and cannon. Word was that they would all be pouring through a narrow gap in the woods. If that was true, he thought, it would be bad. It was hard to tell exactly how far away the firing was, but Addison figured not more than a mile. If that. His throat went dry, his heart pounded, and his hands shook almost uncontrollably. He'd been in a number of big battles including Antietam, but he felt that somehow this one would be different. The knots in his stomach hurt. The sour taste of bile rose in his throat as he searched frantically for the 4th, but he couldn't see the battle flags. He knew his brother was out there somewhere in the mist, and Addison wished and prayed that they could be together.

An unholy and unnerving roar followed the order to charge the Rebel position behind the salient. A sound issued from Addison's throat, but he didn't recognize it as his own voice. The Rebels answered with their high-pitched yell. Men began to fall with gurgles and grunts as the Confederates found the range. A man next to Addison collapsed with a shriek when a ball hit him in the groin and dropped him writhing in unbearable agony. Addison looked down at him for a moment and screamed louder. As he reloaded his weapon, he began to laugh hysterically. He didn't remember firing the rifle, but it was empty and he was almost at the breastworks. Soldiers behind him were rushing forward as though they couldn't see their own men in front of them.

Addison feared being skewered from behind by a bayonet and kept looking over his shoulder at the bearded man behind him who resembled the crazy man that lived up the hill outside of Frankfort. All the kids were afraid of him and scattered like falling maple leaves whenever he came out of his house to yell at them.

"For Maine and the Union!" yelled a young flag bearer next to Addison. No sooner were the words out of his mouth than he was struck by several rounds that ripped his face apart and tore open his throat. He fell mute to the bloody ground and was trampled by the hordes behind him. Addison bent over to try to help him, but recoiled in horror as the boy's face fell to pieces when he tried to turn him over. Another soldier snatched up the shredded colors and ran screaming toward the Rebel line.

With a final rush, the Union boys burst through the Rebel position and discovered that they had captured a Confederate general and several pieces of artillery. The mud and the bloody slime slowed their advance and the advantage was lost. With the units in turmoil, Addison and Lemuel's units ended up near each other.

"Lemuel, Lemuel! Are you in here?" screamed Addison above the din.

No answer came, but there were a dozen different units milling about in the salient, hopelessly confused, and beginning to panic without the command structure.

"Addison! Over here, brother! I'm over here by the artillery pieces! Come here quick!"

Addison shoved and scrambled his way toward his brother, oblivious to the Rebel fire that fortunately was beginning to diminish as the Confederates fell back to their reserve position.

For a moment, the brothers embraced, but a new fusillade erupted from the ridge where Lee was watching the snarled Federal troops attempting to reorganize. Union officers rode their horses into the fray, screaming orders to confused men who didn't recognize anyone around them and some of whom instinctively fired at anyone who came toward them. The plan to break through the "mule shoe" salient had been successful, but the forward motion had been lost when the Federals tried to decide what to do with the captured artillery pieces that were bogged down in the mire.

The battle now turned on what the two great generals, Grant and Lee, would do. Lee was determined to hold his ground and rebuild his defenses. Grant was determined to use his greater materiel and numbers to overwhelm Lee and march into Richmond. As Confederate Generals Gordon and Rodes advanced to the mule shoe, they effectively stopped further penetration by the Federals. This was merely a prelude to the horror and savagery that would follow as both Lee and Grant poured men into the narrow confines of the salient which might as well have been a meat grinder.

"Addison, stay by me! That's my commander over there. Follow him!"

The two brothers struggled to keep the commander in sight through the fog, and followed him out of the salient before they realized that they were again on the outside of the "mule shoe".

"Lemuel, we're out of there! Let's try to find the rest of the Maine boys and regroup!"

"There's no time, Addy! Turn around and shoot, boy!"

"Lemmy, I can't go back in there again! Those Rebs have regrouped and are forming a new line toward the back!"

"Turn around, Addison, damn you! Turn around and fight! There's our boys over there! Hurry! Follow me! Follow me!"

Addison felt the tears burning his cheeks, but he didn't care anymore. Lem had as much as called him a coward. Did his own brother really believe that he had run at Antietam? Everyone in the 7th knew what had happened that day. Lots of boys had taken one in the back, sometimes from their own troops. Even one officer had been shot by mistake. Some boy with a quick trigger finger had shot him in the back. Addison didn't know if the officer had lived or not, but it had shaken up the troops.

With his eyes blurred with tears and sobs sticking in his windpipe, Addison stumbled toward the officer and tried to watch where Lemuel was going. For the moment he'd forgotten about the Rebels. He just wanted to be next to his brother. As he crouched among the mangled, twisted bodies of blue and gray soldiers with the dull glimmer of death on their faces, he thought about his mother and how her heart would break if they didn't both make it home. He wanted his father to be proud of him, but he longed for the days at his mother's knee when he was safe and happy – days long before this horrible war. Somewhere out there in the South were his blood cousins, sons of his father's brother. Maybe they weren't here at Spotsylvania, but they were out there in gray uniforms. They could even be here somewhere. What if he shot one of his own kin? How could he know?

A man fell dead next to him and then another and anther. Addison screamed Lemuel's name, but couldn't see him anywhere. The fighting had renewed and he was in the thick of it. His hands shook as he tried to reload.

"Get down, boy! Get down! Load your weapon before you move again!"

Addison looked up into the intense blue eyes of the officer who was leaning over him.

"Unnhh!" the officer groaned as a round hit him in the neck, tore open his jugular, and ripped through his windpipe. Clutching his throat, unable to speak or breathe, the officer floundered and flopped around on the ground, his eyes wide with terror. He reached a bloody hand out to Addison and gurgled some command that no one living could understand. The wound bubbled and frothed as the life spurted out of the dying man. Finally, blessedly, he lay still. Addison, struck dumb with horror, tried to move his legs but they didn't respond. The boy lurched to his feet and called out to his brother.

Suddenly, Addison was caught in a stampede of troops, all screaming and hollering as they surged toward the point of the "mule shoe" where the fighting was fierce. Addison was hurled along and could barely keep his feet, let alone his rifle. As the two sides met, the din rose to an unearthly howling clash of men and weapons, as though the end of the world were at hand, and the demons of hell had all been unleashed for a final assault on mortal man.

Addison fired his rifle at a gray uniform in front of him and quickly reloaded. Seconds ticked by as he fumbled with the paper patch and cap. Hurry, Addison, hurry, he whispered.

The battle raged around him. Ball and artillery were whining and whizzing past him like a cloud of biting black flies in his father's hayfields. Addison saw the muzzles of the defenders' rifles and muskets through the abatis as he lunged toward the thickest snarl of men in front of him.

The fog cleared unmercifully for a moment, and the soldiers beheld hell in all its rage and gore. The scene made even seasoned soldiers vomit. Bodies were stacked four and five high – many blown to pieces. Some just lumps of gore and flesh where they had been hit repeatedly. Defenders had cocked the stiffened hands of the dead into cups to hold their balls and caps. So much blood had spilled in the trenches that some men actually drowned in the blood or suffocated in the bloody muck if they were unlucky enough to fall face down.

As the two sides, like insane combatants, struggled in mortal combat, hand to hand, musket or rifle butt to butt, and body against body, men fell dead or wounded every second. The shrill screams of the wounded were soon muffled by the dead and dying bodies falling on top of them in the muck. Cries for help were grimly ignored in the desperate fight to take the "shoe". Federals fired point blank over the top of the abatis, and Rebel defenders fired through cracks straight into the bellies and groins of the attackers.

Out of the mist, Josh appeared next to Addison, and the two fought savagely against the Rebs. Josh, already wounded in the left arm, fired and reloaded clumsily only with his right, clasping the rifle between his thighs.

"Geez, Josh, let me help ya with that," Addison mumbled as he tried to keep his head down. The ground shook as a roar of double-charged canister shot knocked Addison to the ground, amid splinters of logs and fence rails. Miraculously, only the concussion had knocked him down, but his ears rang and he could hardly see.

"Josh, Josh! Where are you?" Addison screamed above the din. He crawled among the shattered crumpled corpses searching for his friend. Then he heard an eerie moan like a wounded animal.

"No, no, no!" Addison wailed when he found the source of the unearthly noise. What was left of Josh was a mass of flesh, blood, and broken bones protruding through bloody blue cloth. The eyebrows, eyes, and nose were gone and the skull cracked, but somehow the brain clung to its function until friend found friend and released him.

"Ahhhh!" groaned Addison, rocking back and forth on his knees as he picked up Josh's weapon and reloaded it along with his own. In a mad dash toward oblivion, Addison threw himself at the abatis and fired both weapons point blank into the frenzied faces on the other side. As he screamed, "For the Union!" a barrage of canister and musket fire riddled his body. Only his boots were untouched. His shattered remains fell across the battlements, impaled on a sharpened tree limb. Body after body fell on top of him in a senseless onslaught until the abatis was buried in flesh and no longer of any use. The battle surged in and out of the "shoe", but the fighting around what the soldiers were already calling the "bloody angle" was the most savage.

*****

While the battle ebbed and flowed, some officers clustered around the camp looking for Major Hyde. When they found the young major, he was clearly exhausted.

"Are you going to sign the letter, Thomas? Everyone else is. We need to do it now. We can't have a coward like that leading our boys. Mason is a damned coward, Thomas. He pretended to be hurt and lay on the ground while young soldiers and a couple of officers kneeled around him to protect him. Sign the letter."

A mockingbird sat silently in a nearby tree. She had no songs to sing.

*****

Letter from J. W. Channing, Capt 7th ME to John L. Hodsdon, Adjt. Gen State of Maine
June 27th 1864 from Camp of the 7th Maine Vols.
Five miles south of Petersburg, VA.
Sir:

Being in a kind of bivouac camp for a few days, the thought occurred to me that you would like to hear from the 7th. Events passed very rapidly out here nowadays, whole regiments – aye, even brigades are swept out of existence in a few moments. Our regiments have suffered their share in this Campaign. Maine men are not at discount in this army. Everybody speaks in the highest praise of them, but it would not do to have too many of them in this Army at once, for they would have all of the fighting to do.

An officer said to me the other day that the best troops in this army came from the extremes of the Union – that is from Maine and Minnesota.

We left camp at Brandy Station with four hundred and seventy-nine (479) rifles. By this morning's report I have but one hundred and forty-two (142) available for line of battle. We have lost three hundred and thirty-seven (337) men and

officers – killed wounded and missing. This will
include some 20 sent to the Hospital. Seven of the
officers are dead – eight are absent wounded and
eight are still on duty with the Regt. Four of them
have been wounded, some of them three times, but
still they would not leave the regt. We have been
in all of the battles of our Corps. besides being
twice detached to support the 2nd Corps. While
doing so on the 12th of May, we lost one hundred
and thirty eight (138) men and officers.

Perhaps a small sketch of our fight on the 5th
May would not be out of place here, as it will show
that the right man is not always put in the right
place.

The 6th Corps was on the right and our
Division on the right of the Corps. The 7th ME held
the extreme flank in echelon behind the 49th NY
Vols. We were facing by the rear rank at the time
– At 5 pm our skirmishers were driven in all along
the Brigade front. On came the foe overturning
everything in their path. It was evident that we
must front to back or be taken in flank. Quick as
lightening came the order, change front to rear on
tenths company – then came the order tenths
company about face- right wheel – halt – about
face, commence firing. The movement was
executed as steady as if we were on parade. Our
fire began to check the advance of the enemy.
In fact, we began to gain ground when all at once
the right wing began to fall back. Good God what
was the reason of this? It is according to orders!

Who gave the order? Col. Mason. Then we will
not obey such orders! Forward men – all others
may go back but the 7th Maine – never were the
words Maj. Jones. The men answered us with a
cheer. Forward we went driving everything before
us – taking some two hundred prisoners. But
where was the gallant Colonel who had boasted so
much about what he was going to do and to show
us? He was lying on the ground. I went to him
and asked him if he was wounded. He said that he
was. After the firing ceased he arose, and did not
seem much hurt. Is Colonel Mason a coward? was
the question asked by the officers who had stood
by him through everything. Wait – we shall not
have so long. On the 6th inst. we were under fire
all day. About 6 pm we were ordered back to take
a position on the left of the 3rd division in some
works which had been put up during the afternoon.
Just after dusk the enemy charged our line but
were driven back. They met with better success on
our right. The 3rd Div gave way at the Rebel yell –
while our brave colonel went with them. He, Sir,
who pretended so much, ran away from his
regiment and left us alone in our glory. We were
surrounded on all sides by the enemy – but as firm
as the rock bound coast of their native State stood
the 7th Maine ....backed by the rest of Neills
Brigade.

They charged us again and again but each
time were hurled back in confusion. Gen. John
Sedgwick said that our Brigade saved the Corps

and the Corps the Army. During this time where was the man whose place was there? He had taken the horse of Gen Neill's orderly and gone with the stragglers, and when asked by some of our men who had been swept away by the stampede of the 3rd Division where the Regiment was, he said they were all taken prisoner. He then made a speech to the men congratulating them on their lucky escape. Such a man is Col E. Mason. Is he fit to command the 7th? We have sent him the following letter.

Camp of the 7th ME Vol
In the Trenches before Petersburg VA
June 21st 1864
Col. E. C. Mason
7th Regt, Maine Vol. Inf

Sir,

At a meeting of the officers called by ourself on the evening of the 10th Ma near Spottsylvania Court House Va. You stated that the Officers of the regt. had lost all confidence in you – you intended to make all the amends in your power and would therefore tender your resignation. It was not the time nor place and we not the proper persons to accept such a resignation. But events having since transpired rendering the cessation of our connection with this regiment decisionable, we take the present opportunity to state that our views perfectly coincide with yours expressed on the 10th inst.

Hoping that it will be carried into effect at your earliest convenience

We are Sir,
Very respectfully
Your obt srvts

As darkness descended on the nightmarish scene, it was here that Lemuel came looking for his younger brother. Ignoring commands to leave the field with the 4th, he searched for hours among the thousands of dead and dying, sometimes finding twitching, kicking, wounded underneath four or five corpses. His mind was numb with horror and fear, because Addison had not answered his "hoo, hoo, hoo" call when he called again and again for his little brother. In one space about twelve by fifteen feet he counted one hundred fifty bodies. It was a mad scene, something out of a disturbed child's worst night terrors.

Lemuel heard a horrifying scream. When he turned toward the sound, he saw a vulture tearing at the wounded belly of a Rebel soldier whose arms were pinned under two dead bodies. A black vulture had already plucked out the man's eyes. Lemuel kicked the bird off the Rebel soldier and shot the scavenger, then moved the bodies off to free the dying man. A Reb grabbed his ankle as he stepped over the wounded man.

"Help me, Sergeant! A little water, please! Just a sip. No more. I promise. I'm dead anyhow. Please, for the love of heaven, give me some water."

Lemuel looked at his canteen and thought about his brother. Addison might need it. Lemuel just shook his head and steeled himself against the sobs as he walked on.

Thousands of bodies littered the battlefield. Part of Lemuel's unit had been up on the ridge helping with the artillery. A commissary sergeant, Lemuel was not always in the thick of the battle. Addison, with the 7th Maine, was. Some bodies were no longer recognizable as human. What the shell and shot hadn't accomplished, the vultures and hogs were working on. Even some starving farm dogs, no longer domesticated, had joined in.

Lemuel turned and instinctively ducked when he heard the shrill scream. Another Rebel soldier lay on his back, arms pinned under dead comrades. A large boar hog was tearing at the belly wound. Lemuel shot the hog and gave the Reb a scant sip of water. Although the sergeant had seen many horrors, this repeated scene made him vomit.

"Oh dear God, Addison! Where are you? Hoo, hoo, hoo! Can you hear me, boy? I'm coming for you! Answer me, damn it, boy!"

The stench of rotting human and equine bodies was overpowering. Some bodies had been there for several days and there hadn't been time or timber to burn the horses, some of whose bellies were bloated and bursting.

Lemuel covered his nose with his sleeve and squatted, peering into the smoke that hung over the fields. He heard a strange sound, vaguely human, emanating from the brush and duck-walked toward it, keeping his head low.

The sight that greeted his bleary eyes was appalling. A blue-coated sergeant with both legs shattered was sitting on a dead body and leaning back against a tree stump. Clearly crazed from a severe head wound, he was yelling at the top of his lungs, preaching to an imagined Sunday School class. Lemuel could make out only a few words, but he muttered "amen, preacher, amen" and shuffled off.

As Lemuel and others sought their dead and dying family members and comrades, a Confederate band behind the Rebel lines began to play "Nearer My God to Thee". As they finished their rendition, the Union band responded with "The Dead March" from Handel's SAUL. The effect was both chilling and soothing to the souls of the survivors, as though a host of angels grieving for the dead were playing a requiem.

The shattered trees still shuddered, clung tenaciously to the remains of rocks and soil, holding the broken body of the Earth with their tattered limbs and tangled roots. Huge rocks had been dislodged from their ancient places in the ground, strewn about the battlefield, and flung carelessly as though the Titans had been playing at bowls.

"Hoo, hoo, hoo," Lemuel called again.

A form in a green uniform, clutching a Sharps .52 caliber sharpshooter rifle, rose from a pile of bodies, a ghost in the gathering gloom.

James Moody heard Lemuel calling for his brother and staggered toward the lantern and the voice.

"Halloo? Halloo? Who's looking for Addison Grant?" called the Penobscot sharpshooter. "Are you his brother Lemuel?"

"Who's that using Addison's name? Who are you?"

"I'm with the 7th Maine. If you're looking for Addison Grant, he should be over here somewhere near the "shoe". I'll help you look, Sergeant."

Lemuel found what was left of Addison's body around midnight as he and James staggered along the battlement and pulled up the bloodied shattered faces stacked in front of and on top of the abatis. He sank to his knees in the gore around him. Blood of Rebel and Federal ran together and soaked into the ground, now hallowed. Exhausted, Lemuel surveyed the nightmare that stretched out as far as he could see. The control of the "mule shoe" was uncertain, but he could hear the Rebel soldiers quietly pulling back to their new line of defense. Would they repeat this macabre dance tomorrow? Who would bury these thousands of dead soldiers? The victor customarily buried the dead, but who had won? Lemuel wept long and hard, away from his post as commissary sergeant, but right now no one seemed to care.

The family had no money with which to return the body for burial in the family plot in Winterport, and Lemuel knew what he had to do. He stumbled over dead bodies as he went back to camp looking for any tools he could use to bury his brother. One dying soldier even grabbed his foot and begged for a drink of water. Lemuel had forgotten his canteen back by the "mule shoe" and yanked his foot loose.

"Sorry, soldier. I'm sorry. Don't have any on me."

He went on in a daze, putting one foot in front of the other in a mechanical march. He'd be damned if they were going to throw Addy into a pit with a ton of rotting human meat, unrecognized, unheralded, unknown, to be dug up later, feasted on by boars and half-wild dogs.

After dragging away dozens of bodies, Lemuel prepared to bury his brother in a small clear spot on the field where he had fallen. He couldn't move the mangled corpse without having it fall apart in his hands, so he had tried to move him to the only tree that hadn't been blown apart by the blasts of cannon and rifle, but Addison was so riddled with shot that the only thing holding his remains together was his bloody belt. Lemuel took off the Grant crest and pinned it to a piece of Addison's shredded uniform.

"Craig elachie, little brother, craig elachie."

Lemuel took off his cap and sat mindlessly on a stack of bodies he had created to clear a space for his brother's grave. He wept, even howled in his grief, clutched the penny rug around his neck that his dear Annie had made for him, and wished himself home. The last thing he remembered saying to his brother that horrible day was that he should turn and fight. Lemuel hadn't been able to keep track of Addison after they had found each other. How would he tell his grieving mother that he hadn't been able to protect her youngest son?

Next to Lemuel was a stump. It was all that remained of a two foot diameter oak that had been felled not by cannon but by thousands of rounds of small arms fire. He would use that for a marker so he could hopefully find Addison again when the war was over.

As Lemuel sat on the stack of bodies, he hung his head in abject grief. How could he bear this? He should have protected his younger brother. He should have done as Addison asked and slipped from his unit to the 7th.

"Oh Addison, Addison!" he howled. "Why couldn't you take care of yourself for just a few more weeks? You could have gone home a hero like you wanted, like you deserved."

"Lemuel," a voice said softly. "You must return to your unit. You could be charged with desertion, Lemuel. Lemuel. Lemuel."

James Moody put his hand on Lemuel's shoulder and tried to bring him back to the present. He handed Lemuel a blood-soaked letter that Addison had written to his mother.

"I'll stay here with the grave, Lemuel. He won't be alone. I'm a sharpshooter so no one knows if I'm dead or alive anyway. A few hours won't matter. Go back to your unit. You've done all you can do here. Besides, Lemuel, you can see that Addison died charging the "shoe". He died a hero. A man's death is personal, Lemuel. It's his own. In the end it's the very last thing he can claim as his own. By the way, here's a jar of blueberry jam that was in Addison's haversack. I guess your mother made it? He was saving it for the trip home."

Lemuel knew the man was right, but he didn't want to go back to the 4th. He couldn't bear to leave his little brother, but he must. Without a word, Lemuel put his hand on the dirt that covered Addison, gasped for breath, and turned away to return to the 4th. He turned back and held up the light so he could better see the man who had helped him.

"Thank you. You said you are Penobscot. What's your name? I'm so sorry I didn't ask before."

"My name is James. James Moody. I knew your brother."

"Thank you James. I'll remember your kindness.

*****

For a moment, Addison didn't quite know what had happened to him. The blood and dirt were gone from his body and he was all in white. There seemed to be a light coming from somewhere up above, but it wasn't the moon. He spoke to his brother, but Lemuel didn't hear him. He felt another presence and turned to look. It was Emma! His dearest Emma stood before him! He reached out for her in mindless joy.

"Emma, Emma, you're alive! How did you get here?"

He reached for her, but something was different. He knew he was touching her, but it almost felt like he wasn't touching her either.

"Emma! What's wrong? What's happening to us?"

"Addison, my love, listen to me. We're both dead, my dear, but now we can be together forever. Come with me. I need to talk with you. You have more to do, and we may be separated for a time, but I'll be watching you. You're going to have to help your brother when his time comes."

"What do you mean, Emma? I don't understand! What's going to happen to Lem? Can we stop it?"

"No, my love, we cannot stop it, but you can help him. Come with me."

Addison looked back at his grieving brother for a moment and turned to follow Emma who likewise seemed to be dressed in white. He understood now that they were both dead, but he could only follow her and hope she knew what to do. She had been dead longer than he.

*****

Julia Grant had not heard from Addison for weeks. The longer she went without that precious contact, the harder it was. She had had one letter from Lemuel recently, but nothing more. One afternoon she stood looking out the window of the farmhouse – her mind wandering, wondering. Down the road she saw a single rider with his head bowed. She could not bear to watch the post rider, so she turned her back hoping he would not turn up their rocky sandy road.

"Not today, not today," she whispered. "Oh, please God, not today."

The rider dismounted and took a letter from his saddlebag. With a deep almost mournful sigh, he removed his hat and turned it in his hands, then slowly walked toward the door. Joseph had heard him coming and hurried to intercept him. With tear-filled eyes, the rider put the letter almost reverently into Joseph's hand and looked at the ground.

Joseph grabbed the man's arms and shook him

"Which one, man. Which one? I have to know before I go into that house," Joseph whispered.

"Addison, Joseph. It's Addison. He died at Spotsylvania. A hero. He was a hero, Joseph. I'm so very sorry. Is there anything I can do? Anything at all?"

"No. No. That's all right. Thank you."

Joseph put his trembling hand on the doorknob and hesitated.

How would he tell Julia? With a deep sigh, he opened the door and saw his wife standing by the window. She had seen the rider remove his hat and hand Joseph a letter.

"Which one, Joseph? Which one? Surely not both? I couldn't bear that."

Joseph looked out the window and watched the carrier of dreadful news ride away. This time he sat up straight in the saddle with his hat over his heart. Joseph, the already grief-stricken father put his arm around his wife and pulled her to him. As he drew a deep breath and started to speak, Julia stopped him. She gasped and breathed out the words.

"Not today, husband. Not today. Perhaps tomorrow, but not today. Let my sweet boys live one more day. Just one more day." She turned back to stare out the window.

"Not today."

Perhaps the death rider, that bearer of unbearable news, would not come again. Maybe he could devour the news like sin eaters of olden days. It was a mistake. Someone else's son. Not hers. Surely not hers.

Joseph choked back a sob and stepped outside. The sun was slipping behind the Dixmont hills. The grieving father stumbled to the barn and dropped to his knees in the hay. A howl of grief erupted from his throat.

"Why Addison? Why did I let you go? Dear God, I should never have let you go."

*****

CHAPTER 14

When his unit was released, Lemuel went home to Frankfort. He was anxious to see his sweetheart Annie, but not his father.

As Lemuel stepped through the front door, he looked over at his father who was sitting by the fireplace.

"Evenin', father. I thought you might have met me at the train," Lemuel said with a sharp edge to his voice.

They had never really gotten on well. Addison was the favorite, the patriot. Lemuel, being the older, had been encouraged to carry the Grant crest into the war, but he had always been the rowdy prankster, the rule breaker. Busted to Private more than once, including the day he went looking for Addison.

"Sorry, Lemuel. I forgot you were coming today. Your mother is still grieving over Addison, so she didn't want to go and see all the young soldiers getting off the train. Glad you made it home ok. I'll be needing you in the hayfields. We need to think about getting one of those new-fangled hay balers. Not quite sold on them, but I guess it makes storing the hay easier. Not just loose in the barn like we've always done. We can talk about it tomorrow. John down the road has one and likes it pretty well.

"Say, boy, you weren't wounded anywhere were you? Being a commissary sergeant, you weren't in the thick of things as much as Addison."

Lemuel snorted.

"Hell, yes, father. I was in the thick of it. I didn't sit on my butt watching from the sidelines!"

"Good heavens, boy. Watch your language! Your mother is in hearing. I didn't raise you to cuss!"

"Sorry, mother. I was wounded a time or two. Do you think Addison was the only hero in this family? Him being shot in the back at Antietam and re-enlisting just to prove he wasn't a coward? I'm the one that had to bury what was left of him at Spotsylvania."

"Of course, Lemuel. I know you were a good soldier. Wouldn't have made sergeant so young elsewise."

"Don't know as that's true exactly. Addison's commanding officer, Major Hyde, was scarcely older than us. Good man, but really young. Real young."

"Are you going to go see Annie, son? She'd have been there when you came home, but her father's been real sick. And with her mother dead and all, she's taking care of him. 'Spect she's anxious to see you. Give your mother a kiss, and come back as soon as you can. I'll have dinner set on."

Lemuel kissed his mother and hurried off to Annie's house. He knocked as he opened the door, and grabbed her in a hard embrace. He inhaled the rose water smell of her red hair and felt the silkiness of the curls spilling down her back. Annie squealed as she threw her arms around his neck. Lemuel spun her off the floor and whirled around.

"Oh, Annie, I do love you. I missed you so much."

"I missed you, too, Lemuel. Sorry I couldn't meet you at the train, but Daddy is really sick. At least you got home safe. Must have been terrible finding Addison like that. Your parents were thankful that you took care of him. When this awful war is over, maybe you can help us find his grave, so we can pay our respects."

"Not sure I want to go back there, Annie. I guess we can do that some day. It'll be hard looking at all that again. It was horrible, just horrible."

Annie hugged her sweetheart, and silently thanked God that he had returned with only a few minor wounds. At least one of the brothers had survived to come home.

Lemuel turned to look out the window, bowed his head for a moment, and turned back to face Annie.

"Annie, I've made a decision. Thought about it a lot during the war. Now that Addison is gone, I don't think I can stand to be around my folks anymore. I need to do something else. Addison was the farmer boy, not me. I'm thinking I'll sign on a ship as first mate. After a few trips, I'll have enough shares to buy us our own place. That is, if you'll have me. Will you marry me, Annie?"

Annie gasped and covered her mouth with her hands.

"Oh, Lemuel, I thought you'd never ask me! Of course I'll marry you, but must you go to sea? A lot of Maine men never come back. She's a cold mistress, the sea."

"I know, but I'll pick a good ship, Annie, and a good captain. I'll be fine. It's the only way I know to get enough money put by to get us a place of our own. We can get married before I leave. That way, you'll get my military pension and my shares from the ship if anything happens to me."

"You might have asked me first, Lemuel."

"Well, I'm asking you now, woman. It's something I just have to do. I hope you'll understand. There's a new ship being built right now at Treat's. I plan to find the captain and sign on if the job is open."

Annie shook her head. Most houses had a widow's walk for good reason. The jealous Atlantic Ocean with her cold green water took many men to the bottom. Working at sea was a hard, dangerous life. The young woman shuddered as she thought about her own brothers and cousins who had been lost. She had thought that choosing a farmer would be safer. But now. She stared at Lemuel. She knew it was no use trying to change his mind.

"The tales of that awful, pitiless sea,
With all its terror and mystery,
The dim, dark sea, so like unto death,
That divides and yet unites humankind."
-Longfellow, "The Golden Legend" (1851)

CHAPTER 15

Lemuel got in his time on the sea, and once he got over his seasickness and found his sea legs, he loved sailing. No two trips were ever the same. The smell of the icy Labrador current in the far north, and the sweeter scent of the Gulf Stream along the coast made the trips a more interesting voyage. The fish were different as were the marine mammals and the birds. He learned all their names and recorded them in a small diary along with sketches of each. He sketched the ships he saw as well as sights along the coast. On one particularly long and dreary trip through bad weather and waves, the ship was trailed by an unusual gathering of sharks. They unnerved Lemuel, and he wondered if they were all man-eaters.

When he felt that he had enough experience to ask for the first mate's position with Capt. Averill, he tracked him down in Frankfort where the captain kept a small house. He had never married. Said the sea was mistress enough for him. *The Warren* was nearly finished being refitted, so Lemuel suspected that the captain would be in town buying supplies. He passed a man that he was sure would be the ship's carpenter carrying some tools as he shuffled along to the dock.

"Pardon me, sir, but are you *The Warren's* carpenter? I'm looking for the captain. Do you know where he might be?"

"Hah! Looking for the captain, now, are ye? Well, lad, we've a full complement of crew, and while your clothes tell me ye've been asea some, ye be having a strong smell of the cowyards! Don't think the captain can use ye. I'm also the coffin builder, boy. Hate to have to build one for ye. Git back to yer farm." He spat in the dust as he walked away, and Lemuel resisted the urge to spit back at him.

Captain Averill was standing on his front porch looking at the Penobscot River when Lemuel came up the walk. The path was lined with large shells that held back masses of wildflowers – primroses, brown-eyed susans, queen anne's lace, bleeding hearts and a few that Lemuel didn't know.

"Morning, Captain. Don't know if you recollect me or not, but I'm Lemuel Grant. We spoke some time ago about a possible place for me on your ship. You said you'd consider me for first mate, sir. I've got some experience now. Been all the way down the coast once, sir. Seen some rough water, too. May I talk to you, please?"

The captain continued to look past Lemuel and pulled some more on his briar pipe. His blue eyes had faded some over the years, and his complexion was ruddy and pocked. Lemuel wondered if the captain had ever had smallpox or worse. Other terrible diseases lurked in foreign ports and sailors had a reputation. Captain Averill stood a good six foot or better, the boy gauged. Not an once of fat anywhere that Lemuel could see. Wasn't sure about his age. The sea took its toll of a man's looks.

When the captain finally spoke to stop Lemuel's fidgeting, he still didn't look at the somewhat nervous young man in front of him.

"Ever taken a ship down river, boy? Out of port, I mean. Among the host of ships of all sizes and drafts. Can you handle the sails now? If I were sick could you take the helm and not crash into other ships or the rocks in some foreign harbor? Wind's tricky on the rivers and harbors, boy. Well?"

Lemuel held his breath for a moment. Truth was, he'd only helped at the helm going down river and tacking down east to get back to port. Never had the helm alone. He decided that the truth was the only course.

"Well, sir, I've stood by and helped the mates. I believe I can do it myself if need be. There's always plenty to learn, of course. I'm a quick study, captain. I work hard, I drink little or not at all, and I don't use tobacco."

"Ah, sober lad, are ya, boy? Good. 'Course there's many a good sailor who likes his grog and t'baccy. Don't hold that against him if he's sober on deck. Let's walk to the ship and see if she'll have ya, boy. She'll be sailing out of St. Andrews, New Brunswick, flying the Union Jack, ye know. Believe I told you that Webster Treat still owns her, and at 695 tons, two decks and three masts, she be quite a bark. She be 146 feet in length, her beam be 32 feet and the draft is 19 feet. Let's see how they're doin' finishing up fitting out this lady here."

The captain and Lemuel scurried up the swaying plank that held her tenuously to the shore, and stepped aboard.

"Captain on deck, you lot. Look alive!" the carpenter bellowed. The few crewmen who were aboard stepped smartly into line while the captain walked past them. A few dared to snigger at Lemuel. Everyone in town seemed to know that he coveted the mate's job. And every man aboard ship that day knew he had no real experience as mate. What was the captain thinking?

"Damned cowyard tars," muttered an Irish Newfoundlander seaman named Big Mike. "What the hell a farm boy know about the sea? Ah well, ye can't tell the mind of a squid, bye? Looks like a damned gilderoy to me with his fine coat. Wonder where de captain cotched this'n. We'll see soon enough what this chucklehead knows if'n he don't be getting us kilt first."

The ship rolled slightly as though testing the river currents. She had launched with a dramatic roar the day they finished her. Lemuel remembered that some superstitions connected to launching dealt with direction, sails, and such, but he couldn't remember what they were. And he wasn't about to ask the captain.

Captain Averill scowled at a loose piece of oakum and yelled for the carpenter.

"What's this, for the love of Mike! Loose oakum on deck, man? Would ye be hopin' I'd fall over it some night in the dark and crack my noggin? Fix that right now! And don't let me see another bit of slovenly work – not on my ship!"

Lemuel realized that he had been holding his breath while the captain ranted about a bit of oakum. He'd not be an easy man to work for. Still he had a wonderful reputation for knowing the sea and storms, and always bringing his ships in safely. He'd be a great man to work for if one wanted experience and learning about the sea and ships.

When the day came to decide, Captain Averill picked Lemuel for first mate. "I like the cut of your jib, boy, and a bit of brashness to ye. The crew will settle down after a bit and know that you've enough experience on the sea and at war to lead men. They'll just have to get used to you is all. You're my first mate."

Lemuel was overjoyed. He shook the captain's hand and signed the ship's papers. His share would be settled before they sailed. It would depend some on where they were to go and what they would carry.

Annie cried when Lemuel told her he had signed on. The wedding was a bit rushed and Annie pouted some. Her father grieved a bit. At least she had found a good man from an old family. The Grants had been there longer than Maine had been Maine. Annie begged to see the ship once it was re- fitted inside and out, but Lemuel frowned and shook his head.

"No, Annie! Captain – and most sailors – think a woman is bad luck on board a ship. He won't allow it. And to boot, you have red hair, woman! That's double bad luck!"

"What foolishness is this, Lemuel?" she snapped in reply. "Why can't I see the ship? Do you think I'm bad luck, too? Does that mean the captain's wife has never been on board either? I don't believe that."

She stamped her foot for emphasis. Annie's flaming red hair and green eyes were what had initially attracted Lemuel to his wife, but there was a temper under all that red hair. He couldn't help smiling at his beautiful wife. He hoped that the wound he had received in the war would not keep him from siring children.

"Annie, I've got to go back to the ship. I hate to leave you, but I have to go. Maybe this will be my last voyage. Father wants me to take over the farm. With my share on this trip, I'll have the money to build us a proper house and you won't have to live with my parents. I know it's not much of a life, Annie. I'm sorry I haven't as yet done better by you. We'll talk more about this when I get back. We're heading to Buenos Aires and then Antwerp. Cap'n says with Antwerp opening back up again, we'll get a lot of new merchandise to bring back home. Just be patient with me a little longer. I'll come home to you and we'll make plans. Just be patient, please. I love you so. We'll start our family, I promise. And no, you cannot come aboard the ship."

Annie teared up, but said nothing.

"We'll see about that," she muttered under her breath.

Lemuel hurried back to the ship to prepare her for sailing. Since Big Mike and the crew were still ashore, visiting family and a nearby tavern, Lemuel thought he had the ship to himself until they returned. He didn't know that the captain was below decks in his quarters. The new first mate stood on the bridge and wondered what it would be like to be a captain. He felt the ship stir under him, rocking to and fro, seducing him with her rhythmic motion.

Lemuel loved the powerful salt smell of the sea, the capricious wavelets and the roar of storms in the open ocean, the snap and smack of the sails when the wind shifted. He even loved the fear and the salt spray stinging his face, the whales that breeched and dolphins that rode the bow waves. He was even mesmerized by the sharks as their menacing fins sliced through the waves. They had their place which was often trailing in the ship's wake, waiting. A man who died at sea was buried at sea, and the sharks soon found his body. Lemuel shivered at the thought. The hairs stood up on the back of his neck as he tried not to think too much about the sharks, especially the Oceanic Whitetips, open ocean monsters that could taste a drop of blood from miles away, and who sometimes trailed behind ships to feast on their refuse.

*****

A few hours later, a figure in a dark, hooded cloak stepped out of the darkness and fell in behind the straggle of men returning to the ship. They were reeling and staggering from one too many pints, singing and laughing loudly. The crew didn't notice the person who had slipped into their wake, not even when they waddled up the gangplank like a gaggle of geese.

When they reached the deck, the cloaked interloper quietly stepped back into the shadows and hid behind some boxes of goods that were to be loaded below decks in the morning. When all was quiet and the men were in their bunks below, Annie dropped her cloak and stood up. After looking around her, she sidled crab-wise toward the bridge.

As she tiptoed around the deck in her husband's loose britches, Annie tripped over the piece of oakum that had worked loose from a deck seam and she fell. Lemuel, who had gone below decks working on the ship's log, heard the thud and scrambled up to see what had happened. Annie had twisted her ankle severely and looked up from her tears to see her husband standing over her in a rage of disbelief.

"What on earth are you doing on this ship, woman?" he snarled at her. "Do you want me to lose my position?"

He leaned down to pick her up and carry her ashore, but it was too late. The captain had heard the noise and came up on deck from his quarters.

"Who is this, Mister Grant?" he bellowed at Lemuel.

"It's my wife, sir. I'm very sorry, sir. She followed me back to the ship and came aboard. I'll carry her off and take her home immediately. It won't happen again, sir."

"You've cursed this ship, you stupid cow! Get off, get off, I say!" The captain had lowered his voice to a hiss, hoping the crew was too drunk to hear.

The first mate carried his trembling wife ashore, hoping to be off before anyone else saw a woman on board, but Big Mike had heard the commotion, tiptoed out of the crew's quarters in the fo'c'sle and had come topside. He was leaning against the bulwark in the shadows. When he went below and told a few of the crewmen what had happened, several men immediately threatened to quit the ship's company, contract or no, but the captain persuaded them to stay. After all, the woman had been dressed as a man, so surely the curse wouldn't hold. He, the captain, was certainly staying aboard the ship.

When Lemuel returned to the ship, Big Mike stopped him as he boarded.

"A word wi' ye, sir, if you please."

"Yes, Mike, what is it?"

"Well, sir, I was topside when ye hoisted yer missus and took her away. Since I'm Irish meself I don't hold with red-headed women being bad luck, but the others…can't say fer them. But at any rate, sir, beggin' yer pardon of course, a woman is a jinker, bad luck on a ship fer sure and certain."

Lemuel held his breath and tried to think. Inspiration struck.

"Um, Mike, a woman is of course bad luck on a ship, but she was dressed in britches like a man, don't you see? So that doesn't count as being a woman aboard ship."

Big Mike cocked his head and stared at the first mate. There was no doubt that a woman had been aboard the ship, but the ship was moored and not at sea. Maybe the curse wouldn't apply in that case. He didn't know about the britches.

"Well, sir, a woman's a jinker fer sure. There's no way about it. I won't talk of it more with the others lest they get crazy when they sober up and we have a manus asea. I just hope I'll not be dreaming of horses this night."

"Manus? Horses?"

"Aye, sir. Manus is a mutiny, ye know, and dreamin' of horses means death. Goodnight to yer, sir."

*****

Earlier that same week, during a visit to his parents, Lemuel had leaned on the railing of the bridge that crossed the Cattamawawa Stream in Frankfort, staring at the black ducks for whom the Indians had named this gentle, tame stream. He stared at the water and wondered what he was doing, signing on *The Warren* and leaving a new bride home alone. She would stay with the Grants until Lemuel returned, but still, she would be lonely.

Some black ducks quacked at him and clustered below the bridge, paddling and jostling for the best spot. Lemuel absentmindedly pulled a piece of bread from his pocket and tore it to pieces, dropping them all into the water.

His thoughts turned to Addison when the ducks gave up on him and paddled downstream to a popular picnic spot. He wept.

"Oh Addy, if only you could have lasted through just two more battles, if you'd hung on for a few more weeks, you'd have come home safely. Why couldn't you have looked out for yourself better? If only we hadn't listened to all the big talk and the speeches, not fallen for the fancy uniforms, we might both be staring down into this stream and talking of fishing. Our poor mother. How she grieves, Addison."

Addison's ghost who was sitting on the railing watching the ducks, put his face in his hands. He had watched his unit fight at Cold Harbor and watched his brother head home after that, his enlistment up. He had sailed unseen with Lemuel up and down the coast, and sat in the crow's nest a time or two.

Addison swiped at his brother's cap and knocked it into the water. His skills had improved at last.

"Dadburnit! If I didn't know better, I'd think that scamp was hereabouts. He was always knocking my cap off!"

Lemuel stood perfectly still and listened as though there might be a message from Addison in the suddenly cold breeze. Ridiculous, he thought to himself. I don't believe in ghosts.

A nearby oven bird flicked her tail and sang "teacher, teacher, teacher."

*****

Once the ship was laden with goods -- mostly timber for Buenos Aires and the crew was properly signed on, the captain gave the order to sail. Lemuel watched the tide turning and calculated the time of sailing. It would be several hours until the ship could draft enough water to pick up an offshore breeze. The captain always avoided sailing out in the first or third quarter of the moon, thus avoiding the sluggish neap tide that resulted from the sun, moon, and Earth being at right angles. It was a celestial tug-of-war that neither man nor ship had any business mucking about in. Lemuel loved to watch the tide flowing back to the sea. There was a raw power and a briny smell to it that excited him, made his heart pound.

When the tide swelled and rocked the ship, Lemuel made ready to sail. The captain always took his ship out of the harbor before giving it to his first mate. Maneuvering through the ships and sloops that crowded the Penobscot was difficult at best and no place for an inexperienced hand at the helm. Sometimes the capricious wind would suddenly drop or would gust just at a critical moment as the captain was easing her out of port and into the crowded river.

A few of the men still grumbled among themselves about the ship having been cursed by a woman, but after a few weeks they would be too tired and too busy with shipboard chores to think much about it. Lemuel prayed that they would just forget about it. After all, how could the presence of his sweet Annie possibly curse a ship?

Lemuel wondered if he were skilled enough, competent enough. He hoped that Big Mike and the others would work with him and that he could earn their trust. And he prayed.

"Please, dear God, let nothing happen to the captain on this voyage. I'm not ready yet by far. God bless us all."

He shielded his eyes and stared up at the bright blue sky. Looked like they were going to have great sailing weather, at least to Buenos Aires. The stream was quite predictable, and they didn't have to tack too hard to stay on course. Not like sailing down east and tacking upwind to get back to Bangor. The British flag snapped and fluttered in the breeze, and the bark nosed her way down the river.

The trip from Bangor to Buenos Aires was largely uneventful. The voyage home through the North Atlantic ought to be reasonably safe, thought Lemuel as they approached the Buenos Aires harbor. Hurricanes rarely made their way up the coast as far as Maine, but the Atlantic could be fierce. God willing, they should be well on their way home by July. Lemuel shuddered to think what it would mean if God were not willing. The entire crew had heard about Annie, and the non-

Irish Newfoundlanders had been horrified to learn
that not only had a woman been aboard ship, she
had been redheaded to boot.

"Mr. Grant, sir," Mike asked one day as he
stood playing with a piece of knotted string. "Do
ye know, sir, if there be any witch hazel tucked
aboard this ship, and was she first turned into the
sun when she launched? And was there an old sail
on the mast with the new ones, sir? It's important.
Could ye be asking the cap'n for me, sir?"

"Mike, how could my sweet wife curse this
ship? I don't hold with all that," Lemuel mused.
"And Mike, what the devil are you doing with that
string?"

"Why, Mr. Grant sir, it's nobut a piece of
string with knots and loops to catch and hold the
wind, sir. When ye have need of the wind, ye let
go the knots and loops, sir.

"Ye'd best be believin' these things, Mr.
Grant. It's not just blather and balderdash.
There's things in the world we'll not be
understandin' – banshees and dreams and tokens,
sir. See this bit o' haddock fin I wear around me
neck, sir? It's against the rheumatism. If I take it
off, sir, I'll be that crippled with it."

Lemuel thoughtfully clasped the penny rug
necklace that Annie had made for him before he
went to war and wondered. He had survived the
war. Addison had died. Lemuel had vowed to
wear it always, and tucked it back inside his shirt.

The ship's cat, a gray tabby that was a fine mouser, rubbed against his leg.

"Off with ye, cat. Get below. Go find the cap'n. I think I'll call you Jonesy. Best not let the crew hear that, I guess! And you, ratter dog, you're Beggar. That fits. I know you're the boy's dog."

The little rat terrier's claws clicked on the deck as he trotted off in search of the cabin boy. Lemuel was constantly learning about the strange, superstitious beliefs of his mostly Newfoundland crew. Redheaded women, coiling ropes against the sun, crossing knives on the table. All these were bad luck as was mentioning the dreaded Davy Jones. Lemuel was sure there must be some good luck tokens, but he hadn't heard those yet. The crew was obsessed with bad luck for the moment.

From Buenos Aires to Antwerp was a long trip, boring and usually uneventful unless a rogue wave rushed out of the vast expanse of ocean and smashed into a ship broadside. Many a man had been washed overboard by such a wave. It was impossible to guess from whence or when they might appear. The lookout could only do his best to warn the ship's crew. Some rogues were 100 feet high – monsters that could swallow a ship. Mariners spoke of "the hole in the sea", referring to the incredibly deep trough that would lie in front of the wave. They seemed to appear when currents and winds collided. Only the seamen believed in them. Most captains laughed it off – at least in front of the owners. Sometimes a small flock of seabirds would suddenly rise from the sea when a rogue threatened, but it could also be hungry sharks. Hard to tell.

The open water sharks were able to sense food for dozens of miles, people said. The brutal Oceanic Whitetips were the worst. Whenever a ship went down, they would come. Perhaps not right away, but they would come. A few drops of blood and struggling, drowning men would bring them.

The trip home from Antwerp began routinely, with the ship taking on cargo, food stores, water and rum. The crewmembers were entitled to rum. Their contracts clearly stated that. Each man got a ration a day.

The first mate shielded his eyes against the bright sun and stared up at the azure blue sky.

"Well, Mike, it looks like a fine day for sailing. The stream is with us and the wind is up. We should make good time. Wish the captain was feeling better, though. I think he may have a fever."

Mike mumbled something about ticky mattresses and closed his blue-green eyes as he crossed himself and prayed to be protected against the typhus.

"I hope mac Lir is about somewheres. We may have need of healing," Mike muttered.

Lemuel looked about for the captain and grabbed the young cabin boy by the arm. He was the captain's nephew and this was his first voyage. His mother had been reluctant, but her brother promised to take good care of the boy.

*****

"Don't be mollycoddling the boy, now," he had snapped at his sister. "Never letting him do anything the least exciting. This will be a trip he will always remember. Have a little faith in me, woman, I've been a captain for many years and never lost a ship yet."

"But, my brother, you have lost crewmen. The sea is treacherous. She took my husband, you'll remember. I'll not have her taking my son as well."

"Mother, I shall be fine," said the boy. "It will be a grand adventure, don't you see? And I'm already twelve. I haven't ever done anything exciting. I'm not too young to learn a trade. Perhaps someday I'll captain a great ship myself. My uncle will keep me safe. It's not like I'm shipping off with strangers. Please let me go, mother. I'll take my terrier dog Beggar with me. He won't let any rats bite me. Please?"

Mary bowed her head and exhaled a great, deep sigh. Her only son stood before her, shifting from one foot to the other, waiting for her answer.

"Very well, Richard. I shall let you go this once, but I'm not sure there will ever be another time. Mind your prayers and your scriptures, and be careful. The sea is dangerous. Remember that it killed your father."

Captain Averill doffed his cap and made a grand bow.

"My dear sister, you will not regret this decision. Your boy will return a man and with a trade. We'll all be back before you know it."

*****

Lemuel asked the boy where his uncle, the captain, was.

"I don't know, Mr. Grant, but I'll hurry down to the cabin and see if he's there. I've been helping Big Mike swab the deck. My uncle has not been feeling well, and I think he has a fever. I'll run quick and see about him. Just a minute, sir."

Lemuel stared up at the creaking masts and then down at the deck. He couldn't shake an uneasy feeling that something was not quite right. In fact, something felt very wrong.

"Damned if I know what the trouble is," he muttered to himself. "Hope the cap'n is all right. We need to leave soon. Tides will be wrong otherwise. Where's that boy?"

Breathless, Richard scrambled up the ladder to the deck and ran to Lemuel.

"Mr. Grant, sir, Mr. Grant!" he said gasping. "There's something wrong with my uncle. I can't wake him!"

Lemuel rushed down to the captain's private cabin and pounded on the door. Protocol be damned, he thought, and opened the door. The captain looked deathly pale and was sweating profusely. The ship's cat was curled up behind his knees and Beggar was lying on the small blue and gray braided rug that the captain's sister had made for him.

"Captain Averill, sir! Wake up! It's time to sail for home. Can you stand, sir? Are you ill?"

The captain stirred and tried to sit up, but fell back on his bed.

"I'm really not feeling well, Mr. Grant. I think you'll have to take her seaward. Can you handle her? I just feel so weak. I don't know what's wrong, but I don't trust these doctors here. They'll want to bleed me or some fool thing. Get me home. Help me, Mr. Grant. I must tell the crew that you'll be taking her out of port. I just need some rest is all."

The captain staggered to his feet, and Lemuel could feel the heat of the older man's body right through his clothing as he took his elbow.

"You're burning with fever, sir! Are you sure you don't want to see a doctor here?"

"Mr. Grant. I've sailed in all kinds of weather sick or well, and never delayed my ship. Get me on deck!"

Lemuel and the boy helped the ailing, palsied captain to the deck and called the crew.

"I have something to announce to you all, men. Mr. Grant will take the ship out and be sailing for a while. You must obey him as you would me. I'm not feeling myself just now and need rest," said the captain in a quavering voice.

"Beggin' yer pardon, Mr. Grant," said Big Mike who dared not address his captain directly. "Would ye tell the captain that we'd be thinkin' that perhaps 'twould be somat to think on. There be some good doctors hereabouts, sir. We'd narn o' us want to lose such a good man to some fever. Besides, sir, what if it's the typhus he's cotched from an old mattress? We could all die from it at sea. The ship would be lost. What do ye think, sir?"

Lemuel knew they were probably right. The captain was trembling and weak, and he had a high fever. Could this stubborn, strong-willed man be persuaded to get medical help? What if it was indeed typhus? Many died of it while at sea. He knew the captain was anxious to get home and was planning to retire and give up his captain's papers. But if he sailed from Antwerp this day, they might all die. *The Warren* could end up a ghost ship, adrift with a crew of dead men to tend her. At the very least, Lemuel wasn't sure he was experienced enough to captain the ship all the way to Maine. What if they ran onto a big storm or one crept up on them from behind?

"Captain, sir. I believe that the crew may have a point. Would it not be prudent to see a physician here before we leave port? I promise I won't let them bleed you or give you anything you don't want to take. Just for a day, sir? We made excellent time on the crossing from Buenos Aires and have a day to spare. Please, sir? You wouldn't want your nephew to catch some fever, sir, would you? And with no ship's doctor this trip, sir, well…"

The captain sputtered and wheezed, but was too weak to protest further.

"Big Mike, you're in charge for now. I'm taking the captain ashore to find a doctor," said Lemuel.

"By Molly and the saints," Big Mike whispered to the crew as Lemuel took the captain ashore. "The cap'n looked rawny, bye? And his hair – what there's of it left – was all mops and brooms! He's always been a bit binicky and hard to please, but I've never seen him like this. It's surely something altogether else, boys. Something altogether else."

In the doctor's office, the captain submitted grumpily to an examination. The doctor shook his head and looked at Lemuel.

"Monsieur. Ce n'est pas bien. Not good. He has fièvre. I have medicine. Make the tea. Peut-être it helps, mais je ne sais pas."

"Did you understand that gibberish, Mr. Grant?"

"Pretty much, sir. We had Zouaves next to us in the war, and we all had to learn some French. And our family has some business in Quebec. I think he just said that you have a fever and he's giving you some powders to make a tea. He doesn't know if it will help, though."

"Mais oui! Yes! Bien. Bonne chance, Capitaine. Au revoir."

The doctor dismissed the captain's fever as *mal de mer* of some sort and gave him some powders folded into white pieces of paper. Lemuel pressed him for a closer examination, but the doctor saw no profit in an old sea captain that he likely would never see again. With misgivings in his heart, Lemuel helped the weak, feverish captain back to the ship and his bed.

"See, Mr. Grant?" the captain whispered softly. "The doctor said it would pass. I just need rest and some herb teas. Richard can take care of me. Take her out, Mr. Grant. Let's go home and not lose any more time here."

Lemuel called Big Mike to his side.

"Mike, I need your help. I'm not too proud to ask for it. I've never sailed a ship this far alone before, and July can be dangerous on the high seas, especially in the North Atlantic. God forbid that there could be a hurricane to boot, but it's happened before. The crew needs to respect my authority as they would the captain himself, but I respect your experience and the crew knows you. Will you help me, Mike?"

Big Mike drew in a breath sharply and breathed out slowly. He clapped his hand over his mouth as his breath came out in a whistle. His eyes grew wide and he held his breath.

"Sorry sir! I didn't mean to whistle!"

Lemuel just stared at him. Another superstition no doubt.

"Mike! Will you help me?" the first mate said with an urgency Mike hadn't seen in the man before.

"Of course, Mr. Grant. I'm that pleased that ye asked my help. We'll be fine."

He turned to the crew that was standing about in little knots of anxious men and yelled at them.

"Get to work, ye lazy monkeys! Set the sails. Mind the mizzenmast, ye lot! We'll be headin' home! Mr. Grant has the helm because Cap'n is sick. I'm bein' the first mate. Quickly, now, or I'll keelhaul the lot of ye!"

The crew scrambled about setting the belaying pins and the sails snapped full with the wind.

"It's a fine day for sailing, Annie," Lemuel shouted. "I'm coming home, woman!"

"By the time we get near home, Mr. Grant, sir, it'll be a full buck moon. What a grand sight that will be over the Penobscot, sir."

"Indeed it will, Mike. Indeed it will. And the sun's setting earlier and earlier. We'll lose a half hour in July. There's something about sailing in the dark if there's no stars, Mike. I've never felt comfortable about that. The water's so dark and cold-looking when there's no starlight nor a moon shining on the sea."

"Ah, Mr. Grant, sir. I can smell the stars if there's clouds. And we've got a good compass, sir, and the gimbal lamp. Don't ye be worryin' narn about that, sir."

"I've got a fierce headache, Mike. Do you have anything for it?"

"Indeed, Mr. Grant! Here, let me show ye. Just walk arse foremost around in a circle, sir. Like this. Garnteed to rid your brain o' the demon."

Lemuel tied off the wheel and tried to walk backwards in a circle. Easier said than done, he thought, but it worked. Amazing. Maybe it was just trying not to fall that did the trick. He'd have to remember that.

"Ok, Mike. The headache seems to be gone, but I have an infection on my arm where I cut it a week or so ago. Doesn't seem to be getting any better. What trick would you have for that?"

Mike just grinned.

"Well, sir, I've somat in me bunk. Let me get it fer ye, sir," he said as he hurried to the fo'c'sle and looked around his bed.

"Arrgh! What a clobber this is. So much cultch! Looks like a great grumpus has swum through this and bashed it all to flinders! Hah! There 'tis!"

Big Mike gathered up his treasured potions, herbs, and bottles and hurried topside.

"Mr. Grant, sir! I've got it. Where be ye?"

Lemuel had gone down to check on the captain again and hollered an answer.

"I'm down here, Mike! In the Captain's quarters."

"Aye, sir. Stay where ye be at, and I'll come where you're to, sir!"

Lemuel shook his head and smiled. Mike removed his cap and tapped on the Captain's door.

"Here I be, sirs. Beggin' your pardon, Cap'n, but Mr. Grant has need of me potions, sir."

The captain nodded weakly and closed his eyes. The cat stretched herself and curled up again. The little terrier only watched as Lemuel tiptoed out of the cabin and went above decks.

"What have you got there, Mike? Smells awful! Tell me what it is before you touch that arm!"

"Well, sir, it's all garnteed to work or I'll keelhaul me ownself!"

Lemuel knew that the salt water he'd sloshed on his arm hadn't helped much this time, and his arm kept him awake at night. He was ready to try about anything, and Mike's trick seemed to have gotten rid of his headache.

"Sir, here's me potions and simples. Might I see your arm, sir?"

Lemuel took off his jacket and rolled up his undergarment sleeve.

"That's lookin' bad, sir, if ye don't mind my saying so. I'm sure I have somat that'll help ye. I know this smells awful, sir, but 'twill work if'n ye give it a try. Might I, sir?"

Lemuel nodded and turned his head – most particularly his nose – away.

"What on earth is that stuff, anyway, Mike?"

"Well, sir, 'tis powdered seashells and dried seaweed since we're asea, and moldy bread for a poultice. And this here is a jar o' goose grease. Wonderful stuff!"

Lemuel gagged at the smell of the rancid goose grease, but Mike persisted. He wrapped the whole gunky mess with a clean rag and tied it tightly.

"We'll watch it, sir, and I'll be changing the poultice every day or so, but I'm afraid ye can no wear your mate's jacket, sir. Might I, sir, since I'm acting first mate?" Mike asked with his eyes fixed on the coat.

Lemuel turned his head away to cover up his grin and then turned back to the big man.

"Well now, Mike. What will the crew think to see you with a mate's coat on? And I suppose you'll be wanting my cap as well?"

"Oh no, sir! I wouldn't dream o' that, sir. If I wear your coat, the crew will know I'm fer sure acting mate, and they'll know you're cap'n, sir, until Cap'n Averill is well, don't ye see, sir? I'll be that careful wi' your coat, sir, that ye'll never know 'twas on me back, sir."

"Hmmm. Well, Mike, I guess that would be all right. But be careful with it! You're broader through the back and belly than I am, you know!"

The burly Newfoundlander picked up the jacket with great reverence and brushed a bit of dirt off the sleeve. He combed his hair and beard with grimy fingers and scowled. Mike hung the precious garment on a hook and hoisted a bucket of seawater on deck. He grabbed a piece of lye soap and washed his hair and face and whatever parts of himself he could reach, then dried his hands on his filthy britches. He couldn't remember the last time he had actually bathed, but this was a special occasion.

"Might I, Mr. Grant?" Mike asked with his sweat-stained, slightly tattered cap clutched in his hands.

"Yes, Mike, only as I said, be careful."

"Aye, sir, aye!"

Mike wiped his hands again on his britches which, like his body, hadn't been washed in many weeks, and then he carefully took the jacket off the hook. He measured it against his chest, and cautiously stuck one ham of a fist into the left sleeve. It was more than a bit tight, so he stood for a moment clearly weighing the risk of ripping a seam against the greater good of wearing the prized badge of rank.

Lemuel chuckled in spite of himself and helped Mike ease into the other sleeve. He wasn't about to tell the big man that he had already

ordered a new jacket to replace the one that was
beginning to fade. It would be ready for him when
they returned home.

"Bit tight, Mike, don't you think?"

"Aye, sir, but I'll be very, very careful wi'
it."

The crew was agape when they saw Big
Mike wearing the mate's jacket that the seaman
could not button, but they parted as Mike strolled
through their ranks.

"Here you lot! Get busy! We've a ship to
sail!"

Once more, Lemuel checked on the captain
and told the cabin boy to tell him at once if there
was any change in his uncle's condition. Richard
nodded, but his face showed fear, and his lower lip
trembled. The terrier didn't raise his head, but his
eyes followed Lemuel up the ladder and the little
dog shuddered briefly and whimpered.

"All hands on deck and step lively!" yelled
Mike, assembling the crew. "We've got a ship to
sail home, boys, and we've never let Cap'n down,
have we?"

"No, Mike!" roared the crew. A few added
"sir", not quite sure if the coat warranted the added
respect.

"Well, lads, the cap'n is terrible sick, Mr.
Grant is acting cap'n, and I'm acting first mate.
We'll do like we always do. We'll be the best
crew on the seven seas and take *The Warren* home.
Let's be at it! Haul anchor!"

The new acting captain strode to the wheel, looked once at the compass in the binnacle, looked up at the sails and stared hard at the mizzenmast that creaked oddly for a moment as the sails filled. He couldn't see anything wrong and neither could Mike when he asked him quietly to look at the mast.

Oh well, thought Lemuel. Here I am, master of this good ship.

He caressed the wheel, and leaned forward. As he turned her with the wind and eased her out of the harbor, Lemuel felt the helm answer his hand. He was her master. She was his for a time, like a star-crossed lover. He only hoped that she would not jilt him or be a jealous mistress bent on disobeying him and humiliating him before his crew.

By the middle of July, he expected that they would be tacking down east and heading for the mouth of the Penobscot. He reminded himself to be mindful of the tidal river and not get caught in the ebb like the patriots had in the American Revolution. Brits darn near captured the lot of them, he thought, and would have, too, if the rebellious men of the new land had not scuttled their own ships, including the original *Warren* off Frankfort Marsh.

Lemuel looked over the crew and chuckled at Mike's clean hair and beard, and the jacket whose seams strained to contain all the brawny muscles on the older seaman's body. It would be a miracle if the jacket survived Mike's wild gestures. Lemuel wanted to get home so badly, he could hardly wait. He envisioned himself rowing ahead of the ship, stroking, pulling, urging her on.

"Hurry, you witch! I must get home to my wife, to my Annie!" he whispered to the ship. He was so happy at the thought of going home, that he began to whistle one of his favorite tunes.

Big Mike raced to the wheel and without a thought about protocol grabbed Lemuel's arm.

"Mr. Grant, sir, stop! Don't ye know it's the most worstest bad luck to whistle aboard a ship at sea, sir? Don't do that, sir! Beggin' yer pardon, sir, fer grabbin' yer arm, but I had to stop ye!"

"Bad luck, Mike? Isn't there anything that's *good* luck? Is there anything else I should know before I cause a shipwreck?"

Mike just stared at him and frowned.

"Well, sir, the other day I put me shirt on inside out by mistake. There's some say that's good luck. Mostly we worry about bad luck, sir. Good luck takes care of itself."

Lemuel promised he would not whistle again – at least not where Mike or the crew could hear him. Whistling bad luck? What poppycock. If all the strange superstitions were true, there'd never be a ship that finished her voyage anywhere. What nonsense. Even the soldiers he'd fought with in the war were not this superstitious. Lemuel wondered if humming at least was permitted aboard ship. He laughed to himself and began to hum under his breath. Then ever so quietly so no one but the ship could hear him, he again began to whistle. *The Warren* suddenly lurched as a small rogue wave swept under her keel, and almost knocked Lemuel to the deck. Mike turned and stared at his acting captain. Lemuel waved to his first mate to signal that all was well.

      Mike turned away and watched the rogue wave with a mind all its own go contrary to the swells. He looked heavenward, muttered something only God could hear and crossed himself several times. A cold breeze blew low across the deck and Mike shivered. Was that a whiff of sulfur or smoke he caught just then? He looked up in the rigging to see if Davy Jones himself might be up there, but there was nothing. At least not anything he could see. He didn't hear the low raspy chuckle.

CHAPTER 16

As first mate, Lemuel had been used to great responsibilities aboard the bark. The captain had depended on him to keep things running smoothly, and to keep watch even though the crewmen were experienced and reasonably tame. Some of the men gave him the chills, but they knew their ropes and lashes. He could only hope that with the captain sick in bed, if a problem cropped up he would be able to count on them to behave and do their parts. He was positive that he could count on Big Mike.

In July, the Atlantic was unpredictable at best and absolutely terrifying at her worst. Maine men knew the sea, and the Grants knew the sea better than most. Lemuel's lineage harked back to a long line of sea captains and Scots warriors, and he felt at ease on the swells even though he had been a farmer and a soldier most of his life so far. The sky was clear and cloudless at the moment, but that could change in an instant, and the sea

with it. A peculiar chill had been blowing across
the deck now and then for a day or so, and the sails
would slacken and then suddenly snap to and
billow full of the wind's unseen energy. Big Mike
must be busy with his knotted strings, Lemuel
laughed when the sails blew full. He hardly had to
look aloft to know what the square-rigged sails
were doing, but he was troubled by the
mizzenmast rigged fore and aft. Not quite right,
but he couldn't put his finger on the problem.
Something just didn't feel, or perhaps sound, right.

     The trip from Bangor to Buenos Aires to
Antwerp had been without serious incident or even
foul weather to speak of, but the ship was now
sailing into an area notorious among seamen.
Many a good ship had been lost in this part of the
North Atlantic and all hands with her. If the big
open-water sharks didn't get you, the icy water in
the Labrador Current would in quick order. As
they sailed toward Newfoundland and the Grand
Banks before heading down the coast, Lemuel
grew increasingly uneasy. He looked for signs in
the water and in the sky and found none. No storm
petrels or deepwater sea birds greeted his gaze as
he searched the sky and the ocean. Maybe he was
just tired after such a long sailing. He smiled as he
thought about the old seaman's superstitions
concerning the storm petrels, but wondered to
himself if they could be true. He really didn't
believe in reincarnation, but many of the men who
sailed with him did. Especially Big Mike.

To sailors, the appearance of storm petrels meant foul weather and death. Petrels were known to crash onto ships' decks by the hundreds sometimes, like lemmings leaping off cliffs, but Lemuel couldn't see how a bird's strange behavior could signal a storm. Surely, many birds like the Maine seagulls were driven inland by approaching storms, but to crash onto a deck? Lemuel shook his head in bewilderment and walked the decks again as he did every hour, looking for anything amiss.

Without warning, a bird crashed onto the deck right in front of Lemuel. Catholic sailors, and some who weren't, crossed themselves and fumbled for rosaries, while the others stared at the dead bird and rolled their eyes heavenward looking for more birds.

"Sure'n it be a storm petrel, Mr. Grant," Big Mike whispered in hushed, almost reverent tones. "That's not a good sign, sir. Not good a'tall," he said in his hushed Irish Newfoundland brogue, as he crossed himself again against the evil the bird had brought aboard.

"'Twas that damned redheaded woman done this, for sure and certain," another crewman muttered. "And the cap'n is sick, to boot."

"There's only the one bird," Lemuel snapped at Big Mike as he threw the limp body overboard. A dark triangular fin surfaced behind the bird, and there was a swirl where the bird had been floating, now ripped from the surface of the sea.

Nothing more happened for many days and then the weather changed abruptly. Clouds blew in and the sky darkened.

"Mackerel skies and mares' tails make a sailor furl his sails," chanted Mike as he stared at the changing sky. As the ship surged into the swells, Lemuel and the entire crew felt the first droplets of rain. The seamen stood by, anticipating orders to haul down some of the sheets. The bark was a good ship, but she could be a handful in this kind of wind. She was heavy-laden and a little slow to the helm, like a woman with child. In the distance, thunderclaps grew louder as the storm gathered strength and rolled across the ocean straight toward the ship.

"She'll be catching us broadside, dontcha know, sir," Mike said as he walked across the deck. "Should we wake the captain, sir?"

Lemuel bit his tongue and resisted the urge to remind his crewman that he was the captain for now, as he considered the wisdom in his first mate's question.

"All right, Mike, I'll go below and check on the captain. You take the helm and watch that storm."

Lemuel tapped on the door as he opened it and stepped into the captain's cabin. Richard was sitting on his uncle's bed, holding the sick man's hot hand.

"He's not moved in a long time, Mr. Grant. He's hotter than my mother's wood stove and sweating. When he was awake he said he had a terrible headache and his stomach hurt. What do you think it is? The doctor should have given him better medicine in Antwerp. He just seemed anxious to get rid of him. Is he going to die, Mr. Grant?" Richard whispered.

Lemuel touched his captain's forehead and felt the heat.

"Captain Averill, sir. Please wake up. We've got a bad storm that's going to catch us abeam, sir. Do we run or do we turn into it, sir?"

The captain struggled to open his eyes and stared at Lemuel as if in a dream state. When he finally spoke, his voice was weak and raspy and there was a foul odor on his breath.

"A storm, Mr. Grant? And it's coming out of the north?"

"No sir, actually it's coming from the south of us, and it looks like more than just a squall. Are you strong enough to go topside for a minute and take a look at it? To tell us what you want us to do?"

The captain struggled to his feet and almost fell over. With help from Richard and Lemuel he managed to get up the ladder to the deck. Lemuel had to put his hands in places he never would have dared had the captain been well. Big Mike had the wheel. When he saw the captain he tried his best to get the first mate's jacket off his brawny body.

It wouldn't do for the captain to see him in that coat. As he struggled with it a seam ripped open with a loud tearing sound, but the captain didn't notice. He was looking at the sky.

"There's been a storm petrel hit the deck two days ago, sir," said Lemuel.

He no sooner said that then another bird hit the deck. That bird was followed by another and another. The frightened sailors crossed themselves or made whatever signs their various religious beliefs or superstitions required in the face of evil omens. Most called themselves Christian if they had to put a name to it. Lemuel was devoutly Christian, but also knew that the sea seemed to have its own religion. Almost as though some ancient gods ruled the waters and were allowed to wreak havoc or at least mischief among mortal seamen.

"A storm moving upon us from the south is not normal, Mr. Grant. It could even be a hurricane prowling up the coast. I fear we're in for it. Strike the sheets and come about. We've no choice but to ride it out aweather. We don't want to get pushed onto the shoals. In this deeper water, we stand a better chance."

The petrels falling on the deck made Lemuel nervous. He and the captain would have their hands full with a frightened crew as it was, without bad omens falling from the sky. Lemuel knew that sailors believed the storm petrels were reincarnated souls of sailors lost at sea and come to claim new bodies or take the men down to the bottom.

Then there was the myth about Davy Jones – or was it? Saucer-eyed and horned, the specter of the legendary ruler of all that was evil in the seas, Davy Jones was believed to appear on any ship that was going to wreck or right before a hurricane. Legend said that he would ride the rigging of doomed ships with blue smoke pouring from his nostrils. Lemuel wished he hadn't named the cat Jonesy. Mike had fussed at him for being so ignorant of the ways of the sea and seamen.

"And would ye be tryin' to get us drowned, sir? Do ye not know about Davy Jones? Welshman, they say. Whatever he be, he's the divil incarnate, Mr. Grant. Don't be muckin' about with things ye no understand, sir."

Under his breath, Mike still hoped that mac Lir might be about somewhere.

The sky that had been merely overcast now grew dark and glowered down at the lone ship. Like a child having a tantrum, the wind picked up the wave crests and hurled them at the ship.

"Batten down the hatches and make fast! Strike the sails!" Lemuel yelled above the wind that was now whining in the topsails. "Sorry, cap'n. I should have asked you. Beg pardon."

"Quite right, Mr. Grant, but you gave the right orders. Help me get to the wheel."

Big Mike yielded the ship to her captain and backed away. Lemuel hoped the captain didn't

notice the jacket and hadn't heard the ripping
seam.

"It's all right, Mike. No harm done," said
Lemuel without looking at Mike. He stepped
between the seaman and the captain and behind his
back signaled Mike to get away. Another sailor
helped the big man get the jacket off and stowed,
and Mike turned to face the captain and first mate,
waiting for orders.

The creaking ship began to wallow slightly
as the keel cut into the seas and the ocean fell
away from the rudder in the troughs.

"Are we anywhere near the West Quoddy
Head Light?" the captain queried his mate. "I
suppose we may not be able to tell for sure with
this storm unless we can see her flash her
characteristics which are two white flashes every
fifteen seconds, but it would be smart to make for
the easternmost point if we can. That new steam
whistle they installed last year on the West
Quoddy light is so loud it sounds like a steam
engine, and the new lights can be seen near twenty
miles out from shore. Never had to sail for West
Quoddy before, but I'll try for it first. Help me
with the helm here, Mr. Grant. I'm not myself just
now."

Lemuel was enormously relieved to hand
over the helm and go back to being first mate. At
least someone who had more experience than he in
dealing with Atlantic storms was now in
command. Hurricanes were almost unheard of in

these waters, but he remembered hearing of two ships lost off the coast of northern Maine in hurricanes: the *Bowditch* in July of '61 and the schooner *Helen Eliza* just last September. Only the captain somehow survived the *Bowditch*, and one lone sailor survived the wreck of the *Helen Eliza*. Lemuel tried to shake off the growing sense of dread and threw himself into his work.

The captain asked for the last known position by instrument and shook his head.

"We're closer than I want to be to the shelf and the shoals, Mr. Grant! How did this happen? These waters are tricky enough to navigate without this storm! Don't want to have to deal with shoaling waves!"

The heavy ship groaned as she cleared wave after wave and the masts creaked in protest. A stinging saltwater spray whipped by the wind took away the crew's breath as they struggled with the balky bark.

Adrenaline surged through their veins as the captain and crew strove mightily to make *The Warren* behave and heed the helm.

*****

The captain considered dumping his cargo to lighten the foundering ship, but he had made such a good profit for the owner that he hesitated for fear that the good he had done would be wiped out by disaster. Still, it was an option he must consider to save the ship and the men. He was responsible for their lives, too, he thought as he fought the wheel. Exhausted, he finally tied it off long enough to rest his trembling arms.

The sickness that had come over him in Antwerp was getting worse, and the fever made his eyes ache. He bent over to clear the fog from his brain and blacked out, dropping like a sack of Maine potatoes.

*****

With the wheel tied and the storm raging, the ship slowly began to turn. When the first wave caught the ship broadside, Lemuel knew they were in desperate trouble and he leaned into the raging gale to get to the captain's side. It took two men to untie the stubborn wheel and two more to get the captain into his cabin. He was unconscious and unresponsive, and the men struggled back to their posts. The captain would have to wait or they would all be on the bottom of the ocean. Lemuel took the wheel.

"Annie, Annie, Annie!" Lemuel chanted trying to make mental contact with his beloved wife. "I love you, Annie! I love you! Do you hear me? God help us!"

As the first mate fought to right the ship, a new terror loomed ahead. The Grand Banks area was notorious for something besides sudden squalls and big storms. The area was also known for dense fog as air masses passed over the colliding warm Gulf and frigid Labrador currents.

And there were the shoaling waves. Lemuel set one man to the bell, the ship's soul, sounding a warning to any who might be in the fog fighting to get to safe harbor, although Lemuel doubted the bell could be heard over the roar of the storm. There were some coves and inlets along the coast, but most were guarded by huge rock formations, and Lemuel couldn't see the lighthouses for the fog.

"Come about, you witch!" Lemuel screamed at the ship. "Come about, come about!" he raged at her, but the ship with her 695 tons lumbered on with a mind of her own.

The storm had blown *The Warren* off course more than Lemuel had guessed and they were too far north, heading straight into the shoals off Newfoundland. If they got into shallow water the ship would be impossible to control. If only the captain hadn't gotten so sick, they might not have drifted off course.

Lemuel tried to look at the compass but the rain was now torrential. He could hardly see anything, what with the wind howling and driving rain and salt water into his face. The fog obscured the big waves until they slammed into the ship, and Lemuel hardly had time to count the seconds between swells. Rain hammered his back and legs and puddled on the face of the compass, making it almost unreadable. The first mate screamed to the cabin boy to come to his aid, but the sobbing boy cowered in the doorway to the ladder below decks, shaking his head vigorously.

"Come to me, damn you, boy, or we're all going to die! Come here and read this compass to me!"

The gimbal lamp swung wildly and went out as the terrified boy crept sobbing and shaking toward the wheel.

"Yes, sir, Mr. Grant. What do you want me to do?" the boy screamed into the wind.

"Read me the compass, boy! Lean over it and block the rain! What's our course?"

"It, it says noreast, sir!" the boy stammered. "I think the needle must be stuck, sir!"

"Noreast? Noreast?" Lemuel shouted at the cringing boy. "Are you sure? That's impossible!"

The boy shook uncontrollably and could hardly speak or move, but he leaned over the compass again and nodded to Lemuel. The reading made no sense to the first mate. Even with the storm they should have been heading south by southwest into the weather and out of the North Atlantic. Where were they? What should he do? Had the storm turned the ship?

"Big Mike! Mike! Come here and help me, man! Grab this wheel!" Lemuel shrieked above the roar of the storm.

The seaman fought through the blinding sheets of rain and reached for the wheel while Lemuel lashed the boy to the huge brass binnacle. Richard, who was slightly built, could easily be washed overboard in this storm. Since the boy was the captain's nephew, Lemuel knew the captain would never forgive him if the boy were injured.

This storm ignored the ancient lore of seamen and the waves relentlessly pounded the bark as though the sea and her countless tons of ferocious green and black water could by sheer force make the bark come to heel, to be done with as pleased the storm and the sea.

"Look out, sir!" yelled Mike as the mizzenmast creaked ominously. "She'll be coming down on yer, Mr. Grant! Mind the boy, sir!"

As the mizzenmast fulfilled the prophecy of the old sailor, Lemuel dove to cover the boy and took the brunt of part of the broken mast and its sails across his back. He screamed to the crew to come to his aid at once, and they wrestled the wreckage of the broken mast and sails to one side, freeing the boy and the badly injured first mate. Mike had ducked out of the way. Lemuel could not stand erect and one leg was numb. He guessed that his right shoulder might be dislocated or even broken but couldn't take time to assess the damage. As they moved to the side, another piece of mast crashed down and shattered the compass.

"It's smashed to flinders and smithereens, Mr. Grant," screamed Mike. For the first time, Lemuel saw a flicker of fear cross the face of his Newfoundland crewman.

"I believe it's time to talk to the cap'n again, sir."

"Yes, Mike, you're right. Hold onto the boy here and what's left of the wheel, and I'll see about the captain."

"Please let me go, sir. Let me go to my uncle. The ship's going down isn't it, sir, and no one knows where we are. We're all going to drown! I don't want to get eaten alive by a shark!" the cabin boy said with terror contorting his youthful face.

Lemuel hesitated for a moment and then dragged the shaking boy below deck to check on the captain. The mate knew that they were likely to go down, unless his captain could somehow save them. Maybe the captain knew some trick that would keep the ship afloat until they weathered the storm. Surely the captain had been in such a situation before.

"Captain, captain!" Lemuel yelled at the inert form on the cot. "Wake up, sir, wake up! We're about to founder, sir!"

Captain Averill could not hear him because the fever had taken him during the storm. When he tried to rouse the man by shaking him, Lemuel felt the telltale stiffening in the body. He had seen enough death to recognize its face. More than enough death.

The first mate knew that time was short, and he cast about for something that would float. In his haste, he knocked over the squatty crystal inkwell that the captain's sister had given him. It shattered when it hit the floor and a sudden roll of the ship caused the ship's log and papers to slip off the captain's desk and land in the puddle of ink. For an instant, Lemuel started to pick them up, but time was running out.

The sea will not get this boy, he vowed. The captain's trunk might do if it were empty. Feverishly he emptied the captain's trunk and jammed the hasp closed with a penknife.

"Here, boy, let me have your hands!" Lemuel said with urgency. He quickly fashioned two slipknots at either end of a length of rope that would fit around the trunk and slid them onto the boy's wrists.

"Stay atop the trunk whichever way she rolls, boy! Stay with it no matter what! Someone will find you."

The boy gibbered in terror and could scarcely understand what Lemuel was telling him. He tried to shake his uncle awake and clung to the lifeless body. Beggar leaned against the boy's leg and shook with fear. He heard the terror and urgency in the human voices.

"I can't leave my uncle, Mr. Grant! I'll wake him up for you. You'll see!" he said, clinging to the stiffening body and yelling at his uncle. The terrified tabby crawled under the covers and hissed at the boy.

"Come on, boy! He's dead!" Big Mike yelled at the boy as he burst into the cabin. "Off with yez now! Your uncle is dead and there's naught fer it but to be savin' yerself, boy! Mr.

Grant, the ship is foundering and the wheel's broke in half, sir. Let's go! We've got to abandon her to the sea or she'll suck us down wi' her!"

As the storm raged around the ship, *The Warren* began to creak and groan as timbers cracked and the boards split down the middle. The steering sails stayed gamely aloft until the ship slowly swung broadside to the troughs and the wind shifted against her.

"Jump! All hands abandon ship!" Lemuel bellowed. "The captain is dead. Get clear of the ship or she'll take you down with her to the bottom!"

"Wait, Mr. Grant? Where's my dog? Where's Beggar?" cried Richard.

"I don't know, boy! There's no time!"

"Beggar, Beggar! Where are you? Come here, boy!"

The little brown and white terrier slid across the slippery sloping deck toward his boy just as Lemuel and Mike threw the trunk over the side. Each man held a trembling boy's hand as they jumped into the churning water.

Beggar whined and ran frantically up and down the deck as the boy screamed for him to jump. Finally he leaped over the side and scrabbled and clawed at the trunk, trying to scramble onto it with the boy. The water was icy cold and after a minute or two and a few whimpers the little dog sank out of sight.

"Beggar, oh Beggar, where are you?" the boy wailed.

"He's gone, child. I'm that sorry, boy," whispered Mike through chattering teeth.

The sea began to swallow its prey, and monstrous icy waves pounded the ship and her crew as if to drive them to the bottom. The ship went down with a haunting moan and eerie creaks and turned slowly, prow first, in the eddy it was digging for its grave. Most of the crewmen were sucked down into the maelstrom. The tabby cat and the dead captain in his bed alone were left aboard.

As the ocean poured down the ladder and sought him out in his quarters, the water erased the ship's log and all the papers, and made a slurry of black ink mixed with salt water. A picture of the captain's sister as well as the bedraggled cat drowned in the slurry as the sea washed over the captain's cot. Like a hungry animal it roared through the ship and filled every space. Bodies of drowned sailors accompanied the ship down through the icy water as she and her captain headed for the crushing depths. A cold sea does not give up her dead.

Lemuel and Mike managed to get the boy onto the trunk and each one pulled the rope under the trunk until the boy was centered on top with his arms outstretched. For a short time the men hung on as the storm raged around them and the blinding rain beat their heads and backs. The icy seawater caused both to shudder and shake uncontrollably. After a few minutes in the frigid sea, the men's eyes glazed over and they released their death grips on the rope. The boy who was near madness called out to them but they were gone. His wrists had chafed from the tight ropes and his frantic struggles, and a few drops of blood had dripped into the water. Far away, a monstrous fish with peculiar white-tipped long rounded fins began a methodical zigzag course back and forth across the faint blood trail, coming closer and closer to the debris and a boy tied on a sea chest.

After hours of watery siege, the storm abated and the sun rose on the third day. The sea calmed itself and quietly burped up pieces of the shattered ship and some of the dead crewmen who had tied themselves to bits of wood. The ship was gone as was every man, but the boy lived, tied to the sea chest the carpenter had crafted for the captain.

Now only the boy was left, rocking on top of the wooden trunk. As the sun warmed his back, the boy struggled to free himself and called repeatedly for his uncle and his dog. The fog had cleared, but the boy was nearly blind from the lashing rain and seawater. As he slipped back into unconsciousness, a large dark form circled beneath him.

The storm had driven most of the fish into much deeper water, and the dark thing circling under the boy had not eaten in some time. A

curious kittiwake flew down and settled on the
water near the trunk, interested in both the trunk
and the form on top of it. Perhaps it was
something to eat. Shearwaters floated aloft
watching the scene below and squawking at the
huge fish circling closer and closer. Gannets who
had been diving like shimmering knives into the
sea to grab fish suddenly broke from the surface
with a rush and flew squeaking to the flock
hanging in the sky.

The sea erupted as the Oceanic Whitetip
lunged to the surface and grabbed the kittiwake,
shaking it like a rag doll as she rolled over into the
depths. The pregnant predator returned once to
bump the trunk and then cruised among the frigid
bodies of *The Warren's* crew. Her peculiar
rounded dorsal fin zigzagged through the debris.
There was a feast there and the blood would soon
draw other predators.

The shark bumped the bodies of the dead
crewmen. Persistent, the Whitetip again circled
around as though anticipating the meal. Then she
stopped, turned toward the trunk and sank below
the surface. The ghost of Addison Grant appeared.

"No!" said Addison. "You shall not have
the boy!"

For an instant, Addison forgot that he, too,
was dead. What could he do to protect the boy
from this horror? When he remembered that he
was a ghost, Addison slipped below the waves and
faced the shark. He didn't know for a moment if

the shark could even see him. No one in his family had. The monster shark stopped circling the trunk and appeared to be looking straight at Addison.

For a few moments the shark hung motionless in the water, then started pronking, lowering her long rounded pectoral fins and arching her already somewhat arched back. She continued the display, as though warning Addison away from what was hers. Addison tried to blow bubbles at the animal but could not. Waving his arms and trying to yell had no effect either. What else could he do, he thought frantically. The shark stopped her display and sank into the blackness. Addison was relieved. The boy would be safe for now!

With no warning, the shark reappeared out of the dark depths and charged Addison at full speed with jaws agape. Instinctively Addison threw up his arms and tried to hit the shark, but the fish swam right through him and hit the sea chest, flipping it over. With the weight of the boy the chest was top-heavy. Addison tried to turn the trunk over and save the struggling drowning boy but he could not move it.

"Why can't I do this?" he shouted. "Someone help me!"

"I'll try, brother, but I just figured out that I'm dead," said Lemuel, appearing next to him. "Tell me what to do!"

"Help me, Lemuel! Help me turn this thing over! Just try! Try!"

The shark had moved away again into the debris field, but was watching the commotion by the box.

Addison tried to untie the boy but could not make his fingers work the knots. The best he had been able to do so far was to knock off his brother's cap by the stream in Frankfort. This was so much more important!

While the two fumbled with the chest, the struggling child expelled his last bit of air and drowned.

"Stop Addison, stop. The boy is gone. At least I kept part of my promise. He didn't get eaten alive by a shark. The chest was the only thing I could see that would float. If only I could have done something better for him."

The two brothers stayed by the boy, grieving at their inability to save him, determined that the Whitetip should not get him. The sea would keep her secrets. The force of the monster shark's attack had broken a corner of the trunk and water began to leak into the chest. As the two brothers watched, the inverted chest filled with water and with the boy lashed to its top, it sank into the depths after its captain.

"Let's go, little brother. There's nothing more we can do here. Let's go home. Maybe you can teach me how to knock a cap off. That was you, wasn't it? At the stream?" Lemuel asked.

"Don't think I'm much of a teacher, Lem. I couldn't do anything to save that boy, not when it counted. And yes, it was me. Trying to talk you out of your fool idea of sailing on a ship. Especially on a ship named for one that our ancestor burned and sank. Now neither of us is alive to help Ma and Pa."

"And who will take care of my Annie, I wonder. I never thought I'd die on a ship."

Addison smiled a grim smile.

"Actually, Lem, you weren't on the ship. You drowned, remember?"

"Let's go home, Addison. Let's just go home. Maybe we can learn to do something to help out. How did you knock my cap off? Show me how you did that."

Far away from the wrecked ship the West Quoddy Light steam whistle wailed like a banshee and the lantern flashed its powerful beacon out to sea, like Rachel searching, mourning for her children.   None on the shattered ship were left alive to see or hear, but a saucer-eyed horned specter sat on the splintered masts, tilted his head back and blew blue smoke from his flared nostrils.

"Ha, ha, mac Lir! Do ye hear me now, Manannan mac Lir, son of Lir? So ye think ye be king of the oceans, do ye? Ye and yer magic ship "Wave Sweeper" with no sails may have saved King Arthur and seen him safe to Afallach of Avalon, but ye'll no be saving these ones here! They be mine!"

Then Davy Jones laughed an unholy, screeching, shrieking laugh like fingernails on a chalkboard and dove after the boy. There would be plenty of company at the bottom of the sea this night.

Rachel who mourned did not find the children who died young, and the willows of the brook wept and faded.

CHAPTER 17

When the rider had brought the notice that Addison had died at Spotsylvania, Julia had collapsed with grief. She saw the post rider dismount and take off his cap before knocking on the door. It was a re-enactment of the nightmares she had had since Lemuel first enlisted.

When the post rider again approached her house, dread overcame her and she sank, pale and perspiring, into the overstuffed chair by the fireplace. Joseph just stared at her for a moment and then walked to the door like a man in a trance. He opened the door before there was a knock.

"Mr. Grant, sir. There's word about Lemuel, sir. I'm sorry," he said as he handed Joseph the letter. "I'm so sorry," he repeated as he stepped back and bowed slightly. He turned his hat slowly in his hands, wishing he were not the one to bring such dreadful news. When Joseph just stood staring at the paper, the post rider backed away respectfully and mounted his black gelding.

Joseph read the terse message about *The Warren* being lost with all hands somewhere in the North Atlantic. The ship had been overdue for several weeks along with one other in the same area. Fishermen had also reported an unusual storm in the north. As Joseph stepped back into the room where his wife sat staring into the fireplace and barely breathing, Julia looked up at her husband. She held her breath and put her delicate hands over her ears. Then she exhaled until there was no air left.

"Don't tell me just yet, Joseph. I don't think I can bear it. Don't tell me I have lost both of my sons. Let it not be true for just a few minutes more. Please."

Joseph nodded and sat heavily in the chair that his own father had made. He folded the paper carefully and put it in his vest pocket. He gasped in grief and the tears started flowing down his cheeks. Unable to control his emotions, he just said Lemuel's name over and over again. Neither parent could help the other and they sat frozen in time and space, until the physical grief subsided somewhat and they were left with broken hearts and the pain of unbearable loss.

Joseph went to his knees and bowed his head on the floor.

"Why, God, why? How can you take both of our boys from us? For what purpose? They were both good boys. Why are you punishing us like this?"

Addison and Lemuel stood mute in the corner. They hadn't meant to die. It just happened. They didn't expect it. They surely didn't plan it. Addison moved to his mother's side and his heart ached for her. He wanted to hold her while she wept. He reached out to stroke her hair but he could not touch her, so he knelt by her side as he had when he was a boy.

"Oh mother, I'm so sorry. I wish I hadn't died. I wish Lemmy hadn't died. If we'd only known, we'd have done differently, mother. We love you."

Lemuel stood behind his father who was now prostrate with grief.

"I'm sorry, father. I'm so sorry. I couldn't save the ship. Maybe the captain could have if he hadn't died, but I couldn't. I couldn't even save the little cabin boy. I didn't even do that right," he said as he bowed his head.

"Addison, I've got to go to Annie. I'll be back later. Just call 'hoo, hoo, hoo'. I'll find you."

Addison looked up at his brother and wished with all his heart that they hadn't died.

*****

Lemuel got to Annie just as the messenger rode up to her father's house where she had been visiting for a few days, since her widowed father was lonely. Her father stepped off the porch and spoke to the post rider. This time there was only a verbal message. Annie looked out the window and saw the dismounted rider standing with his hat in his hands. Her father bowed his head and put his hand over his mouth, then turned back to the house. When he reached the porch, he stopped and leaned over, holding the rail. Annie saw the contorted face and the tears and knew instantly that she was now a widow.

The terrible nightmares she had been having were harbingers of evil news. She could not know that her husband's ghost was standing behind her, longing to hold her and comfort her, wanting not to be dead.

He stayed with her for hours, standing in the corner of the room, head down, wishing he could pound something. How had Addison knocked his cap off? Even Addison wasn't sure, but there must be a way. It had happened. He had felt it. Even sensed Addison's presence, he remembered. He walked over to the picture Annie had placed on the mantel. They had spent money they really didn't have to buy a portrait when they were married. Lemuel deliberately tried to knock the picture down, but nothing happened. Again and again he swung at it until finally in a fit of frustration he connected and the picture fell to the floor.

Annie gasped and stared at the tintype.

"Lemuel? Lemuel? Are you here, my love?" she whispered. She looked quickly around the room. Her eyes told her nobody was here, but her heart told her otherwise. She closed her eyes and tried to use every sense she had and even one she wasn't sure existed. She reached out with her spirit, trying to connect.

"Lemuel, if you're here, I want you to know that I am carrying your baby. I will do my best to raise this baby alone. I don't intend to remarry, ever. I can take in sewing. I was a good seamstress, made all my own clothes, remember? And your mother will help me. I know she will."

Annie's father had been watching his only daughter, now a widow, talking to her dead husband. He stepped over to her and put his arm around her.

"It's almost as though he were still here, isn't it Annie?" he said with tears streaming down his face.

Annie hugged her father. She knew that the pain over the death of his wife was still keen and fresh, like a raw new wound.

"I'll be all right, father. Really I will. I wish there was a body to bury, though. It would be easier."

Lemuel bowed his head and walked through the wall, much to his surprise. He had learned a new skill. The thought that his sweet Annie would birth a child without him near to comfort her, and would raise the child alone broke his heart. Although he could not bear to think of her with another man, he hoped that she would remarry.

CHAPTER 18

Joseph covered his grief for a time and tried to farm, but his heart was not in it. Julia sat by the window, holding pictures of her two dead sons, and said little. Annie came every day to cook, clean, and do the washing, but she could not engage Julia in conversation. That worried her, so one day she sat directly in front of her dead husband's mother, took both of her hands, and spoke gently.

"Mother. Look at me. I have something to tell you. I'm carrying Lemuel's baby. I'll need your help. I have no one else. Will you help me with the baby?"

With pain in her eyes, Julia unfixed her stare and looked into Annie's teary eyes. She nodded her head and wept.

"I'll help you with the baby. I'm sorry that you will have to raise the child without Lemuel, but I'll help you all I can. I've appreciated all the help you've been. Coming every day like you have. I should have been able to deal with all this, but…"

"That's all right Mother Grant. I didn't mind. It took my mind off Lemuel a little bit. Look out the window at the hayfields, mother. The boys loved to play out there in the summer, didn't they?"

"Yes, dear. I think about that often. Joseph does, too. It pains him to work the fields without his sons."

"When is the baby due, dear?" Julia asked.

"Sometime in the fall, the doctor says," Annie replied.

"Ah. Well, the fall is a nice time to have a baby, dear. Not too hot, and it gives the baby time to grow some before the winter comes. That's nice. I'll look forward to Christmas with a new baby in the house. Perhaps your father will feel like having Christmas dinner with us by then. Thank you for telling me. You've been like a daughter to me. My own are grown and gone, married and with their own children and homes to care for. Yes, I'll be looking forward to seeing Lemuel's child. I can start making things now. Would you like me to do that, dear?"

Annie nodded and smiled. She was glad she had been able to get Julia to engage. Maybe going on board the ship had cursed it. She never spoke of it, but she could not help wondering. If she had indeed cursed the ship and thereby caused her husband's death, at least she would have his child.

*****

Joseph knew that he was in desperate trouble and tried to keep working the fields. Neighbors pitied him for the loss of his two sons, and they helped with the haying and the blueberry fields. They repaired the broken harness and shod the Percheron team whose feet had suffered during the last few weeks. The team had nasty quarter cracks in their hooves from lack of trimming, but the town blacksmith and farrier made special shoes for them and came weekly to see how the horses fared. Slowly, the lameness and soreness faded, and with proper worming and grooming, the horses again sported shiny coats and good flesh. The hames and collars were even a little tight around their stout black necks.

Joseph, embarrassed that his neighbors were doing so much for him tried to rally, but Julia often heard him weeping in the night when he thought she was asleep. His own father had suffered greatly from depression and it was widely believed that he had not died of a heart attack but rather had hung himself in the barn. Only his widow and the doctor knew the truth. The casket had been closed at the funeral, leading to further speculation.

One day, Joseph quietly asked a friend to drive him to Bangor to the doctor. Julia packed a lunch for the trip, expecting that they would be back the next morning. When the friend came back without Joseph, Julia asked where her husband was. The family doctor was in the carriage, and took Julia in the house, while the family friend put away the driving mare and saddled his own horse that he had left in the Grant barn. The doctor's bay saddle horse had been tied on behind the carriage.

"Julia, my dear," began the doctor with a slight clearing of his throat. "Your husband is not well. He suffers from grief over the loss of your two boys, and can't seem to come out of it. We've decided to put him in the State Hospital in Bangor for a time, and see if we can help him. Not much is known about this condition, and I understand his own father apparently suffered from it as well."

Julia, stunned and surprised by this turn of events, made arrangements for the neighbors to continue to help her with the farm. Annie couldn't because she was with child, but there were some around town needing jobs. Many had been in the war and were suffering from injuries sustained in battle. They couldn't handle a man's portion of work, but they could help, and that would make all the difference.

As often as she could, she went to Bangor, but when winter storms came, she often didn't see Joseph for weeks at a time. She had food stored and women neighbors checked on her often to see that she had meat and flour.

One sunny late summer day, Joseph asked the hospital for a furlough to visit family members in Palmyra, suggesting to the doctors that perhaps a visit with family might help break the depression that gripped his heart and soul. Somewhat reluctantly, the doctors agreed, and Joseph hired a horse and carriage to go to Palmyra for a visit. Oddly cheerful, Joseph made the trip fairly quickly and had a most enjoyable visit with what remained of his family in the North. He believed that he would never again see his family in the South. Mail was still erratic and undependable. He missed his brothers and sisters and grieved over the separation the war had wrought.

Joseph did not return to the hospital. Instead, he drove to his family farm and stayed a while with Julia who was overjoyed at first to see him released from the hospital. When he told her that it was only a furlough, she began to worry. Why was he wanting to go about visiting family and friends? She quizzed him as only she could, and he confessed that the depression was still deep and that his mind was filled with dark thoughts that he could not vanquish. Julia prayed that the fresh air, the apple orchard, and the visits to family and to her would be able to do for him what the doctors obviously were not able to accomplish. Not much was known about mental deficiencies and depression, but doctors were convinced that like idiocy it tended to run in families.

"Julia, my dear, would you please fix me your wonderful green apple pie? The food at the hospital is terrible, and if I can't take it in with me when I return, at least I can have the pleasure of

252		Bury Thy Brother

eating the whole thing on the way back to Bangor."

"But, Joseph, I haven't any green apples here in the house. I'll get some from the orchard. Just a moment."

"No, no, dear! Let me do that for you! It's the least I can do. You just get the stove hot. There's plenty of wood in the box. I won't be long."

"Oh, I almost forgot," he said as he pulled a piece of paper from his pocket. "Here's the name of the man I rented the horse and carriage from, just in case anything untoward should occur on the drive back to the hospital, dear. I don't expect that anything will happen, but then we didn't think anything would happen to our sons, either. And you remember that I've gone over all our personal records with you. I did that before I went to Bangor, so I believe everything is in apple pie order, if you'll pardon my joke. I'll be back soon enough.

"Don't fret if I don't come back immediately, dear, for I always loved to sit in the apple orchard and think. Give me a bit of time, will you?" Joseph said as he kissed her cheek and gave her a bear hug. "I'll be back soon."

He picked up his favorite hickory walking stick, and put on his favorite plaid cap and deerskin gloves. As he went out the door, Joseph tipped his hat to his wife and smiled. He seems almost too happy, she thought.

When he didn't come back right away, Julia didn't fret, but when the sun was low in the sky and still Joseph had not returned, a vague feeling that something was terribly wrong began to plague her thoughts as she busied herself in the kitchen. If he didn't return soon, the piecrust would dry out, dinner would be ready, and there would be no time for pie.

"Oh dear," said Julia as she put on a heavy wool cloak. Even though it was summer, the evenings were still chilly.

"I do hope he hasn't fallen or something. He looked weak and pale from being in the hospital, even though he drove to Palmyra and then here."

Her stomach began to churn as a post rider passed her on the road and tipped his hat to her. A messenger of death, she thought, and tried to block the past images. The orchard was a good mile away, near the back of the farm, and the ground was rough. Julia twisted her ankle and nearly fell, but a growing dread drove her on. She was sure he didn't have a firearm with him, but that thought was little comfort as she limped down the dirt road. Joseph had suffered so much in his life that he often told her he didn't see how he could bear much more. He had lost two brothers, a sister, two infant children, two young sons, and even his father at an early age. The war had killed some and separated others. Torn families apart it had.

When word came that Lemuel was lost at sea, Joseph had collapsed into such sadness and grief that Julia became angry with him. After all, Lemuel was her son, too, and Joseph gave her no support in her own grief. Before that, it had been even worse when Addison died.

By the time Julia reached the apple orchard, her ankle hurt a great deal and was quite swollen, but fear forced her onward.

"Joseph? Are you out here, Joseph?" she called in a voice growing shrill with desperation. "Joseph! Answer me, please! Where are you?" When she saw the dark figure swinging slowly from the branch of an old, taller apple tree, Julia gasped. The sun was nearly down and darkness was creeping across the ground toward her as the sun cast ever-lengthening shadows. A bat flew past her hair and she heard a barn owl hoo, hoo, hoo nearby. She hobbled to her husband to see if he might still be alive, but she could tell from the color of his face that he was dead. His eyes stared at nothing. He had soiled his clothing in death and torn his shirt as he had climbed out on the limb, but his coat was neatly hung on a branch nearby and the walking stick was propped against the apple tree.

Julia tried to untie the rope, but her husband's weight made it impossible. There was nothing she could do.

"Oh Joseph! How could you do this to me? How dare you die, too, and leave me with all this pain. No, Joseph, oh no!"

As she sank to the ground at his feet, Julia wept and wailed in disbelief and despair. She was alone. Her two sons stood unseen behind her with heads bowed in fervent prayer for their dead father and their widowed mother.

People in town were polite and even respectful of her grief, but the whispers started almost immediately. A family of cowards, some said. God is punishing them, some said. Runs in the family, don't you know. His father killed himself, too, they say. Finally, the torrent of whispers abated and people forgot and went on to other subjects. Stale rumors aren't nearly as exciting as new ones.

Julia withdrew to her sitting room and her collection of pictures of her dead sons and her husband. She rarely visited the burial plot. It brought back too many painful, almost unbearable memories. There were two empty places where no bodies lay to whom one could pay respects. There were only markers. Two sons whose lives had been cut horribly short. And there was her husband's simple marker.

The bereaved mother and now widow could not bear to look at the town's war memorial that listed the honored dead on bronze plates. Lemuel's name was not there, they said, because he had survived the war even though he had been

lost at sea. Addison's name was not there because
he had been branded a coward.

One day, Julia stood by the window that
looked out over the cemetery. Her thin, bony
hands brushed aside the yellowed lace curtains.
Across the back of her hands, blue veins stood out
like the veins on a dying maple leaf. She had aged
terribly in the year since her husband's macabre
dance of death in the apple orchard and now
looked twenty years older than she was. The
shadow of the war monument crept slowly toward
the Grant family plot. Julia watched its inexorable,
inevitable progress.

Annie visited her often, trying to interest her
mother-in-law in the baby son whom she had
named Lemuel in honor of her dead husband.
Occasionally, Annie saw a flash of life in Julia's
sad eyes, but mostly she was distant and stared out
the window. Annie stopped coming finally,
worried that she was upsetting Julia and bringing
back painful memories of how things were before
the war.

This day was different. Julia was waiting
for someone. She had seen a copy of the Bangor
paper a month or so previously in which Addison's
letter to his father had been published. She still
didn't know who sent the letter, but it appeared on
July 4th as an example of a patriotic boy's desire to
serve his country. Julia had teared up when she
read it. How ironic that someone finally was
calling him a hero. A few weeks after publication,

another letter appeared – this one from a man named N. S. Fales. He had been with Addison at Antietam and praised the boy's courage in battle. When Julia saw that letter, her heart leapt with hope. She had to find Mr. Fales. The paper gave her his address and she sent for him.

Julia stood by the window hoping to see the man she knew must hold the clue to Addison's story. Fales was late, and her hopes began to fade. Surely he would come? He knew how important his information must be. She had told him in her letter. She had to sit down at last, because she had so much pain in her back. Julia picked up Addison's picture and held it tightly to her breast. Was this finally going to be the missing piece of the puzzle? Would this man be able to clear Addison's name of the false charge of cowardice?

Julia moved to the dining table with all the letters stacked in piles by date and by son. Mementoes were laid carefully in rows as though awaiting review. For a moment, it was more than she could bear to look at, and tears streaked her pale, wrinkled cheeks. She dabbed at the tears with an heirloom handkerchief her mother had made from fine linen to which she had added two inches of tatting as a border. Julia loved to knit, but did not have her mother's patience for cut work and tatting, so all the fine linens in Julia's house had been lovingly and patiently made by her mother and grandmother who understood her impatience, but they made certain that the Grant home would have proper linens.

When the knock came at the front door, followed by the bell ringing in the hall, Julia rose slowly and painfully from her chair, stood a moment with her hand on the table to get her balance, and straightened her back as she walked as gracefully as she could to the door. On the other side of the door would be the answers to many questions and an ally in her now lone battle to restore her son's honor.

"Afternoon, ma'am," the man said with a slight bow and a doffed hat. "Sorry I'm late, but my horse lost a shoe, and I had to find a smithy."

"That's perfectly all right. I was just re-reading some of Addison's and Lemuel's letters," Julia said. "It's very hard for me to look at them sometimes, but I'm hopeful that you will have something to tell me. Please sit down here at the table."

The man who looked much older than she knew he must be, stared for a moment at Julia, and then followed her gaze out the window. He knew the story of the war monument that did not have Addison's name on it. And he knew the truth.

"Ma'am, my name is N. S. Fales," he said respectfully, "and I was with Addison in the 7th when he was wounded at Antietam Creek."

During the long afternoon as she had waited, Julia occasionally felt that she was not alone. Indeed she was not, for both of her sons were

standing behind her chair, waiting to hear what
Fales would have to say. They looked at the letters
and the mementoes and smiled. She had kept
everything. Even the jar of blueberry jam which
now was moldy.

    N. S. Fales told her the story of Antietam
and how he had found Addison weeping in the
medical tent, not from the severe pain, but because
he had been shot in the back and his father would
think he was a coward.

    Fales told her about the drunken colonel and
the slaughter of a large number of the boys who
were sent alone onto a battlefield into the teeth of
the Rebel sharpshooters. When he was finished
with his story, Julia was sobbing. Her mother's
heart told her that what he was saying was true,
and she clasped his hand with both of hers.

    "Thank you, Mr. Fales, thank you. I knew
my son was not a coward, but his father…"
Fales nodded. He had felt guilty himself for
having survived the battle unscathed.

    "What can I do to help you, ma'am?" he
said softly. "Can I talk to the townspeople,
perhaps? Maybe they'll believe me because I was
there."

    "Yes, perhaps that would help," the weeping
mother answered.

    "I'll stay with the parson tonight, Mrs.
Grant. I've already talked with him. He knew
Addison before the war. Perhaps he can help me

find the right people who can correct this dreadful wrong. Goodnight, ma'am. I hope I can help."

Julia watched him ride back toward the town and sighed. She had hope again, but she also knew the townspeople. One man was not going to change their minds. At least she now knew the whole story and was sure Mr. Fales was telling the truth. Why would he have gone to all this trouble if he were not?

Fales did his best, but the town fathers simply stared at him as he told his story. They had seen Addison's letter and his letter in the paper, but it didn't change their minds. They held fast to the lie because it was familiar. Change didn't come easily to these river town people. People were what they were.

Lemuel and Addison listened to Fales trying to change the minds and hearts of the town leaders. Only the parson was inclined to believe the best about Addison, but even his voice was stilled by the stony silence in the room. Someone else would have to take up the gauntlet. Addison only knew one other who might succeed.

CHAPTER 19

Georgia had been good to Lemuel P. Grant. He would be eternally grateful that he had listened to his inner voice and gone south to work on the railroads. From the time he was a young man, he had loved the railroads and worked hard in Maine to make a name for himself. When the opportunity presented itself to go to Georgia, Lemuel was ecstatic and happily prepared to leave the family homestead.

Joseph was heart-sick when his younger brother told him he was leaving. The two were very close, almost like twins. They would frequently finish each other's sentences and burst into gales of laughter. Joseph could hardly bear to see his brother off on the train south, but at least the rest of the family was still there, working the hayfields and the blueberries. The work was hard, but it took Joseph's mind off his brother's leaving. He wondered when and if they would ever meet again.

Lemuel P., as people called him, quickly earned a reputation for hard work, honesty, integrity and intelligent planning. He rose in the ranks of the railroad world, having started as a lowly rod man at age nineteen for the Philadelphia and Reading Railroad and rising to Chief Engineer of the Atlanta and West Point Railroad in 1853. He showed mathematical genius even though he had almost no formal education, and was regarded as one of the ablest engineers in Georgia.

Opportunities presented themselves and Lemuel took advantage of them. Chances to buy property where the railroads were likely to go eventually afforded Lemuel P. great wealth and status in the area. He was a railroad man through and through.

Vague rumors of war began to drift about like the persistent wisps of smoke that trail behind a train long after the roar and belching has passed. Lemuel paid little heed to the rumors and continued building the railroads. Eventually two other brothers and one sister came south because times were hard in the North Country, and at least there were jobs in the South.

All of the brothers worried some about leaving Joseph behind, but someone had to stay and help their widowed mother with the farm or they would lose it, and Joseph was the one best suited due to his love of the land and skills at farming. When the hay didn't make for one reason or another – usually rain – then the family could fall back on the blueberry fields, except for the time fire destroyed the entire crop.

Tragedy struck the southern branch of the family almost immediately. James Hervey, one of Lemuel P.'s brothers, lost a young son, and the letter to Lemuel nearly broke his heart.

"We have lost our darling boy," the sad letter began, and L.P. grieved. He thought of a younger brother and an uncle who had both died young. His father had also died young but no one talked about that. The boys were never exactly sure what had happened to him. He had fallen from a hayloft in the barn his mother had said, but the rumors flew anyway. Suicide, some said.

The days ran together in the South, and Lemuel P. was engrossed in building the railroads. With so much responsibility, Lemuel had little time to think about or write to the family still in the North. Besides, almost all of his siblings except Joseph were in the South. Lemuel hoped that they hadn't made a mistake leaving Joseph there alone. Their mother was a strong woman, but Joseph did not handle stress well. Hopefully the blueberry fields would do well enough to sustain them along with the hay harvests. Lemuel tapped his fingers on the table and said to no one in particular, well at least they can eat the blueberries and the horses can eat the hay.

When the war finally came, L.P. Grant was stunned. How could this have happened? He agonized over whether or not they should all go back to the North, but when they discussed it, his brothers realized that everything they had, including their wives and children, were in the South.

For a long time, the war seemed distant, on some other continent. Everyone said it would be over soon. But it wasn't. Finally the war crept to their doorsteps, skulking about the countryside like a hungry wolf.

CHAPTER 20

When the generals asked Lemuel P. if he would accept a colonelcy as the war neared Atlanta, he declined, but said he would accept the rank of Captain. That seemed appropriate for a man they were asking to build the defenses around the city. "Uncle Billy" Sherman was headed for Atlanta, and the southern generals knew that he could ill afford to leave Atlanta standing in his wake. He would destroy the city that was the railroad hub of the South. The South could only fortify the city and pray.

After the war, L. P. and his son John finessed the carpetbaggers and with tact, cunning, and diplomacy managed to keep most of their property out of the hands of the vultures. L. P.'s thoughts soon turned to the North and what remained of his family up there.

"John, I have to go to Maine," he said one afternoon as he stared out the window of the house the Federals had spared, because they found Masonic emblems and materials in an attic trunk.

By Sherman's orders, the soldiers were not to loot or damage any property belonging to a brother Mason.

"My brother's sons are dead and now so is my brother Joseph. If I could have gone up there sooner, perhaps I could have saved him. I was so immersed in my own problems that I never realized how desperate he was. I must see to his widow. She will need my help and advice. Look what this terrible war has cost just our own family, John," Lemuel said as he turned back to his desk, sighed, and sat down.

"Father, we had no choice," said John who walked to the window and stared into the garden his mother had planted.

"We could not have gone back to Maine, even if we thought that was the right thing to do. Our home was in the South. Or at least my home was. I was born here. I'm a Southerner. You had the railroads to protect. It was just too hard watching those Union boys turning the tracks into bowties,"

"I guess you're right, John. I had spent my adult life building those railroads. The South needed them to survive, but then the war came. Surely there must have been another way to resolve the problems without nearly destroying what my own grandfather fought to create in the Revolution? Why did so many have to die? Why did Atlanta have to die in the flames? It will take a huge effort to rebuild her. At least they spared my property. I'll make sure that my good fortune is shared. We must, like the Phoenix, arise from the ashes, my son. We must build an even better Atlanta. Right now, I'll have to see about a pass to leave the city and go north. You take care of things here until I return," L.P. said as he hugged his oldest son.

John reached into his jacket pocket and pulled out a letter.

"You'd better read this, father," he said as he handed the letter to L. P.   The next day the pass was granted.

*****

When he arrived in Frankfort, Lemuel felt a twinge of sadness for ever having left the farm. The hayfields were in sorry shape, and the blueberries weren't much better. It didn't take long for Nature to reclaim the land. The blueberries had gone wild and were small, not plump and juicy, like their domesticated brothers. The weedy hayfields wanted fertilizing, but they could come back after one or two hayings, he thought. The blueberries would take longer. Maybe the whole year. Julia greeted her brother-in-law with eagerness and hope.

"Oh, Lemuel, dear Lemuel! I'm so very happy to see you! I'm sorry that I haven't much to offer you except a bed and a bit of food. Times have been difficult since Joseph's death."

Julia teared up and stared hard at the floor. She gasped, attempting to control her emotions,

but she totally lost her composure when Lemuel
stepped to her side and put his arms around her.

"There, there, my dear sister-in-law. All
will be well. Sit down here in father's old chair,
and tell me exactly what is going on and what I
can do to help you. You know that I have
managed to save most of what I had in Atlanta.
I've been greatly blessed. My own family is
grown and established. Let me help you."

"Oh Lemuel, I scarce know where to begin.
You've seen the fields. The neighbors helped as
much as they could for a while, but they have their
own lands and families to care for. I don't blame
them for not continuing to help us. My daughter-
in-law comes at least once a week to help me make
bread or to tend the vegetable garden, but she has a
child to care for and an aging father to see to. She
does what she can, but of course she can't work
the fields."

Lemuel turned away pretending to look out
the window at the hayfields. His eyes brimmed
with tears as he listened to his brother's widow
describe the situation. His heart was breaking.
Even though the war had not been fought here in
Maine, its claws had reached even here and rent
the fabric of this peaceful land. Most of the
families had lost at least a son; others had lost a
husband; still others had lost both or worse.

"Julia," Lemuel said as he turned back.

"Julia, we must sit down together and
determine what you are going to need and what I

can do to help. Your troubles are over, at least financially, but we must make a plan. I must ask some very personal questions. I hope that you understand that I am not prying, but I must know exactly where things stand, my dear. I will help you."

Julia wept openly, no longer trying to hide her feelings. She sobbed until she had no energy left.

"Oh Lemuel, if only you could have been here before Joseph…..died. Perhaps you could have helped him. But perhaps not. The doctors in Bangor tried to help him overcome the terrible sadness that plagued him without mercy, and they couldn't stop him from taking his own life. You know that I was the one who found him. It was terrible. I shall never be able to erase that dreadful scene from my memory. How could he do that to me?"

"He must have known that I would be the one. How could he? I have not been able to forgive him yet for dying and leaving me with all this grief. How did he think I would survive and run the farm without him? I'm not like his mother. She was a strong woman raised on a farm. I was born in town. Lemuel, how could he have done that? Did he not love me? If only I had gone out to the orchard sooner, perhaps I might have stopped him."

Lemuel took her hand, raised her face to his and spoke gently to his distraught sister by marriage.

"Dear Julia," he began, knowing that he had no answers.

"Dear Julia, I cannot tell you that I understand your pain, but I can tell you that I, too, have suffered loss. My own dear wife was taken with the fever not too long after the war began. Perhaps it was the stress of war or just fate. I don't know. I can tell you that I still miss her. My lovely Jane lost her husband in a botched robbery attempt. Perhaps you already knew that. I was never sure which letters got through and which did not. Almost no letters got through during the war, of course. And after the war, travel out of the South was severely limited – why, I am not really sure. It made no sense to me. And then those dreadful carpetbaggers who sacked the South. Or what was left of her. At any rate, I can share your grief. God has blessed me with the means. I just need to know what is wanted."

Because Julia was in such a state and embarrassed by her red, swollen eyes, she declined to go to town for dinner, so Lemuel drove Julia's carriage to town and bought food. Everyone was very curious about Lemuel P. Grant, and begged for details about conditions in the South. Rumors abounded about the success of L.P.'s home-grown success story, the founder of Atlanta. Even the newspaper editor asked for an interview that

Lemuel politely put off for another day. He had to get back to the farm.

After dinner, while Annie cleared away the dishes and put water on to boil, Julia brought all of her papers and records from the bedroom and spread them out on the table. With a few pointed questions and because he had years of experience as the president of more than one railroad, Lemuel quickly sized up the situation and organized the papers into piles that made sense to him. What he found troubled him. Julia was in danger of losing the farm for unpaid taxes, she owed money to nearly everyone in town from the grocer to the smithy, and she had almost no income at all.

"Lemuel, I'm sorry that things are in such a jumble. I just haven't known what to do. I couldn't see any solution. I know I'm in terrible financial trouble, but there wasn't anything I could do. Can you help me, Lemuel?"

"Of course I can and I shall help you, dear Julia. I just needed to know where things stood. It's bad, but we shall fix it! First thing in the morning, I want you to accompany me to the bank."

"Oh dear! Do I have to go, Lemuel? Can't you go without me? I'll be so embarrassed!"

"No, Julia, I will not go without you. The banker must know that you are in agreement with my plans, and I want to be sure that this is a man you can trust. I will require that he report to me on a very regular basis as to what moneys have been used and what remains. I intend to set up a kind of trust for you, but you must be careful with it, dear. It will be sufficient for a comfortable life and will enable you to get the farm going again. I shall see to that myself before I ever leave you."

The next morning, Lemuel hitched up the buggy he had rented in town and drove Julia to the bank. The banker had heard through the town gossip that the founder of Atlanta was in town visiting Julia Grant. The banker, Mr. Peabody, recognized Julia when she stepped down from the buggy, but not the very well-dressed gentleman who handed her down and on whose arm she now approached his front door.

Mr. Peabody smoothed back his hair, nervously checked his pocket watch as if he had appointments, and sat down again at his desk, pretending to be busy with papers. He quickly thought back over his relationship with the Grant family, wondering what he could have done differently and what this very wealthy man wanted with his bank.

Lemuel opened the door for Julia and followed her into the bank. He quickly noted that there was but one teller window and one teller who spoke to him at once. Lemuel was certain that the nervous fellow sitting at the corner desk was undoubtedly the president, but he decided to play the game and see what developed. Julia had already told him that the bank president's name was Peabody.

"Good morning, sir. What can the bank do for you today?"

"Well, I have some business to transact, young man. I believe that the president of the bank will need to be involved."

"Um, sir, he's quite busy at the moment. Perhaps I may be of assistance, sir?" the young man said uncertainly. He had been trained not to bother the president unless the customer was very important, and he didn't know who this man was. He did know, however, that the woman with him had an unpaid loan and no money. So he smirked. That was a mistake.

"Young man, I gather that you do not know who I am, but then you probably are not important enough to have access to the rumor mill," Lemuel said with a chill in his voice that could have frozen Hades. "I am certain, however, that Mr. Peabody does know who I am, and may have guessed that I came here from Atlanta to help my brother's widow in her hour of need. He also no doubt knows that I own most of Atlanta. But since he is so busy, we'll go to Bangor and conduct our business with a larger bank that has an adequate staff."

Julia gasped, but Lemuel took her arm and headed for the door, doing his very best not to laugh at the consternation he had left in his wake.

The bank president leaped to his feet.

"Wait, Mr. Grant, sir. Please wait! I'm sure our bank can handle whatever business you need to transact. That young man is new, sir, and I'll have words with him after I have helped you, sir."

Julia stared at the president but bit her tongue. The boy in fact was not new, and treated her with contempt whenever she set foot in the bank. Lemuel obviously had a plan, so she kept still.

Lemuel turned with his hand still on the doorknob. He carried a walking stick with a gold knob on it and rapped it on the floor in a show of displeasure.

"Mr. Peabody, I believe it is?"

"Yes, sir, and you are Mr. Grant?"

"I believe that has already been established, sir."

"Of course, sir, of course. Won't you and Mrs. Grant please sit down here at my desk."

"Mr. Peabody, I am not accustomed to conducting my personal business in the full view and hearing of anyone who happens to walk into the bank. Perhaps this is a mistake, after all," he said, rising from his chair.

"Oh, I beg your pardon, sir. We do have a small office over there with a door we can close. Perhaps that would suit you better, sir?"

Julia had never seen the bank president fawning and gushing over anyone before. He had met his match in Lemuel P. Grant.

"Did you say small office, Mr. Peabody? Small? Does it have any furniture in it? At least a proper chair for my sister-in-law? Good heavens, man! A bank such as this would never survive in Atlanta. Still, if that's the best you can do....and it would be more convenient for Julia to not have to go to Bangor for her banking needs. Well, let's discuss why I have come here."

"Certainly, Mr. Grant, certainly. Julia, please take my chair at the desk, and I'll sit over here with Mr. Grant."

"Mr. Peabody," Lemuel said with an icy stare. "Mr. Peabody, I do not wish to *ever* hear you call my sister-in-law by her first name. You will refer to her properly as Mrs. Grant. Is that quite clear? Were you raised in a barn, sir?"

Peabody flushed a bright crimson red and stammered his response.

"I beg your pardon, ma'am. I shall not make such an error again. It's just that we have known one another a good time, and I believe that I have shown you every courtesy in the past, Mrs. Grant. I shall be most careful in the future not to offend you."

Lemuel smiled slightly in spite of himself and laid a leather case on the desk. He removed a sheaf of papers and pushed them across the desk to the bank president.

"These were drawn up my solicitor in Atlanta, sir. I'm sure you will find them all in order. They create an account for Mrs. Grant that she may use as long as she lives. The funds will transfer by courier from Atlanta. I have brought sufficient to open it for her – say, one thousand dollars? I believe that will be sufficient for some time. I also will buy her note on the farm from you today and pay the back taxes. This way no one can cheat her out of her property because officially I will own it. The tax bills will come to me. She will be safe from any questionable dealings. Can you think of anything else, Julia? Is there anything you need that I have overlooked?"

Julia simply stared at her magnanimous brother-in-law with mouth agape. She was gasping for breath and looked as though she might faint. Fanning herself vigorously, she simply shook her head.

Mr. Peabody was speechless. One thousand dollars was a good deal of money.

"Oh, one more thing, Mr. Peabody. I can see by your expression that you are already investing the money to your own advancement. You will not do anything with this money other than keep it in your safe for Julia. I will come from Atlanta unannounced from time to time and check on this. So far, you have only annoyed me. You would not enjoy dealing with me if I were angry. Is this clear, sir?"

Peabody nodded his head so hard, one might have feared that it would separate from his scrawny neck. Lemuel nodded.

"Very good. One thing more. About this teller here whom you have assured me is new. Of course, I don't believe that for one minute, but I require one thing more. Call him into this office at once, please. I need to hear him apologize to Mrs. Grant and assure me that his rude behavior will never be repeated."

The bank president hurried out to the teller's cage and dragged the young man into the office. The boy gulped loudly and asked Lemuel what he could do to assist him. Lemuel demanded and got the apology, and the young man – bowing and stammering – backed out of the office as though in the presence of royalty.

"Well, Julia, if there is nothing more, I believe we are finished here. Mr. Peabody, I trust that I can depend on you to be as solicitous and careful on Julia's behalf as you would be if I were still standing by your desk, sir?"

"Oh my, yes sir! You certainly may depend on me to be particularly careful as to her affairs. Yes indeed, sir. Yes indeed!"

Lemuel saw his sister-in-law out the door and noted with satisfaction that her head was noticeably higher, and there was a relaxed look on her face that he had not seen since he arrived. Her cheeks were flushed with pleasure and relief, and she now carried herself with dignity and grace as she had when he first met her. He remembered thinking that his brother Joseph had chosen well.

Lemuel knew that going to the cemetery would be very difficult and painful for Julia, but he had to go with or without her. He had to see the monument for himself and he had to pay his respects to the family that the war had destroyed.

"Julia, my dear," he said as he picked up the reins and chirped to the driving horse.

"Yes, Lemuel?"

"I want to go to the cemetery tomorrow. Will you come with me, please? I know it will be painful, but there are some things I need to know. If Addison's and Lemuel's names are still not on the monument as I suspect, then I need to try to rectify that. Failing that, I have another plan that I prefer not to discuss at this time. Perhaps it will not be necessary. We'll see. I'll stay at the hotel here tonight and leave first thing in the morning, right after we have a nice breakfast. I'll pick you up."

"Oh my, yes, Lemuel! I'm just sorry that I'm such poor company these days. Even my daughter-in-law Annie can't seem to rouse my spirits.

"What you have done for me today, though, is just now sinking in. You have been so unbelievably generous in setting up that account for me and restoring my property that I scarce know what to say. I didn't expect that, Lemuel. I thought you would talk to the banker and arrange for more time to catch things up. I don't think that a simple "thank you" is nearly enough, but I don't know what else to say, dear brother."

"No need to say anything more, Julia. I'm just very thankful that I am in a position to be of help. Despite the war and the destruction of Atlanta and the railroads, I have been greatly blessed. It behooves me to share and do good with it."

They traveled in silence to the hotel. Julia still could scarce believe her good fortune, and smiled at Lemuel as he handed her down from the carriage. A stable boy of about twelve years of age, nicely dressed, and very polite stood ready to take the horse and carriage to the livery, and having been richly rewarded in advance for tending to this chore, he doffed his cap to his benefactor and to the lady.

"I'll have the carriage ready in the morning, sir. Will you be leaving after breakfast, sir?"

Lemuel nodded and watched the boy drive the carriage down the street.

"Very nice young lad. Reminds me of me when I was about his age. I believe he'll do very well for himself," Lemuel said as he offered his arm to Julia. He wished he dared suggest that enough time had passed for her to stop wearing widow's weeds, but perhaps the opportunity would present itself before he left. For now, it was just as well, since townsfolk were likely to gossip about them both staying in the hotel. Ah well. Not much one could do about people with such limited mental capacity, he thought.

The dinner was served in the private dining room and the staff hovered politely at a distance, standing quietly with their hands folded. None of them had seen such a wealthy, important guest since the end of the war. There were no more

Union officers in fancy dress frequenting the hotel since the war ended, and times were hard. Many had lost their farms and homes. Jobs were few and far between these days.

Lemuel waited patiently while Julia enjoyed every bite of food, savoring the moment and the attention. She barely had to look at her water glass and it was immediately refilled. The candles cast a soft light on the crisply starched and ironed linens, and the fresh wildflowers added a sweet floral note to the atmosphere. Lemuel had requested flowers. He knew that his brother had not been able to afford hotels and fancy meals. A vague melancholy crept over him as he thought about his childhood and his decision to go to the South.

If only there had been some way to avoid the war. He personally had not seen as much of the slaughter as his son John had, but he had seen his beloved Atlanta die of starvation and disease. Sherman had seen to that. Even the breastworks Lemuel built had only served to delay the inevitable. What a tragic waste. Jeff Davis had not wanted the war or the secession. He had bowed his head and wept at his desk when it became painfully clear that there seemed to be no other alternative. And Lee and Grant had been friends. How could they have taken opposite sides in such a horrific war? Lemuel put his head in his hands and sighed.

"Are you alright, Lemuel, dear?" Julia asked with concern. The trip to Maine had been very hard on him. His health was not the best, she had learned from the few and far between letters from Atlanta.

"Yes, dear, yes. I'm fine. Just quite tired. I was thinking about how close Joseph and I were as children, and how delightful it was to work the land. I have a farm in Georgia, but I live in the city. I do miss country life. One can grow food and preserve it; there are animals to tend, eggs to candle, chickens to pluck, hams to smoke…I do miss all that. I purchase most of my food already smoked and plucked and candled these days. Perhaps it's a result of the war. We had so little to eat during the siege of Atlanta. It was quite horrible. Little children starving for want of a crust of bread or a cup of soup. Horrible."

Julia could only imagine. Times had been very difficult in Maine, too, but there was nearly always enough food. If only the war had been avoided. If only men had sat down and resolved to fix things that were wrong, instead of going to war and slaughtering each other. Surely there must have been some solution other than killing each other. She wondered where the next generation of young men would come from? Hundreds of thousands lay buried in trenches on the battlefields. She smiled briefly. Now if women, mothers had been in charge, perhaps things would have been different.

"Why are you smiling, dear? Some private thought, perhaps?"

"No, Lemuel. I was just wondering what would have happened if mothers had been in charge instead of men."

She looked into his eyes and hoped she had not offended him. His smile told her she had not. Still, perhaps she should keep such thoughts to herself for now.

The morning dawned in a spectacular display of rose and gold over the hills. The stable boy was waiting for them when they finished a sumptuous breakfast. The sideboard was loaded with eggs, ham, jonnycakes, maple syrup, butter, and bacon.

"Ah, no grits," Lemuel said and laughed out loud. He really hadn't expected any, but one could always hope.

He tipped the young boy a few extra coins and smiled at the astonishment in the lad's face.

"Oh sir, you needn't do that! You've already paid me, sir," he stammered with a quizzical look. "I don't need more, sir."

Lemuel looked into the surprised face and put his hand on the boy's shoulder.

"Boy, you remind me of myself when I was your age. You work hard and look for opportunities to prosper honestly. You'll be an important man someday. Just remember to say your prayers, go to church every week, and mind your manners. Especially at home. I imagine your mother is a good cook, too, by the look of you."

The boy bowed his head and dug his toe in the dirt.

"Sir, both of my parents died of the grippe two years ago. I have no family at all. The influenza took them all. Somehow I lived. The stable master lets me sleep in the haymow, and the cook at the hotel lets me eat the scraps every day. I'm quite lucky, sir. I have a roof and food to eat and a means of making some money. I'll heed your advice, though, sir. I surely will. Thank you."

"Boy, you stay in touch with me through Mrs. Grant here. I'll give you her address in Frankfort, and any mail you send to me can go through her. How would that be? When you're older, perhaps I can find a job for you with my railroad. You work hard, keep out of trouble, and remember me, will you, boy?"

"Yes sir. Thank you, sir"

The boy waved at them until they were out of sight. The livery owner had overheard the last part of the conversation and put his hand on the boy's shoulder.

"Do ya ken who that gentleman is, laddie?" he said with a heavy Scots accent. "Ye've made yeself a fine friend there, laddie. A fine friend. That man came fra Frankfort, went south afore the war, he did, and became a rich man. Some say he owns all of Atlanta, Georgia. I do ken that he's a good man, boy. Ye couldna do worse than have him for a friend. Aye, laddie, aye."

When Lemuel and Julia arrived home, Annie hurried out to meet them. Lunch was on the table and Lemuel was ready for that. The trip to Bangor and back had taken longer than he remembered, and he tired easily these days.

After he had seen to the horse, he joined the women for lunch and enjoyed listening to the chatter of female voices. Lemuel finished his meal and walked over to the door. The cemetery that had been carved out of an ancient bit of forest stood on a small hill and looked about the same, except that it wanted tending. The chokecherry trees and the wildflowers were edging their way back into the space, as were the lichens who seemed bent on obliterating what humans had carved into the ancient gravestones dating back to the American Revolution.

The towering war memorial was on top of the grassy slope above the Grant plot that now had more markers than when he lived here. Saddened by omnipresent death, he excused himself and said he would like to be alone in the cemetery for a few minutes. Annie understood his need to grieve alone for his brother and his nephews, and she gently laid her hand on Julia's arm. War had touched every life in some way or another.

Years lay heavy on Lemuel's shoulders, and his white beard and hair marked his age and experiences. War aged a man, he thought. The path up to the Grant plot seemed steeper and longer. His heart raced a bit as he swung the cane in front of his footfalls. He had to stop. With one hand on an old tombstone, he placed his right hand over his heart and tried to will his heart to slow down. Perhaps deeper, slower breaths would help, he thought. After a few minutes, he resumed the now torturous climb up the hill.

When he arrived at the Grant plot on his left, he could not help sobbing with grief. There was a new marker for Joseph, but nothing was carved into it. Julia had no money with which to commission the work. Lemuel knew Julia was embarrassed, but Lemuel turned his thoughts to his brother.

"Oh Joseph, my dear, dear brother. We should never have left you alone up here. One of us should have stayed. I'm so sorry. We were so anxious to make a good life and the money was so tempting. You were willing and we took advantage of that. And then there was the war."

Lemuel looked around for any other markers for his nephews and found none. With a gasp, he tried to stem the flow of tears, but they flooded his faded blue eyes and flowed down into his beard. After a few minutes he regained his composure. He knelt by his brother's stone, laid his black beaver hat on the grass, and raised his right hand as if making a solemn oath.

"Joseph, I promise you that I will take care of Julia until the day she dies. And I will either get your sons' names on the memorial or build another

one in their honor. This I swear to you, brother.
This I swear. As God is my witness."

With the aid of his cane, Lemuel struggled
to his feet and pulled a piece of paper from his coat
pocket. A stub of pencil recorded the names and
dates of the few Grants noted in the plot. The
family Bible would yield the rest. Before he left to
return to the house, Lemuel paused.

"And if it be possible in this life, Joseph, I
will clear your son Addison's name. There must
be some way."

Lemuel could not see the two ghosts
standing by their father's stone. Arm in arm they
stood and listened to their uncle's oath of fealty to
the quest, the mission to right the wrong. With
bowed heads they prayed together that he would
succeed, that someone, somehow would clear the
name of a brave young soldier falsely accused of
cowardice. And that someone would care enough
to put a marker for each of the two lost ones, that
they might not be forgotten.

As he limped back down the path, Lemuel
felt his age and knew that he did not have much
time left in which to do all these things. He feared
that the town would continue its stubborn
insistence that Addison, having been shot in the
back, was a coward and had no right to have his
name inscribed with the honored dead, even
though he had died at Spotsylvania. There was no
body, they would argue. He probably ran away
there, too, they would sneer. They would very

likely also refuse to put his nephew Lemuel's name on the monument either, since he survived the war and died at sea.

Lemuel continued his slow painful walk back to the house but could not keep the memories at bay. They tumbled about like a kaleidoscopic collage, snippets of pictures from his youth. Had he done the right thing by going south to Georgia? Should his brothers and a sister have followed him? Death stalked the whole family, he mused. His brother, a sister, his nephews, one of his sons, his first wife, James Hervey's baby son. He had seen more death and destruction in Atlanta than a man could bear without it tearing away at his very soul. He knew his nephews had seen as bad or worse, but the defenseless civilians in Atlanta had borne the brunt of the savage attacks by Sherman's army and the merciless siege. Lemuel shook his head trying to clear the horrible images from his mind and concentrate on what he had to do for his dead brother's family.

Sleep would not come that night as he rehearsed to himself what he should say to the town elders concerning his two nephews. He must know quickly whether or not they would help him or hinder him. He felt time slipping away from him and wished that he had come sooner. Atlanta had held him to her bosom, crying for help, singing her siren song as she tried to absorb the Reconstruction and fight off the carpetbaggers. She needed his wisdom, his courage, his

remarkable skills at negotiation. Soon he must
return to her side, but now he must channel all his
energy into dealing with the town and its cruel
blindness.

He lay down on the old four-poster bed and
stared out the bedroom window. The moon, full
and glowing like a paler version of her brother sun,
shone its light through the ancient elm tree's
branches, casting eerie shadows that danced on the
wall. As a child, he had feared the dark closet
even though he knew it contained naught but a few
clothes, one pair of church shoes, and a few toy
soldiers. Now he feared death. Not because he
feared dying, but because he feared dying before
he had completed his mission. He had sworn an
oath to his dead brother and that oath was sacred,
divine.

"Craig elachie," he whispered.

CHAPTER 21

They were waiting for him as he was sure they would be. Nothing remained a secret for long in this old river town. As Lemuel stepped into the room at the back of the tiny town hall, he looked each man in the eye, moving deliberately from one man to the next, gauging the strength of the man and his mindset. The early morning sun streamed in through the antique glass window pane with its wavy patterns, and a tiny army of dust particles rose in the stream of light, pulled skyward like the souls of dead soldiers rising to heaven.

"Good morning, gentlemen. Since you have all gathered here so early, I assume that you know why I am here today? May I sit down?"

They nodded with arms folded defensively across their chests and did not rise to greet him, a not-so-subtle declaration of war. Lemuel already felt the heavy hand of intolerance on his shoulder, but he at least had to try.

"What is it you want, Mr. Grant?" one of the men said as he leaned forward on the unbalanced old table.

"Yeah, what do you want, Johnny Reb?" sneered another.

Lemuel had not counted on the possibility that the war was still being fought so far north. That surprised him. The war had ended, for the North at least, some ten years ago.

Lemuel chose to ignore the taunt and stick to business.

"Well, gentlemen, I'm here on a simple enough mission. My nephew Addison's name is not on the war memorial and that omission is causing great pain to his dear mother. As you know, Addison died at the battle of Spotsylvania Court House, and…"

Before he could finish the sentence, an older farmer at the end of the table jumped to his feet.

"We don't know no such a thing! He ran at Antietam, the damned coward, and for all we know he ran again!"

"Excuse me, sir. Addison did not run at Antietam. I was an officer in that war, sir, and I can tell you clearly that the South had some very fine sharpshooters on that battlefield, hiding in an apple orchard. One of his companions wrote a letter to the Bangor paper trying to clear this boy's good name. He was there at the battle himself and was one of only two who were not either wounded or killed."

"Ha! My point exactly!" said the farmer. "Birds of a feather! Prob'ly another coward!"

"Addison's military records are clear. He was badly wounded at Antietam, came home to recover, and reenlisted to fight again for the North. He died at Spotsylvania with most of the rest of the Maine boys. Of course, you wouldn't know because none of you were there, were you?" Lemuel said with mounting fury.

The Southern war hero knew it was now a lost cause. Undertaking any further discussion would be pointless. He rose from his chair and looked at the stubborn men glaring at him. Time was precious. There was another solution to this problem, although not as good.

In the corner of the room stood Addison Grant. The boy soldier hung his head. He had hoped that his uncle's money and reputation and local roots might accomplish that which no one in the family could with military records and righteous demands. His name would still be banned from the war memorial. Who could help him if not his brother, his uncle, or his friend N. S. Fales?

Lemuel P. chose not to tip his hand at this point, excused himself, ignored the guffaws from the town leaders, and left the room. He headed straight to the other side of town where a local stonecutter lived.

It didn't take long to strike a deal with the man. Money talked louder than the town council.

Lemuel commissioned a four-sided monument for the Grant plot that included information about his nephews on the side facing the walking path. He assured the man that he would be well paid, and gave him a handsome advance on the work. More than anyone else would have paid for the entire work. Lemuel was quite sure that there would be some in town who would try their best to intimidate the stonecutter into refusing the commission. Money was the best antidote for that.

He pledged to return again to see the work completed and installed. The monument was to be eight feet tall and would be placed in the center of the plot.

When Lemuel P. returned to the farm, he had the sad duty to tell Julia that he had failed to change the minds of the townspeople, but he also let her know that he had commissioned a monument that would tell the world that Addison was a hero, and that would make certain that no one forgot Lemuel either. The other stones would be finished soon and the plot would be complete.

"Oh, Lemuel. I can't thank you enough. Poor dear Addison told me over and over again that he was not a coward. I believed him, of course, but his father…his father never was sure. And when Addison's friend N. S. Fales came to see me, I was even more certain that Addison had told the truth about that battle. Thank you for helping us, Lemuel. You have saved my life, most likely. I wish you could stay here and counsel me on business matters. I really don't trust the bank president, but I think he fears you and knows that you will come back from time to time to visit me and check on the fund you set up for me. It amused me to see him shake in his boots."

"My dear sister-in-law, I wish I could stay but the South needs me. My family in Georgia needs me. I must return. I assure you that I will come to Maine as often as I can to see how you are doing. I agree that the banker fears me and with good reason. He knows that I am a man of my word."

As painful as it was, Lemuel had to leave Julia. He stopped by to visit his nephew's widow and see her child, and was pleased to learn that a friend of Lemuel's from the old 4th Maine Volunteers lived nearby and was watching over her with more than a passing interest.

"That's good," he whispered to himself. "Life goes on with or without us. The child needs a father, especially with these uncertain times."

Julia drove him to the rail depot and waved until the train was out of sight, chugging down the tracks, spewing ash and smoke into the air and onto the landscape.

Lemuel thought about his life and his present circumstances all the way to Georgia. He had been generous before the war, donating to many charitable causes, but now he realized that there was much to do in order to restore Atlanta to her former glory. Lord only knew how long they would have to abide the carpetbaggers and such vermin, but this, too, would pass. He must be patient. He began to make a list of the needs of the city and her citizens, and he thought long and hard about his family and their needs. He could not slight either group. Somehow he must find ways to care for both.

On the way back to Atlanta, L. P. Grant – as he was fondly known – made a list of things that were needed and what he proposed to do. Some things he could take care of by himself, but for some others he would need some sort of financial consortium to deal with the woes of what had been a nation in secession.

CHAPTER 22

L. P. clicked open his gold pocket watch. Given to him when he retired from the position of General Superintendent of a railroad, he valued this gift more than almost any other possession. He had gone on to become president of several different railroads, but secretly he loved the work of a superintendent better than the social status of a president.

The train was already five minutes late, and L. P. frowned. His trains always ran on time except during the war. What was the country coming to if an engineer couldn't even keep a schedule? People depended on the trains running on time. Commerce depended on it sometimes.

He "tsk'd" a few times and stood up. The wooden bench was uncomfortable at best, and his hips bothered him even more than when he was a younger man.

Ah, he said as he heard the far-off whistle of the steam locomotive. It was hard to believe that the one ton Tiny Tim started all of this.

Nowadays, he thought, the big steam engines would have flattened Tiny Tim.

L. P. settled into the first-class seat. His health wasn't the best and he missed Laura. She had been a wonderful mother and wife, and her death shocked him. Laura had been the picture of health one day and dead of typhoid pneumonia four days later. The doctors were helpless when the fever took her. L. P. remembered with slight shame how he had railed at the doctors, ordering them to save his wife and the mother of his four children. They had been married just over thirty-five years. It wasn't possible that she was gone.

Death had stalked the Grant family, he thought. First his nephew Addison, then nephew Lemuel C., then his brother Joseph by his own hand, and his brother James Hervey whose child had preceded him in death. It was too much. Tears trembled on his face as he thought about Laura. So sudden. So unreal.

As the train rumbled south, L. P. thought about the war. So many thousands dead or wounded. So many lives ruined. So many cities devastated or even burned to the ground like Atlanta. Was the Confederacy right to secede? He wasn't sure. He didn't hold with slavery although he had bought a young Negro girl and made her a house servant. He paid her a decent wage and treated her like one of the family. It had cost him $1,000 to rescue her from a bad situation, and she often expressed her gratitude for his kindness.

When Lincoln freed the slaves, L. P. had offered
her freedom but she refused to leave the family.
Free but bound by loyalty. L. P. shook his head.
How the world had changed since the war erupted.

When the train finally pulled into the station,
L. P. found a carriage for hire and slowly stepped
up into the dark interior. He was so tired. Perhaps
there wouldn't be many more times that he could
make the trip north. It had been good to see Julia
and his nephew's widow Annie. At least he was
able to see to the financial matters, he thought as
he dozed off.

When he arrived at the house, his son John
was waiting for him with a hot dinner. Like his
father and his uncles he had an interest in railroads
as well, and he had already earned the respect and
friendship of Atlanta's elite. His father's money
had helped, but he made his own way.

"Thank you, son. I really appreciate your
kindness. I am extremely tired. My hips are
bothering me a great deal, and I really don't feel
well. I'll eat a little something and then retire if
you don't mind. Tell your lovely wife that I'll see
her tomorrow."

The next morning, L. P. felt a little stronger,
and ate a hearty breakfast. The aromas from the
kitchen had wafted up the stairs and tickled his
nose until he woke and stroked his moustache and
beard. Immediately after his meal, L. P. took
paper and ink and walked with a decided limp into
the library. There was so much to do in Atlanta

that he hardly knew where to start. The
carpetbaggers were everywhere still, and one had
to be careful.

John rapped at the door and called to his
father.

"Father, are you up? Where are you?"

"I'm in the library, John. Come in. I was
just thinking about the city. There's so much to
do."

"You can't do it alone, father. You'll need
the help of all the big money men in Atlanta. At
least there are still a few who survived the war and
the carpetbaggers. The scum. Imagine having to
have permission to go to Maine to see your
family."

"Now, son, don't get upset. All things pass
with time. They won't be here forever."
John stamped his foot in annoyance.

"What are you planning to do, father? And
how are Aunt Julia and Lemuel's widow Annie?"

"I'm not sure yet how to do it, but I know
some of the things we have to do. I straightened
things out for Julia and Annie. They'll be fine
now. But after I'm gone, son, it will be up to you
to watch over them."

L. P. leaned back in the brown leather chair
he had purchased in Boston and had shipped to
Atlanta. There were a few advantages to being the
president of a railroad, he thought with a smile.
He did enjoy traveling and had been as far west as

San Francisco and as far east as Boston, as well as having traveled from Maine to Georgia.

The civil engineer tapped his writing instrument on the table and turned the squatty crystal inkwell around and around. The shape kept the ink from spilling when the train swayed, and L. P. liked the functionality of it. Sea captains had similar inkwells.

"John, I really need to be alone for a bit. I have to think."

"Certainly, father. I understand. We'll bring you supper tonight. How will that suit you?"

"Just fine, son, just fine. That would be wonderful."

John took his father's hand, but didn't grip it the way he used to. His father suffered from some stiffness and swelling, and he had to be careful.

"Oh father, I meant to ask you about something. While you were gone, I looked in the attic to see if there was anything that you needed to bring downstairs. In a trunk, I found your Masonic apron. I know that you were a Mason before the war and of course "Uncle Billy" Sherman's men ransacked all the houses before they torched them. How is it that your house was not burned and that the soldiers didn't touch your belongings or burn your house?"

"Ah, that's an interesting story," said Lemuel. "When Sherman started their marauding march south, he told his officers that they were not to touch the house or belongings of a brother

Mason. So when they found that apron in a trunk, they left my property alone. I almost felt guilty about it when so many others lost everything, but I guess the Lord was watching over some of us. That's why we still have this house, son. We were spared. Now I must repay that debt."

"I'll see you this evening, father. We'll bring you a nice supper."

L. P. Grant leaned back in his chair, turned it about and looked at the beautiful garden. Many houses still didn't have glass windows, and made do with oiled paper. The need in the city was great. And there was one other decision he had to make. There was Jane, the widow of his best friend who was murdered by two freed slaves in a botched robbery back in 1865. Jane had been a widow all these years and a good friend of his late wife, Laura.

It had only been two years since Laura died, but somehow L. P. thought that she would approve. He and Jane had had dinner a few times and Jane was careful to observe all the proprieties since L. P. had only been a widower for two years. She still wore dark dresses and her wedding ring even though it had been more than fifteen years since her beloved James had been brutally murdered by those robbers. They thought he was carrying money from the telegraph office, but he wasn't. So he was killed for nothing. The city had been chaotic right after the war. That was a November that Jane wished she could forget.

L. P. thought about Laura for some time and then thought about his children. What would they think about his remarrying so soon? Everyone loved Jane and admired her for her strength and courage. He had secretly inquired of a few family members, and all were happy for him. But what about John? He had been so attached to his mother, that L. P. wondered if John could accept another woman in his father's house.

He and Jane had talked some of her accepting a position as his housekeeper and later becoming his wife. After all, they were no longer young. There was one problem, though. Jane had a brother Charles who was more than fond of intoxicating drink.

L. P. had found a job for him that paid well after Jane begged for his assistance. L. P. did not relish the thought of having to deal with a sot. Hopefully Jane knew her brother's situation since L. P. hadn't seen the brother in some time, nor heard anything about him. There was much to consider.

The flower gardens behind the house had been tended with love while he was gone. He assumed that Jane's hand was in it. Right now, he needed to get to work. He decided to make a list of the leading citizens of Atlanta – those who still had money. The reclamation of the beautiful city would take a lot of money. Pledges would be needed, and plans. They would have to start with what was the most important. Not all would agree

on that, so L. P. would have hope that most would
see things his way.

Jane had waited an appropriate amount of
time before she tapped at the door. She smoothed
her salt and pepper hair and her dark blue skirts
and held her breath. Her heart was pounding and
her face was flushed.

L. P. turned his chair back around and stared
at the door. He knew it must be Jane, but he
wasn't ready to make his decision yet. Still, he
couldn't leave her standing at the door. He rose
stiffly.

"Hello, Jane. How wonderful you look. I'm
so glad that you came by. Here, sit down on the
divan."

"How was your trip L. P.? Productive, I
hope. How is your sister-in-law? I'm sure she's
been having a difficult time of it. I know I did,
with James having been shot. And of course
you've not been spared yourself. Life can be
cruel, can't it?"

"Yes, Jane. Life can be very cruel. I was
able to help Julia and my nephew Lemuel's
widow. I doubt that they'll have any more trouble
with the bank up there. If they do, I shall just go
back up again and straighten out that banker. An
annoying man. I shall have to keep close watch on
the funds I left for her. I don't entirely trust that
weasel."

L. P. sat down on the divan next to Jane and
took her pale hand, admiring the lovely long

fingers. She had been just 39 years old when her husband was murdered and had never remarried all those lonely years. L. P. had helped her on occasion, but she never asked. Burdened with a sot for a brother, Jane bore her difficulties with grace and patience.

L. P. himself was very lonely and there were times when he thought he could bear no more. Death seemed to stalk his family, and it seemed that just when he had managed to recover from one grief, there stood another.

He had not thought that he would ever remarry, but of late – perhaps due to his illness – he longed for the comfort of a woman about the house. He had an excellent cook and housekeeper to look after him, and attentive children, but that was not the same as having a wife to comfort him in his declining years.

"Jane," he began, and then hesitated for what seemed forever. He cleared his throat and sighed. This was not going well.

"Yes, L. P., what is it?"

"Jane, dear," he began again and stopped. He stared out the window and thought about Laura. How he missed her. No one would ever be able to replace her. Was it fair to ask this woman to share his life when he still loved Laura? Could he learn to care so deeply a second time?

Jane held her breath. A breeze blew the lace curtains that Laura had made with such skill and

love and ruffled the antimacassar that Laura's
mother had made for the back of L. P.'s chair.

L. P. held his breath and returned his gaze to
the widow of his best friend. Surely James would
want him to care for his Jane, even if that meant
marrying her. The aging widower looked deeply
into Jane's dark brown eyes and then stroked the
pale hand across the back of which several blue
veins intersected and then vanished into her
slender wrist.

L. P. began again.

"Jane, there is something I must ask you.
We are neither of us getting any younger, you
know. You've been widowed a very long time.
Over 15 years, I believe?"

Jane simply nodded.

"I lost my dear Laura but two years ago.
Sometimes it seems impossible. Well and happy
one day and dead four days later. I believe you
knew that the doctors called it typhoid pneumonia.
It wasn't fair that she should be taken like that. I
confess that my faith was somewhat shaken. How
could God let that happen, I thought. Then I
realized that many, many others had suffered the
same loss when the typhoid visited us.

"I have been thinking, Jane. We are both
alone. We've known each other many years. I
dare say we know each other as well as any of our
family know us. Do you not think so?"

Jane could only nod. Her heart was
pounding in her chest.

L. P. stood up and limped over to his desk.
He turned to face Jane with tears in his eyes, partly
because he missed Laura and was still grieving for
her, and partly because he was unsure as to exactly
what he could offer this widow some ten years his
junior. He had money and position in Atlanta
society. He had an outstanding reputation as a
man of honor and integrity. But his health was not
good, and the years of traveling through the South
looking for rights of way for the railroad had left
their mark on him. He often feared that yellow
fever or smallpox or some such disease would, like
dirty linens, befoul his body.

"I am an old man, my dear. Even though I
am just 64 years of age, and many men live much
longer these days, I fear that death may find me
sooner than he finds some others. I have lived a
stressful life. Building the railroads and then the
defenses around Atlanta. Even the war itself took
its toll on all of us. I have a question to ask of you
and you need not reply at once. If you need time
to think it over, that is fine. It's an important
decision. I would get down on one knee like a
proper gentleman, but my old bones will not
permit that. My dear Jane, will you do me the
honor to accept my proposal of marriage? I know
you could do better, my dear, but I promise to care
for you and protect you. Will you marry me?"

Jane gasped and flushed like a schoolgirl.
They had discussed the possibility of her becoming
his housekeeper, but she had not foreseen a

proposal of marriage. She fanned herself
vigorously.

"Oh my goodness, L. P.! Are you sure?
What will your children think about this?"

L. P. laughed.

"I've already discussed it with everyone
except my son John. He may resist at first and
think it far too soon, but I am certain that we
should do this. May I court you properly for a
short time? Then we can announce the
engagement. What do you think of that idea?"

"Of course you may court me, L.P. I think
that would be wonderful. I've chosen not to see
anyone since James died. The days turned into
weeks, and the weeks to months, then years. There
was just no one of interest after James. But you, I
know you, L. P. You're a fine and decent man. I
should be honored to be your wife. I know that
you will always love Laura as I still love James,
but we would be good for each other. Yes, yes, I
will marry you."

"Then may I kiss you to seal the bargain? A
handshake seems a bit stiff, don't you think? This
is a merger of sorts, but not a business deal!"

Jane rose from the divan and took L. P.'s
outstretched hands. She raised her face to his, but
giggled when his moustache tickled her cheek.

"If you do not care for a moustache, I shall
have the barber remove it at once, my dear," L. P.
whispered.

"Oh my, no! You look very distinguished in a moustache, L. P. Don't have it shaved off, dear. I shall get used to it with much practice."

Jane giggled and looked at the floor.

L. P. lifted her sweet face to his and kissed her gently on the lips. Something stirred in him that he had not felt since Laura's death. Could he love another? Jane responded eagerly and the kiss became more passionate. Quickly Jane stepped back and fanned herself again.

"L. P., we must be very careful. Since both of us have previously been married, things might get out of hand. It was a lovely kiss though. I believe you are correct. We will be good for each other. I hope your son John does not object. It would no doubt be best if you told him soon when the two of you are alone."

"Yes, Jane, you are quite correct. I will tell John soon."

"L. P., I need to go, my dear. I've been here too long and people will talk. Funny, is it not? Two old people kissing in the parlor!"

CHAPTER 23

John Grant was not happy. His father would remarry after his dear mother was scarcely cold in her grave. It had only been two years. Was his father insane? What would people think? He liked Jane Crew well enough, but still this was so sudden. They had so much to do to rebuild Atlanta, and here was his aged and infirm father courting a much younger woman he intended to marry! John had come to his father's house to reason with him and dissuade him from this awful plan.

"Father, I don't think this is a good idea. Why don't you wait a while? We all know that Jane is a virtuous woman and has remained celibate all these years since James died, but really, Father! It's nearly ludicrous, or worse yet, improper entirely! Furthermore, Father, for heaven's sake do not take her into your home as a housekeeper. If you must have her, then marry her!"

John turned away from his father and leaned against the fireplace mantel.

L. P. smiled and covered his mouth with his monogrammed handkerchief. Laura had made it one Christmas when they were newly married and had little money for gifts. He had treasured it and carried it everywhere with him. He hoped that it would not bother Jane. She was a sensible woman and would realize how much it meant to him. He knew that she had kept many of her dead husband's things. They gave her comfort.

"My son," L. P. began. "I've lived much longer than you have, have suffered much including the loss of my beloved Laura, and I deserve a little peace and a loving companion near the end of this mortal journey. Please do not endeavor to tell me how to live my life. I know well that there are those who will quickly forget my great service and generosity to this city and see only that I am marrying Jane after my wife has been gone but two years. Some will think it too soon. I frankly don't care one whit what they think. Laura would approve.

"I know she was your mother, son, but she was first my wife. I knew her longer than you did. Have a care, son, that you do not attempt to thwart my plans. I will not permit it. I do not wish to become your enemy, nor does Jane. Be a good son and accept my decision. Support me in this. Do not oppose me. Everyone else in the family is happy for me. I hope to have your blessing, but I will proceed with or without it."

John Grant stared at his father. He had never heard him speak in this manner nor with such passion. The son of the great benefactor of Atlanta realized that his father had made up his mind and that there would be no stopping him regardless of what Atlanta society thought about it. He strode to the window and looked out at his late mother's garden. Would she indeed understand his widowed father's needs and great longing for a companion? Was she even watching this from heaven? He turned back to his father who was patiently waiting for his son's answer.

"Very well, father," John said with a deep sigh. "Very well. I suppose you have a right to make this decision regardless of what others may think. I assume you have already asked Jane to marry you."

"Yes, I have asked Jane to marry me, and she said 'yes'," L. P. replied as he watched the blood recede from his son's face.

"Very well, then, I see that I cannot change your mind. Am I the last to know?"

"Yes, John, you are the last to know. I knew you would not be in favor of the union, so I spoke with other family members first to see how the wind blew. Everyone else encouraged me to proceed. Yes, you are the last. As I said, I knew you would oppose it, but I hoped that I could persuade you. Will you give us your blessing?"

John frowned and held his breath. He pulled his black leather driving gloves from his jacket and smacked them against his hand. He did not wish to give his blessing at all, but if he withheld it, there would be tension between him and his father that might never heal. He said a silent prayer that his mother would not be upset by this arrangement and sighed, blowing out the breath that he had held in.

"Well enough then, father. I wish you happiness. When is the wedding?"

"We haven't gotten that far, John. It won't be a big affair as it is the second marriage for both of us, although both of our spouses were taken from us by death. We will very likely have just an intimate wedding with only family and close friends in attendance. I trust you will come?"

"I will come, father. I will come," John said as he stepped to the front door. For a moment, he stood with his hand on the doorknob and stared down at the floor. He wished with all his heart that he could think of some way to change his father's mind, to at least delay things, hoping that his father would not go ahead with this marriage.

"This is difficult for me, father. I feel that you are dishonoring my mother, your wife. I will support you, but I do not approve. I will give my blessing and wish you well, but I wish you would change your mind. There's just no hope of that, is there?"

"No, John. No hope at all. And I would not marry Jane if I thought for one moment that I was dishonoring dear Laura."

John put on his top hat, opened the door, and stepped into the street. His father watched him walk to his carriage and pick up the anchor. The carriage squeaked as he stepped in, and his black mare tossed her head. As he clucked to his horse, John nodded to his father and drove off without looking back.

L. P. shook his head as he closed the door. He had guessed correctly that his son would not be pleased. He blew out his breath to ease the tension and went into the kitchen. The cook had left dinner on the sideboard and he picked at the baked chicken and inhaled the delicious odor of sage.

"I just wish John could see the wisdom in two old people who have each lost a spouse …" L. P. said as his eyes welled with tears. "I just wish he would worry less about what people think and more about Jane's and my own happiness. Ah well. One day, perhaps, one day."

He served himself some chicken and potatoes, and just stared at the carrots. Nothing really looked very good to him, but he needed to eat. He was blessed with a fine cook to look after him, but Jane was also skilled in the kitchen. Her bread was famous all over the city. L. P. hesitated as he prepared to bless the food.

"Lord, please bless what Thy providence has provided. And please bless my son that he will have a change of heart. I feel that I am doing the right thing and so does Jane. Bless us, Father, and please bless this food. Amen."

L. P. leaned back in his chair and again stared out at the garden. A soft breeze blew in through the open window and carried with it the sweet breath of the roses outside. Laura loved roses and made her own toilet water from the petals. The aging widower leaned forward with his forehead on his closed fists and wept.

CHAPTER 24

The wedding went as planned. Jane wore a beige silk dress and carried a bouquet of roses from her own garden. Friends provided food and a cake. The parson told L. P. that he was very happy for them both and hoped they would have many years together. L. P. relaxed after the wedding, but wondered how he would do this night. Could he really love Jane or would he be thinking about Laura? And after all, he was now 64 years old and not well. Could he still perform? Jane was only 55, and there would likely be expectations. Well, he thought to himself, I either can or I can't. I guess we'll find out soon enough!

He needn't have worried. Jane was patient and loving and the marriage was consummated. There was no time just then for a honeymoon, but they had planned for one later when L. P. was feeling stronger. Atlanta still needed him, and even though he had accomplished much, much still remained to be done.

L. P. delighted in doing things to please Jane. He ordered some shoes for her, hand made in Boston. She had to be carefully measured as her feet were delicate. Some time passed and the shoes didn't appear. Jane's husband became irate one morning and penned a scathing complaint to the company. In almost no time at all, the shoes arrived along with an abject apology from the owner of the shoe manufacturer. Enclosed with the shoes was a certificate for a discount of half the price on the next order of shoes. L. P. smiled when he saw that piece of paper.

"Well, Jane, my dear, perhaps I should run for president! If I can produce these results with just one letter, think what I might accomplish in Washington!"

"Good heavens, L. P.! Surely you're not serious?" Jane said with her hand over her heart.

"No, no, my dear! I was jesting! What man in his right mind would want to be president of this country!" laughed L. P. "Jeff Davis didn't even want to be president of the Confederacy. They don't pay enough for all the headaches and stress. There's a good reason why presidents go gray so quickly. I'll take railroading any day, my dear. Not to worry."

After the couple had settled in and began receiving guests, L. P. was pressed into service once again to help rebuild his beloved Atlanta. There were any number of committees begging for his commitment, and boards forming that invited him to participate. As one of the wealthiest citizens, L. P. felt strongly about giving back to the land that had made him rich. After donating land for four churches, including land for a black church, and committing funds to renovate his own church, L. P. was asked by his son John why he was contributing to the Methodists, Baptists, and Presbyterians to build churches. Why not just support his own church?

"John, I must stand up square to the future work. There is so much to be done, that we have to give what we can, where we can, and it doesn't matter whose church you support. They all need us. I gave land to the black people to build their own church only to find out that they didn't have the funds or any way of obtaining the funds to build the building. Now, it wouldn't have made much sense to donate the land unless I also helped build the church, would it?

"Just like when Mrs. Lizzie Murphy needed some place to put her fruit stand. I allowed her to use a piece of land I own on Marietta Street. It didn't cost me anything, but it gave her a chance to earn the money she needed for her and her boy. Do you see, son?"

"Yes, father. I'm sorry. I know that I need to pitch in as well. What can I do?"

Father and son sat down at the table with paper and pen and began to make a list of everything that they knew still needed doing, and a list of boards and committees that were requesting their time and money. L. P. had already donated 100 acres of his best land for a public park near the end of the war. He wanted it named for Laura, but the city just named it Grant Park. L. P. was annoyed, but shrugged it off.

"Have some cookies, son. Jane made these delicious sugar cookies today. John, what would you think if I stood for election to the city council? I've been giving it some thought and I think that I could contribute quite a lot, given my experience."

"Father," John said rather loudly as he took several of the cookies. "What are you thinking? Your health is none too good, and you are already involved with the Young Men's Library Association, serve on the Board of Education, the Board of Directors for the Bank of the State of Georgia, and you're president of the Atlanta and West Point Railroad! Shall I go on? Are you trying to kill yourself? And what about Jane? When will you find any time for her? No, father. It's insane. Please don't do that. Or at best, if you feel you must do it, then resign one of your other positions. You hardly have time eat a meal as things sit now."

L. P. knew that John was right, but he also knew that Atlanta needed him. The city lay in ruins after the war. One true thing that Maj. General William T. Sherman had said was – as best L. P. could recollect – the following statement:

"We have devoured the land – all the people retire before us and desolation is behind. To realize what war is, one should follow our tracks."

"John, the war scattered a comfortable little fortune to the winds. I have since gathered some of the debris and ought to feel grateful to a kind Provider for my present comforts. I need to give back everything I can to rebuild Atlanta. If that means I hardly have time for a meal or a trip to the barber, so be it. I've made my decision. I shall stand for election," L. P. said with a clenched jaw.

"Very well, father. You ask my advice but you seldom listen to me. I don't know why you bother to ask. You always do what you want."

"John, that may be because I'm seeking your approval, not your permission, son! I do like to know what you think, even if I don't agree with you."

L. P. looked down at his pocket watch and whistled.

"My goodness, where has the time gone? I have a board meeting to attend. Please excuse me. I'll perhaps see you tomorrow?"

"Yes, father. I'll be happy to have supper with you. We have much to talk of and plan. And I want to talk to you some more about your plans to stand for election. I still think it's most unwise. I'll stop by tomorrow. Good night, father."

CHAPTER 25

L. P. did stand for election and won, but at a price. His health had begun to deteriorate rapidly and he wondered just how much time he had left. "Father, I really wish you would rest more and work less," said John. "You don't look well at all."

L. P. smiled, doffed his top hat to his worried son and stepped up into the waiting carriage that would take him to an important meeting with his solicitor. There was one more thing he needed to take care of. He knew he probably didn't have a lot of years left to make plans for himself and his family. When he arrived at the attorney's office, he shook hands and sat down in a comfortable leather chair.

"How are you today, Lemuel? You look tired. Are you well?"

"Well, not really, but I need you to do something for me. I want to change my will and add a codicil concerning burial. There's a new cemetery and I wish to purchase a rather large lot for myself and others. I of course wish to be buried with my wife Laura, but also with Jane. I have this little drawing. Let me show you. As we face the monument I want Laura on this side and Janie on the other."

"Why of course, Lemuel," said the lawyer. "That's easily done. What else?"

"Well, Edward, this next item may cause a bit of a stir, but I've already spoken to Jane about it. I want to have her husband's grave moved so that Jane will lie between us, thus."

The attorney was silent for a moment.

"You wish to move her husband's grave to the new cemetery, Lemuel? You wish to have Mr. Crew, then Jane, then yourself, then Laura buried thusly?"

"Quite so," said a relieved Lemuel. That was not as difficult as he thought it would be. He would have to hope that John would not be upset. On the way home, Lemuel rehearsed his speech to John. The mere fact that he felt compelled to do that gave him his answer. John would not be pleased. Ah well. Perhaps not, but it was his own affair, not John's. He could be buried on his mother's side of the plot.

When Lemuel Pratt Grant died, his family was at his bedside, and Atlanta mourned the loss of their generous benefactor. Atlanta would rise again from the destruction and was already healing.

CHAPTER 26

Addison's ghost sat on a stone step leading down from the plateau on Marye's Heights. He had been following his cousin around the cemetery as she searched for his grave. She had seen him before when she was a child, but she would probably not recall the meeting. Addison did. She was his last hope. The last of a generation. Now she had picked up the gauntlet, although she might not know it. She was searching for lost ancestors and family.

It was Memorial Day, and the cemetery was eerily empty. There were no visitors to the cemetery on this special day except his cousin, her sister and those who had died in the Civil War. Many, if not most, of the graves were identified with small stones that bore the identification numbers of the remains buried there. Addison was not there. He knew she would not find him. In the past, he had watched as she searched for him through cemeteries and genealogy records, a family Bible, and oral traditions. She kept going

back to the Winterport cemetery and looking at the
war memorial and the obelisk in the Grant plot.
His cousin was here in this cemetery because she
had been writing about him. When she wrote his
death scene without even visiting the battlefields
where he had fought and died, he could stand it no
longer. He threw books on the floor of her studio
to get her attention. Only a huge dictionary and
books about the Civil War battlefields. Only the
battlefields. Surely she would get the message.

Here she was on this special day searching
in vain for his grave. The rangers had been helpful
and she found the exact spot where he had fallen
wounded at Antietam. Now she searched for the
place where he died at a horrible place called "The
Bloody Angle." The abatises were no longer there
at Spotsylvania, and grass covered the trenches
where so many thousand corpses lay mouldering.

It was time. He had to tell her whatever was
allowed. If she believed in him enough to spend
time trying to find him and clear his name of the
false charge of cowardice when so many had failed
before her, she would see him. She would hear his
voice. He had to try. His cousin, now in her
sixties, began to weep.

"It's Memorial Day. Why is no one here to
pay their respects?" she whispered. "Where are
they?"

Sobbing, she headed for the stone steps that
led down in layer upon layer, tier upon tier of
graves. Embarrassed, she turned her head away

from him and passed him, still sitting on the stone steps.

He could not let this moment pass!

"Cousin," he said rather forcefully. "Cousin, don't look for me. I'm not here. Look at the battlefield and the trench. You will feel my spirit there, for I am not here."

His cousin turned to look at the man on the steps.

"Addison? Are you Addison Grant?" she said in a trembling voice.

Addison nodded his head. They were calling him back. He had to go. She was still his last hope.

"Cousin! Clear my name! Please clear my name. Goodbye. Craig Elachie, my cousin, Craig Elachie."

Addison longed to hug her and thank her, to tell her to keep on, but they were calling him. It was time. As he walked back through the veil of immortality, he was joined by thousands of others, blue and gray, and he added his voice to theirs.

"Shall we gather at the river…" a beautiful hymn written by a preacher in New York to memorialize those who had died in the war and those who had died when a plague attacked the citizens of New York.

Forget them not. They see and hear, and they care.

*****

N.B.

    After Lee's surrender, he attended St. Paul's Episcopal Church in Richmond, Virginia. No longer completely segregated, the church was eerily quiet. After a few minutes, the minister invited the congregation to come to the communion rail. For a time, no one moved. Then a well-dressed black man rose and walked to the front. Still the church was quiet. As a bit of whispering began, an elegant white man with silver hair rose from his seat, walked slowly and painfully to the front where he braced himself on the rail and with a soft grunt knelt on aging knees.

    The black man looked at him and smiled.

    "Thank you, General Lee, thank you," the black man whispered.

THE END

About the author

Barbara M. Lord was born in Boston, Massachusetts. She received her BA from Ohio Wesleyan University with a major in English. She was also a departmental assistant. She started her writing career at TIME/LIFE as a staffer on the publishing side. Prior to that she spent several years in administrative social work as a Program Director for the YWCA, a USO executive director, an Assistant Director for the American Heart Association, Director for the Retired Senior Volunteer Program, and Director for the Association for Retarded Citizens (ARC). She volunteered as a Big Sister in the Big Brother/Big Sister program and was also a volunteer ski instructor for underprivileged children.

While on leave from LIFE, Barbara worked as a Wyoming hunting camp cook one fall. She had fallen in love with the backcountry and would gladly have traded her job at LIFE for a cabin in the wilderness. Perhaps the most important lessons learned were not to tie the pack mule's lead rope to your own saddle horn lest you end up in the drink and also not to ride between a mother moose and her calf!

Barbara and her family enjoy their life in Texas where she lives with her husband, two cats, one German Shepherd, and a retired AQHA show horse. Her children live nearby and all gather for family dinners. Her family has always been there to support her writing, and Barbara has always tried to inspire her children to stretch their minds and to reach for the stars. The family home schooled for several years. She would say to her children "If you reach for the stars and happen to land on the moon, what a wonderful adventure that would be!" Even now she inspires her granddaughter to use her imagination and to find a way to put her dreams on paper.

BURY THY BROTHER is Barbara's first novel, although she has had other pieces published. The next book (AN ANGEL'S QUEST) is nearly finished and can be pre-ordered now. The author dedicated many years to extensive research in order to get both the genealogy and the history of the Civil War correct. The cover picture on the historical novel is her cousin Addison H. Grant who served with the 7th Maine, and whose ghost often visited Barbara begging her to clear his name of the false charge of cowardice. The war tore the family to pieces. Addison and his parents stayed in Maine while part of the family went to Georgia to build the railroads. The first Grant to go south was Lemuel P. Grant, later founder of Atlanta and president of several railroads.

The next book is AN ANGEL'S QUEST—the amazing and true story of Barbara's journey from day one to the eventual publication of this historical novel based on a real family and a horrible war that nearly destroyed our nation. There are myriads of Civil War ghosts who restlessly prowl the battlefields and visit their descendents.

Over 600,000 men and boys died in that war.

BURY THY BROTHER and AN ANGEL'S QUEST
Order Form

Website Orders: www.SkywriterLLC.com

Postal Orders: Lord Skywriter LLC
PO Box 451057
Garland, TX 75045-1057

Please Send _____ Copies of BURY THY BROTHER

Please Send _____ Copies of AN ANGEL'S QUEST

Person Ordering: _____

Company Name: _____

Street Address: _____

City: _____ Prov/State: _____

Postal/Zip Code: _____

Email: _____

Tel No.: (_____) _____-_____

Basic Order:

A) No of Copies   _____ (as per above)

B) Cost Per Copy $_____ ($25 Paperback US)

C) Total Base Cost $_____

D) Taxes 8.25% $_____ (Texas only— D= C X 8.25%)

E)   Shipping $_____ (E = A x $3 postage, packaging)

Total of Order $_____ (Total = C+D+E)

Payments

[] Check enclosed [] Money Order enclosed [] Visa/MC

Credit Card #:_____

Exp. Date: _____/_____   CVV Code: _____

Cardholder Name:_____

Cardholder Signature: _____